TAKING
CONTROL

8/15

TAKING CONTROL

BOOK 2 OF THE KERR CHRONICLES

JEN FREDERICK

 Montlake
Romance

Text copyright © 2015 Jen Frederick
All rights reserved.

Published by Montlake Romance, Seattle

www.apub.com

Amazon, the Amazon logo, and Montlake Romance are trademarks of Amazon.com, Inc., or its affiliates.

ISBN-13: 9781503944664
ISBN-10: 1503944662

Cover design by Shasti O'Leary-Soudant

Printed in the United States of America

To Michelle Kannan, Lisa Schilling Hintz, and Cece Carroll.
Thank you for holding my hand over and over and over.

CHAPTER 1

IAN

"This fella is a Nigerian dwarf goat. We put them in their own pens because they're small and stress can make them sick." The zoo worker gazes adoringly at the slight brunette kneeling at his feet before crouching beside her.

"He's adorable." She rubs the goat's ears. "How old is he?"

"Four years." His hand joins hers by the animal, ostensibly to give the goat a rubdown, but when his fingers accidentally-on-purpose brush hers for the third time, I'm done with being patient because the beautiful brunette he's making calf eyes toward is mine.

As if sensing my impending violence, Victoria—or Tiny as her mother called her—tilts her head and beckons me. "Don't you want to feed the goats, Ian?"

"No." *I want to take you home and make love to you. I want to sink into your body and brand you with mine.* When she smiles and crooks her finger, my feet propel me forward as if she has me on a string.

She's spent too many days and weeks looking sad-eyed and grim after the death of her mother, so if feeding these filthy animals makes her happy, then I'll get down on my three-hundred-dollar jeans and allow some meat to slobber all over my hand. She dribbles a handful of pellets into my palm.

"Thanks." They look like bird turds and smell even worse. Two goats mouth my hand, one nearly biting my finger off.

"Hold your hand flat," she instructs. I straighten my fingers and the goats eat the tiny pellets and then nose around for more. "There. That's better isn't it?"

I turn my head into the fall of her honey brown hair and breathe in its lemon scent. "Yeah, much better."

"Isn't he the cutest thing?"

I look at the pointed furry face with its soft ears. I suppose it's cute as cute things go, but it's dirty here and reminds me of the time I spent poor, hungry, and constantly watching my back down under the Atlantic City boardwalks.

"Lots of cute things in the zoo," the worker winks at Tiny. The worker is about twenty-two. He has a difficult time growing hair on his face, but he's working it hard, beards being trendy for the Brooklyn crowd. Idly I imagine him facedown in the shit-stained hay after I've taught him that winking at a woman whose man is standing two feet away is a dangerous pastime. I'm trying to curb my caveman instincts for Tiny's sake. I highly doubt she'd be happy if I started brawling with a kid at the zoo. I can see the headlines now. *Kerr Gets KO'ed.*

Tiny awkwardly shoves a lock of her hair behind her ear and casts me an uncertain glance. I give her a tight smile. "You ready, babe?"

She nods and rises to her feet. As she brushes her hand against her fit thigh, I slide a possessive arm around her back. "Did you think you had a chance?" I can't help myself.

"Ian Kerr," she hisses.

The worker lifts a hand to shade his face. "Nothing ventured, nothing gained." He shrugs with the insouciance only the young and privileged can carry off.

Punks like this remind me of an older privileged asshole and the urge to punch his lights out has me clenching my fist. Since that would make Tiny angry, I settle for a warning. "Word of caution. Don't trespass on another man's property and you might make it to your quarter century mark without a serious injury."

The boy's mouth flaps open, but Tiny tugs me away before he can regain an ounce of composure.

"Property?" she says with an arched eyebrow.

"I belong to you and you belong to me," I reply. "Two-way street. Besides, would you ever have been interested in a guy like that?"

"He wasn't even flirting with me."

Love makes you blind and weak. "If you say so."

"This was fun." She squeezes my arm and then leans her sweet head against me. "Thank you for bringing me."

I've bought her gems and houses and apartments, but a trip to the zoo is what makes her happy. I knew from the very first moment I saw her on the street that she was different.

I liked the way she carried herself—self-assured and comfortable. I thought her long, light brown hair would look tempting spread out on my pillow. I imagined her thighs would be steel-hard from the biking. She made me laugh when she kicked the doorframe of the store after realizing the shop owner, who needed to sign for the delivery, was missing.

She made me hard when she stared at my lips like she wanted to taste me.

Her unfettered emotions were refreshing. But it was when she ran from me and my direct offer of pleasure that my appetite was whetted.

I was well and truly caught.

I hadn't actively avoided love, but I hadn't sought it out. Why should I? I'd spent most of my thirty-two years fixated on making money. And there were few bedroom doors closed to me. Reasonable attractiveness—made infinitely more so by the thickness of my wallet—ensured that bachelorhood in New York City was easy and entertaining.

Maybe too easy, because her refusal unwittingly transformed her into an irresistible challenge. The more she denied me, the more I wanted her.

Even now, I'm not sure how many walls I've managed to tear down, how far inside the citadel of her heart I stand. It's only when I'm buried inside her that I feel content . . . safe.

There's a danger that she'll wake up from her grief-induced fog and realize that I'm a manipulative asshole who is more trouble than he's worth, but I have time and proximity on my side. I've bought my way into her heart and life. I'll lie, steal, and cheat to stay there because nothing is worth more than her.

The rest of the morning she stays close to me, and while she attracts attention from other men, I manage to keep my temper in check, even in the face of one doughy father looking at her rapaciously as she eats an ice cream cone.

On the ride home, I stew. I manage to hide it well enough that it doesn't affect her. She sighs happily and then falls asleep against me as we make the trip from Brooklyn back to our home in the Meatpacking District.

Our house is a prime example of Tiny not settling in. There's very little of her there.

I went through and cleaned out space in the closet for her, but many of the drawers remain empty, and the hanging space I cleared look bare. Tiny still hasn't let go of her fifth-story walk-up. "My rent is paid," she'd said mulishly when I brought up the topic. She also has belongings at Central Towers, the place where she and her mom lived temporarily before her mom passed away four weeks ago. Tiny went back once, took a look at the bedroom where her mother had slept, and walked back out. I grabbed a few of her things, and we left. She hasn't yet returned—at least as far as I know.

I want us to be so intertwined that you can't tell where my shit ends and her stuff begins. The fact that she's holding part of herself back is terrifying to me. Me, Ian Kerr, the man who makes Wall Street tremble.

I manage to keep the roiling emotions in check even through dinner. But when she's skin to skin with me, I can't hide from her. The sweet welcome of her body is too precious to touch with anything but honesty.

"What's wrong, Ian?" she asks after we fall back onto the rumpled sheets. "And don't say nothing because I can still feel you vibrating and it isn't from me. Is it Richard Howe?"

I jerk back in surprise. "What about him?"

"Maybe if you'd let me help you take him down, I'd feel better. Like I did something for you for a change."

Little furrows appear between her brows. I try to smooth them away with my finger. "Let me worry about Howe."

"But, Ian," she protests. "He's a boil on the ass of humanity. He needs to be gone."

She isn't saying anything I disagree with. I was thirteen when my father died and fifteen when my mother committed suicide. Both events I connect directly to Richard Howe. He needs to be finished, but the last thing I want is for her to become more deeply involved in my revenge scheme—a scheme that I had to revise. Not wanting to hurt Tiny, I couldn't use another woman.

I was wrong to have allowed that shit to even touch her, and now I'm paying for it. Wrapping her in my embrace, I try to rub out the anxiety I feel with long sweeps of my hands down her strained back.

"It's just not something you need to be concerned about."

I feel her open and then shut her mouth. She tries again, her throat a little hoarse with emotion. "I just feel like one of us deserves to have their mother. Cancer stole mine, but he took yours. I want him to suffer. I want him to feel pain. I want him to be afraid to close his eyes at night because of the nightmare we inflict upon him. I hate him. I hate him for you. I hate him for me. I hate him for us."

Though her fierceness makes me love her more, I don't want her even breathing the same air as him. I try to explain this to her.

"I want you to be safe," I say quietly. "To that end, your role in this fiasco is done."

"You can't give up on taking him down," she protests.

"I have no intention of giving up." I just don't want her involved anymore. "But I can't have you flirting with him, touching him. I don't want you to look at him. I don't want him to even think about you in any manner. It ruins me."

"Ian, if you're baiting the hook with another woman, that means you have to spend time with her. And that would ruin me." She stabs a thumb into her chest.

"Which is why we should drop it." Letting go of the past is a bitter and hard pill, but as I told my friend, Kaga, Tiny is far more important to me. At the very least, I need to re-analyze my options.

Her eyes are filled with grief. "I didn't realize what a monster he was. I just can't stand that he's breathing and she's not."

On the last word, her voice catches and the tears she's so valiantly tried to hold back spill over. She's not crying about Howe. It's about loss in general. The loss of her mother. The feeling of being out of control and helpless. I understand all of it.

"I hate that I'm crying. I'm blaming that on Howe too," she says, pressing the heels of her hands against her eyes.

"Crying isn't a sign of weakness."

"Oh, right. I see you bawling all over."

Tiny hates being viewed as fragile.

"Not crying doesn't make me the better person. Just an emotionally deficient one."

When I got to the jail where my mother was being held and was told that she'd hanged herself with the scarf that I'd brought her the day before—at her request—I wanted to howl in grief, but I didn't have anyone to hold me or to stand with me so I swallowed my grief and let it rot me from the inside out.

"You are not deficient," she says fiercely.

"And you are not weak." A sharp, bitter laugh escapes me. "I hate that you even know his name. He shouldn't be allowed to breathe the same air, walk the same streets, eat at the same tables as you."

Her hand squeezes mine in reassurance. I need to pull it together. It is Tiny's mother who has recently passed and she is in need of comfort, yet here she is trying to bolster me with the warmth and solace of her body.

"Is it me? Am I preventing you from taking action?"

Sliding my arm around her waist, I struggle for the right answer. "It's not you. It's never been you."

"Why have you waited so long to pull the trigger on him? Metaphorically speaking," she rushes to add. "I'm not suggesting you should have murdered him or something, but why the kid gloves? The man embezzled money and blamed it on your father. He . . . hurt your mother, and because of him you had to grow up on your own. You've had the power to ruin him for years."

Her explanation of the horror my life turned into after my father's death is laughably euphemistic. My father had a heart attack after being blamed for a seven-figure embezzlement scheme orchestrated by Richard Howe, my father's protégé. My mother killed herself in an Atlantic City jail after prostituting herself to Howe in a stupid and tragic attempt to regain money in the mistaken belief that was all she needed to reenter the world she'd lost when my father died. I'd left that jail with her few effects, vowing revenge, and then I met Tiny.

Somehow the need to have her in my life has superseded my desire for retribution. At least momentarily.

Tiny is correct. Richard Howe is the scum of the earth. The ironic thing is that he is also the one that brought us together.

Until I'd met Tiny, I'd been good at compartmentalization, putting each person or activity in its own separate mental file drawer. Trying to ignore the strength of my developing feelings for her, I thought to use her against Richard. But she wouldn't stay in her little drawer; instead, her influence crept into every aspect of my life.

I was wholly unprepared for the depth of my feelings for Tiny. Or, more likely, I had been denying them. I wanted her but hadn't realized until the moment I saw them together, dancing, that I'd rather burn the whole world down than have another man lay a finger on her.

I tried to swallow down the rage and allow Tiny to lure him in, but as each minute ticked by and he stood close enough to touch her, my anger was stoked hotter and hotter. And when he placed his fucking hands on her, my restraint was ripped to shreds. I wish I had realized sooner that I'd feel that way.

"Do you know what you're doing?" Kaga, one of my few friends, had asked me at the time. "If you walk out there, he's going to know what she means to you."

"If I watch him try to touch her ass one more time, you'll be visiting me in prison," I'd said.

That he even knows her name is my own goddamn fault.

I rub my forehead. "When I first returned to the city, I had these grand ideas that I'd storm his townhome and wrench a confession out of him. It didn't take long to realize that he'd never confess. I kept making money, and in the meantime, I started to buy up his debt. About eight years ago, I had enough of his debt that I could have made it difficult for him, but then his wife approached me at a party. I don't think she remembered me or knew who I was. She just came up out of the blue and started telling me about how she volunteered at a women's crisis hotline and how life changing it was. She asked if I would be interested in donating."

"So she stayed your hand?"

"Yes. Every time I was in a position to do something to Howe, I'd see her at an event. She'd share her latest charitable activities with me. She was doing things that could have helped my mother. She would mention how much she missed my mother." I clenched my fists in frustration. "Would Howe's shame transfer to her? Would she feel the same as my own mother? I found I couldn't act. And I felt sorry for her because

Richard cheated on her regularly. She had to know about his infidelity. Discretion wasn't important to him, although he rarely hunted in their social circles. He preferred the working class, like waitresses, models—which are often one and the same in the city. Women he viewed as disposable. Possibly worse, she loves him. Even now, after all these years, her eyes follow him across a room. Now that I have you, I recognize her longing even more acutely. How deeply devoted she is to him."

"You thought that a scandal would separate her from him."

"Yes, even if it would be painful, if I could decouple her from him before I struck, then I wouldn't have her wounds on my conscience." I shake my head. "I'll think of something else."

She presses her face close to my chest. I feel her trembling. "What is it?" I ask urgently.

"You're amazing, Ian Kerr. Your compassion is inspiring. I don't know if I could be that generous in the same situation." She rains kisses on my shoulders and at the base of my neck.

"If you were another woman, I'd say you were buttering me up for something. But since you won't even take what I'm willing to give you without argument, I'm going to have to ask: Are you on drugs? Because I distinctly remember you calling me an arrogant asshole more than once."

"That was before I realized that you needed my help to correct your character flaws. I'm here now."

"You're like a missionary then, to save me from myself?" I'm only half joking.

"That's right and from all the other women in New York City. I'm sacrificing myself on the altar of Ian Kerr's pleasure in order to prevent heartbreak and sorrow across the city."

"You deserve sainthood." I pull her tight against me and kiss her in gratitude for driving away my moodiness.

"In honor of my impending deification, will you make love to me again?"

"Mmmm," I murmur against her lips. "I'm sorry but no. You're too swollen and tender."

She draws away from me, although the circle of my arms doesn't allow her to get far. "Are you feeling sick? Because I swear I heard you turn me down."

"I'm not turning you down. I'm . . . delaying our gratification until later."

"Delayed gratification is for suckers. I want you now." She looks determined, but I get my way. Always.

I push her back and slide down her body until I'm kneeling between her legs. "I'll take care of you, bunny."

Softly, tenderly, as if she were a virgin, I stroke her delicate lips. Her clit slowly emerges, as if jealous of the attention given to her other body parts. I lick my thumb and rub it lightly across the tip.

"Ian," she moans. My name on her lips in that breathy tone has the same effect as mainlining aphrodisiacs. My already-erect cock throbs in response. I'm starting to believe in soul mates and life in the hereafter, because one lifetime won't be enough with Victoria Corielli.

Sliding my palms under her ass, I lift her to my mouth. I'm too horny right now to lick her slowly. I need to feel her orgasm all over my face, to have her thighs clench my head in a viselike grip, like nothing is ever going to separate the two of us.

I suck at her lips, separating the folds with my tongue. Placing my thumb—wet from her arousal—on her clit, I tease her with tongue and lips until her thighs are moving restlessly beside my head, bumping my ears.

The taste of her is making me wild. My cock is thick and hard and even the expensive sheets are chafing my sensitive skin. *Inside her,* my mental caveman grunts. *Need inside her.* I thrust into the sheets as I devour her.

"Oh shit, Ian." The hand on my head tightens and my scalp begins to protest, but the pain brings a smile to my face. She's getting there. It's heaven down here. I could live here, her juices sustaining me for days. Opening my mouth wide, I engulf her. Every little crevice is explored and sucked until her whole body stiffens and arches in front of me. Her soft walls start to convulse, and her thighs tighten.

"That's it, bunny. Just let go." I lap at her, maintaining the rhythm that brought her to the peak. She pulses her hips against my fingers and mouth. I torture her with my lips, tongue, and fingers until she's crying out my name and pulling and pushing against me at the same time. And then I hold her with fierce pride as she comes down off her orgasmic high.

"Have I told you that I love you?" she whispers and pulls me to her for a fierce kiss. Her teeth nip at mine and then our mouths are fused. For long moments, the only air that we breathe is through each other. Breaking away, she pants and presses soft kisses along my jaw and down my neck.

"Only once today." I smooth her hair back. We've made a mess of it. The long strands are tangled and matted, but she's never looked sexier. My gut tightens at the thought that others have seen her in this just-fucked state.

"What's that look for?" she asks, smoothing a hand across my sweat-dampened skin.

"I'm a jealous fucker." No one but me will ever get to see her this disheveled again.

"Are you just figuring that out, because it was pretty evident a few weeks ago when you dragged me out of the bar by my hair."

"It was by your hand, but if you're okay with the hair dragging, I can pull that off the next time we're out."

She pinches me lightly. "No, I'm not into the hair dragging thing. I'm not against a little hair pulling, though."

"Is that right?" My tone is light, but her words have made my cock harder than marble.

"This can't be comfortable." Her hand dips down to stroke me and I shudder at the caress.

Comfortable? No. "It'll go away if you ignore it," I lie.

"I don't want to ignore it. I want it inside me."

I shake my head. "You're too sore, bunny." I rub a finger over her lips, shiny and plump from our kisses. "I'll hurt you."

"I'll feel worse if you don't," she pleads.

Her gentle begging makes me even harder, and I feel a twinge of guilt that her helpless desire turns me on even more. A decent man wouldn't feel good about hearing his woman beg. Hell, a decent man probably never refers to his companion as *his woman*. But since I raised myself from the age of thirteen, I've developed my own rules and my own code.

I want. I take. I keep.

Tiny belongs to me now, and I'm not letting her go. She's mine to love and to care for.

CHAPTER 2

When I wake up, my cock is rock hard again. Her hand is curled around it, stoking my fire. "No, bunny." I worked her way too hard last night, trying to fuck some demons out of my head. This morning she's probably still sore. It's about as easy as walking into a fifty-mile-per-hour headwind and I'm sweating with the effort, but I manage to put about two inches of distance between us.

"Don't tempt me. You're too sore, and I'd cut off my right nut before I'd hurt you."

"Your right nut? That's some serious talk. Usually a guy only offers his left nut." She erases the two inches and slips a leg over mine. My little head tells me that if I don't impale her within the next five seconds, we're all going to die. I take a few deep breaths to regain some self-control and inch backward.

"You can't talk about another guy's nuts in our bed. It makes me want to mark my territory."

"Come on then, take me." She rolls on her side and strokes a hand down my chest, trailing her fingers across my abdomen and the hard planes of my obliques. Each little kitten touch is making everything harder. Jackknifing out of bed and away from her clever fingers, I head to the bathroom, rubbing my hair in agitation. Soon I'll be rubbing something else, because I won't be able to step foot out of my house without being arrested for public indecency if I don't do something about this goddamn erection.

Behind me, I hear her footsteps.

"Is your dick hard, Ian? Do you want me to lick it?" There's glee in her voice as she mocks me.

Fuck yes.

"No, bunny. I want you to lie down and rest." Inside the shower, I flick on the full array of sprays.

"I'm not an invalid, and you're sucking up at least half the Hudson with that thing," she says.

Turning back, I see her, completely nude, leaning against my black marble vanity. She looks like a goddess. I hit the temperature controls. I'm going to need it to be refrigerator cold inside the shower to get rid of my hard-on.

"Good thing the 'Bruce Wayne fuckpad' has a direct drain back into the river." I use her nickname for my Meatpacking District home.

"How cold is it in there?" She's crept closer to the shower, and I can still see her naked body through the water-spattered glass. I turn the water even colder. "Because I think I can see my breath out here."

She purses her lips and blows, her cheeks hollowed and her lips a perfect circle. I swear she's doing this to purposely torment me. Taking my cock in hand, I lean against the glass with the other and stare at her while I pump my shaft. She drifts toward me until there's nothing separating us but the sheet of glass. The water drives against my back like thin needles but my cock is on fire. Her gaze never wavers from mine and even through the drops of water and the clear glass wall, I can see both her love and her lust.

I don't need her hand on me. I just need to see *her*. She reaches out her hand so that it mirrors mine, the action causing her body to elongate as she stretches. Her breasts press against the glass, the nipples hardening due to the cold, due to me. They're so hard that they resist flattening, instead poking forward like darts and displacing the soft breast tissue surrounding them.

My mouth waters. I've had those precious tits in my mouth a dozen times but I can't wait for a dozen more. I want my tongue flicking against those hard tips. As if she can read my mind, she reaches down and cups one of her breasts. Her fingers roll one hardened nipple between them.

Breathing choppily, I jerk faster until my thighs are shaking and my balls are ready to burst. "I'm going to come now," I pant and she nods her head. In understanding? Agreement? I have no idea, but the orgasm rolls up from the base of my spine until I spurt against the glass and on the floor, my hips pumping into the air. I let loose a groan and Tiny's mouth opens as if she's swallowing the sound. The air is filled with the musky scent of my ejaculate. She licks her fingers and smiles, an evil temptress smile. God, I fucking love her.

Without the adrenaline of arousal, the water is far too cold. I switch the hot on and soap up, lifting the handheld showerhead to wash away the evidence of my jacking off. Tiny has disappeared. I'm simultaneously disappointed and relieved. Disappointed because I want her with me always, and relieved because I don't think my heart can stand another round right now.

As quickly as possible, I finish my shower, sticking my head face-forward into the stream and cleaning off. When I turn off the sprayers, a towel is shoved in my face. "Thanks. What's on your agenda today?" I ask.

"Work. And Sarah called the other day, so we're trying to meet up for lunch. Maybe today."

I exert some self-control so she doesn't see a frown of disappointment that I won't be seeing her until the end of the day. "If I'd known that, I would have allowed you to take advantage of me this morning."

"I guess you'll think twice about turning me down tomorrow morning."

"No doubt."

Tiny is currently working for Jake Tanner, a friend of mine who runs a security firm that provides everything from in-home alarm systems to personal protection services to investigative work. He does a lot of insurance company jobs, which he describes as dull but lucrative.

After Tiny was fired from her bike messenger job for missing work, she took over as his receptionist and dispatcher. He'd recently been given a medical discharge from the Marines and decided to start a security firm instead of rolling around in his family money.

"Sounds like a plan. I'll have Steve drive you."

She fidgets slightly with the lapels of the robe. Tiny isn't really that small, but she's nearly a foot shorter than me and the robe makes her look young—too young to be out in the big, bad city without me. I'd like for her to stay here where it's completely safe. Everything she could ever want can be delivered right to our doorstep. As a former bike courier, she should know that, but I know that if I suggested this plan she'd turn on her heels and walk out.

"What am I doing here, Ian?" she asks finally. Her exhale is so heavy that her entire chest heaves.

"Making sure I don't have to jerk off every day?" I say lightly.

"No, really." She tightens her belt and shoves a hand through her hair. Because of the tangles, her hand gets caught and she jerks it away from her head with a small curse. "I feel like a complete freeloader. I'm working a job that you arranged. I live in your house. I'm driven to work by your driver-slash-bodyguard. You won't let me pay for anything. If you really had your way, I'd be lying on the roof working on a tan." She throws out her arms in exasperation.

I'd known she'd been feeling discontent, but I hadn't realized how deep it went. Worry creeps in and I have the urge to take her back to bed. Imprint myself on her. *That's healthy,* I mock myself silently.

I tip her head up so she looks me in the eyes. "Your mom just died.

You were grieving. Still are. You aren't freeloading. You're allowing me to take care of you, which is a gift." I press a kiss against her forehead but am deeply concerned by the tension in her frame. "Let's take the day off. There are other zoos we haven't visited yet."

"I'm going to work, so you might as well too," she declares. "Besides didn't you say that your guy isn't happy with you? What's his name? Louis?" She trails a hand down the rack of perfectly tailored suits.

"Louis can suck an egg. I pay him a fortune. He should be happy I'm not in the office cracking the whip." I hired Louis Durand out of B school. I had street smarts and good instincts but needed the expertise of someone who'd had an MBA. Louis was a good fit because he lacked the capital and the instincts. From him I was able to glean the necessary information to make sure we didn't run afoul of the regulatory officials. We'd made a good team, constantly searching for the next acquisition to add to my holding company.

My thirst for widening my monetary reach has been waning since I found Tiny. In some ways, I had been completely impoverished before I met her. These days, I wanted to spend my time with her rather than in an office going over endless analyst reports with Louis.

"What are you going to wear today?"

"Dress me," I suggest. She likes looking at my clothes. Anything that makes her happy pleases me.

"Hmmm." Her fine fingers smooth down a light blue suit coat in a linen and wool blend. "Tell me about your stylist. Will I meet him?"

"Personal shopper," I correct her. "The word stylist makes me sound like I belong on Broadway. My suits are made by a Savile Row tailor whose family has been in business since the late 1800s. Twice a year, he brings a battered Louis Vuitton trunk to the city and all of us acolytes trek to The Plaza to be measured, try on muslin prototypes, and put in our orders for the next year. I was introduced to Bakers & Henry via Frank."

"How'd you get to know Frank?"

"I met Frank while he was grifting, selling everything from stolen wallets to, ah, other things, in an effort to feed and clothe his two younger sisters."

Looking at Frank now, you'd never guess that he'd walked the boardwalk in Atlantic City lifting purses and wallets and servicing bored businessmen. He'd taught me how to dress, having an innate fashion sense. He knew that clothes made all the difference to the people with whom you did business. Wear a suit to a drug deal and you'd get shot. Wear jeans to a boardroom and they'd laugh you out. Frank taught me that a hand-stitched suit and French cuffs could get me into places that a gun could not.

Wall Street isn't much different than the boardwalk. The bills are larger and everyone smells better, but that's about it. A hustle is a hustle.

We'd both gotten out of the rat holes, but there was still sand in the crevices of our skin. Frank surmises that the amount of sand we've accumulated is directly responsible for all the pearls we're shitting out—and that I must have taken on more sand than most, since my pearls are more frequent and bigger than everyone else's.

"Where's Frank now?"

"He lives in an apartment on Madison Avenue."

"And his sisters?"

"One's at NYU and the other just graduated from Columbia. She's in grad school now, getting her MBA."

"That's awesome."

"It is."

"This is different." She's moved on from the light blue suit to land on a heather gray with a darker gray check. It's definitely one of my bolder suits because of the strong contrasting lines.

"Frank sold me on that fabric on the basis that only a man with giant balls could wear it and not be embarrassed. I was peer pressured into buying it," I joke.

I'm rewarded with a small laugh. "I like it, and I think your balls are big enough to carry it off."

"I'm glad. My balls like you too."

At her stare, my cock pulses and fills to a half-erect state. She tries to suppress a smile, but the mischievous glint in her eyes reveals how much she enjoys turning me on. It's a mutual pleasure, though. I enjoy the ache because I know the sweet release that follows will be worth it. Plus, I'd rather see her smiling, because she thinks she's torturing me, than sad and grieving. She pulls the dove-gray suit down off the hanger. "Then this one today."

"What else?" I ask, taking the suit from her and pulling off the pants. "Or should I go commando?"

"I like the idea of commando," she says perversely, her hand not so inadvertently brushing against my groin.

My groan sounds overly loud in the dressing room. "Keep doing that and I'll bend you over that bench over there." I jerk my head toward the padded leather bench situated at the end of the island of drawers.

She quirks her lips and this time places her hand on my chest, tracing a fingertip down the center and stopping just above my belly button. My cock surges upward under the loosely tied towel and bobs for her attention. Her fingers delve under the fabric and close gently around the tip. With a swift twist of her hand, my knees weaken. I'm forced to place a hand against one of the shelf supports so I don't fall over.

"Your threats have no power," she mocks. "You already denied me."

"Sweet Jesus." I can't stop my hips from pumping in her tight grip. "I'm already loving my punishment, if that's what this is."

Turning away she lets me go. "Not really, but it is nice to know that you do want me."

"Is there any doubt?" I bury my face in her hair and pull her ass flush against my thick arousal.

"You turned me down this morning." There's a kernel of hurt in her voice which renders me defenseless. If rousing me to the point of pain and sending me out allows her to feel more secure, I'd go out this way every day.

"Oh, bunny, just because I don't want to hurt you." I lick the sensitive part of her skin where her neck and shoulder join. I'd love to put a mark there. One that everyone can see, particularly given that she wants to go to Jake's office where a bunch of former military assholes will be tromping in and out, no doubt hitting on her every five seconds.

She shakes her head. "Shouldn't I be the one to decide if I'm too sore?"

"Sure," I say, but it's my job to protect her from everything, even herself. I keep that sentiment to myself. She wouldn't appreciate it.

With a half-smile, she turns to give me a slight squeeze and then kisses me lightly. "I'm done torturing you. Let's get you dressed."

After kissing her back, I reach around her for a pair of boxer briefs and start to dress, pulling on the slacks and then searching for a shirt. "You're probably right. Louis is turning into a shrew at work since I've started coming in later and leaving earlier."

Tiny hesitates handing me a dark blue dress shirt with white stripes and a burgundy tie speckled with tiny white triangles. "Am I keeping you from something important? Are you losing money because of me?"

Shoving my arms into the shirt, I root around for a black belt. "No. I've been exactly where I wanted to be since I met you. I think we both know I've got enough money to see us through two lifetimes of winters."

Money will never be a problem for either of us.

Accepting my reassurances, she nods. "You don't have to change your life for me."

"Why not? I expect you to change yours for me. I want you to live with me, accept my gifts, allow me to provide for you. It's reasonable for you to expect me to change as well. I want our lives to be different.

That's the point of being together. You are now my life, and I want to see evidence of you here." I wave at the empty shelves and drawers.

"I love how your romantic gestures are all declarations. Accept my gifts, dammit," she mocks. Gesturing for me to stand upright, she starts putting me together, which, unfortunately for the tight fit of my pants, is just as erotic as having her unclothe me.

"Some things can't be changed," I admit. "And me being a dictatorial, overbearing, possessive bastard is one of them. I'd say I was sorry, but it wouldn't be sincere." When her hands bump up against my cock as she's threading the belt through the loops, I tell her, "Just ignore it."

"I guess I love you in spite of your Emperor Napoleon ways." With her tongue pushed again her cheek, presumably so she doesn't start laughing, she finishes buttoning my shirt, leaving the collar upright so that I can fix my tie. It's the one thing she doesn't know how to do, but maybe some night I'll teach her the intricacies of tie knots and how useful they can be.

"Whatever you're thinking about, you should stop or you'll never be able to tuck in your shirt," she observes.

"Can't stop." I lean down to kiss her. "Don't want to stop."

Shrugging, she picks out a pocket square and tucks it into the suit coat. "I think the story about how you met Frank is the most you've ever revealed about yourself. Other than what happened with your mom and dad."

"What is it that you want to know? I'll tell you anything. There will be no secrets between us." I tuck in my shirt and adjust myself. I'll deflate . . . eventually. For now, I'll live with my erection. There are worse things. She hands me a pair of burgundy and blue striped socks and my hand-stitched Italian wingtips, and I sit on the bench to pull them on.

"I want to know everything. I want to know which food is your favorite, what your guilty pleasures are, what movies you like the best."

"Steak, I don't believe in guilty pleasures just pleasure, and *The Godfather* trilogy." I tie my shoes and stride to the full-length mirror at the end of the dressing room. "My turn. For every piece of information you get from me, I want one in return."

"That's fair." She peers over my shoulder as I maneuver the silk length of my tie into a Pratt knot.

"Since I shared with you about Frank, I think it is time for you to tell me why you haven't moved all your things into my home."

She grimaces. "Precisely because it is *your* home."

Her emphasis on the pronoun is not lost on me. "I have no problem selling this place and buying one together with you."

I didn't think her dismay could deepen, but I was wrong. "No, I don't want that. I just . . ." She looks around and then meets my gaze in the mirror. "It doesn't feel like home."

The warehouse once served as home base for my import-export business—which really consisted of facilitating the trade of goods that weren't sanctioned by the government, including things as innocuous as non-FDA-approved cheese to art with curious provenance.

Once I was completely legit, I hired an architect who converted the warehouse into plush, three-level, sun-soaked living quarters for one. The ground level houses the vehicles, the second floor houses the kitchen, exercise equipment, and big screen television. A bedroom and office on the third floor loft completes the space.

I'm asked regularly if I want to sell it. The architect, Adam Markham, is now big time, designing skyscrapers in Dubai and Hong Kong, and the converted warehouse is one of the few residential pieces he's ever done. I'd never had the urge to sell it before, but it'd be gone in a heartbeat if Tiny didn't like it.

I make a mental note to check with my realtor for a more family-friendly residence in the city. Maybe along Central Park. A townhome. I bought property in Long Island for us where we can spend long weekends and most of the summer, but living outside the city on a regular basis wouldn't suit either of us.

Tiny and I love the city, from the green parks to the gray concrete. But I want her to be happy, and if a new residence will accomplish that, it's a small sacrifice to say good-bye to this home.

She hands me my jacket, but I toss it aside. Picking her up, I carry her to the island of mahogany in the middle of the room and set her down. She's inches taller than me, but I can look her in the eyes better.

"If you don't want to move, then make this place your home. Let's buy new furniture. Hell, let's get an architect in here and we'll remake it from the ground up. We'll dig out the basement and put in a pool. We'll plant a palm tree on the roof. I don't care what we do so long as when we're done, you can walk in here and say 'I'm glad to be home.' And if you can't see yourself ever saying that about this place, then we'll sell it." I squeeze her hips for emphasis. "And don't say a word about the cost because I don't give a shit about the cost. You could refurnish the entire Meatpacking District and I'd—" I pause to correct myself "—we'd still be rich as hell."

With a sigh, she curls my hair in her fingers. "Living together, potentially moving, ignoring Howe, not working as much are part of those things that will change? It's a lot for me to take in."

Dealing with her mother's loss goes unstated but hangs there in between the words.

"Do you believe that I love you?" I demand.

"You know I do."

"Then believe every word I say to you is the truth and exactly what I mean."

Before she can answer, I hear her phone ring. The "Bad Company" ringtone signals it's her stepbrother, Malcolm. Tiny assigns ringtones to all of her callers, not that she has many. I enjoy redoing them.

"Bad Company" for her drug-dealing stepbrother; "You've Got a Friend" sung by James Taylor—not the later covers—for her old friend Sarah; the theme from *The Bodyguard* soundtrack for my driver, Steve, who is not so surreptitiously serving as her bodyguard; and last but not least, "Ain't No Other Man" by Christina Aguilera for me.

With pressure against my shoulder, she signals she wants to answer the phone. Reluctantly, I lift her down.

I'm not a fan of Malcolm, but right now I know to step lightly around the subject. She feels tethered to him because he knew her mother. Gritting my teeth, I finish my morning routine. I haven't shaved yet, but the grungy unshaven look is popular and I answer to no one. Generally I shave so my coarse facial hair doesn't scratch Tiny's skin, but perhaps . . . I stroke the side of my face. Maybe I'll see how she likes the different texture tonight.

From the bedroom I hear Tiny's side of the conversation.

"No, I didn't mind that your mom came to the funeral. I thought that was nice of her. How's she doing?"

Malcolm's mother is addicted to gambling, and that's why he's got his hands in so many different criminal pots—or at least that's his excuse. Malcolm and Tiny shared a father for a short time when they were teens, but Mitch Hedder, Malcolm's biological father and Tiny's stepfather, took off and hasn't been seen for a long time.

"No way," she exclaims. "God, I'm sorry. Where's he staying?"

More silence from Tiny's end.

"How's your mom taking it?"

"Yeah, okay, thanks for the warning."

Shrugging into my jacket, I place my phone and wallet in the inside breast pocket and press a button to alert Steve I'll be ready for a pickup in ten minutes.

"What's that all about?"

"Mitch is back in town. And he's staying at The Plaza."

Her worried look tells me this is trouble.

"It's not your problem."

"Malcolm's family."

"No, I'm your family," I counter.

"Mitch was part of my life for six years. My stepdad for four of those years. Malcolm says he wants to talk to me about Mom. I can't deny him that." She sounds anguished, which is exactly what I'm trying to protect her from.

I count to ten in my head. And then backward. This is a tipping point. I either step right or onto a land mine. I can't demand she not meet with him because she's an adult and will do what she wants. I struggle to find a compromise we both can live with. "Then promise me you won't meet him without me."

She nods slowly. "Okay, I promise."

"Thank you." I kiss her slowly, because it's going to have to last me all day.

CHAPTER 3

Not five minutes after I climb into my car, the phone rings. It's Tiny.

"Bunny."

"Can Steve hear you?" she demands.

"Doubt it. But the privacy screen isn't up. Why? Do you want to have phone sex? Because I can be home in five minutes and have you naked in one more."

She smothers a laugh. "No, I just don't want him to know you call me bunny. I get that it's an endearment, and I guess it is sweet, but it sounds weak. I don't want Steve to think I'm weak."

"No one else is going to call you bunny," I reassure her. If they did, my fist would be in their mouth before they pronounced the last syllable. "Besides, why do you care what Steve thinks of you?"

"He's your friend. I want your friends to think I'm good for you and that I'm not some weak chick that needs saving all the time." She makes a gagging sound. "Barf. Who wants that?"

Tiny's neuroses are strange. "Even if Steve thought you were weaker than a newborn, I'd get rid of him before I'd get rid of you." In the rearview mirror, I see Steve raise his eyebrows. Apparently he can hear me. I just shrug in response. Everyone should know where my loyalties lie. "Is that what you called about, or are you in need of something?"

She sighs. "I just got off the phone with Mitch. He wants to see me. He was crying. I couldn't tell him no."

I'm glad we're on the phone so she can't see my glare. "It's been seven years since you last saw him."

"I know." She hesitates and then rushes forward. "He says he has something of hers that I would want."

Of course he would say that. He's manipulating her, but either she doesn't see it or doesn't want to. With as much patience as I can muster, I ask, "When and where?"

"Maybe Friday at The Plaza?" she replies with obvious relief. Not pointing out Mitch Hedder's manipulation was the right tactic, but at some point she will need to acknowledge his motives are not innocent.

"No problem. I've got a several meetings this week, but I believe my last one on Friday is at three."

"And you said you'd stay home today," she chided.

"No meeting is more important than you. Nothing is," I say quietly.

She's silent for a long time, and I begin to think she's hung up on me when she finally says, "I'm trying to wrap my head around that. It's just not something I've felt in a very long time from a man. My mother yes, but no male in my life has ever expressed that to me," she admits.

"You take as long as you want," I reassure her.

"I love you."

I can almost see her biting the side of her lip as she says it, slightly afraid of my response. Her past boyfriends must have been real winners. Someday I'll tell her that a man secure enough in himself isn't afraid to say those words. "Love you too."

"Bye," she says softly.

◆ ◆ ◆

TINY

Ever since Ian Kerr walked into my life, change has been the only constant. Change and his incredible and undeserved devotion to me. I love him, and—worse—I'm addicted to him.

He calls every day to see if I want to have lunch. Invariably, that means we have sex, because we can't be within five feet of each other without wanting to rip each other's clothes off. It's bad enough that I can't look Ian's driver, Steve, in the eye because of all the times I've exited the car with my clothes askew. I need to be able to look into my boss's face without turning all kinds of red.

Besides, Ian's got more important things to do than eat with me. He's in charge of a holding company that is worth a billion dollars. A billion. I can't even fathom that. Ian wants me to stay home and suck on my toes or something. Okay, maybe not suck my toes, but he actually said I could just sit in his converted warehouse and relax. He dragged me to the rooftop, and while it's a cool place and I don't mind spending an hour out there enjoying a cold beer with him after work, the last thing I want to do is sit around and have to think.

If I'm not busy or Ian isn't occupying my attention, then all I can do is think about my mom and start crying. I've cried enough to float an entire armada. I hate that I cried this morning. I tried to pass them off as hate tears. I hate Richard Howe for all the shitty things he's done to Ian. Shitty isn't even the right word for it. More like despicable. If I could read a thesaurus, I'd come up with an even better word.

"What's worse than shitty?" I ask Jake when I go back and hand him the mail.

"Fucking shitty?" He takes the mail and rifles through it. I wonder if he regrets hiring a dyslexic whose reading level is about that of a third grader. He's never complained about my poor writing skills. I wonder if it's because he and Ian are friends.

If I didn't love Ian so goddamn much I'd run away. Run away from this job I don't really like. Run away from the lifestyle that makes me uncomfortable. Run away from the grief of my mother's death. But my love binds me to him more effectively than a pair of gold handcuffs. If losing my mother to cancer was painful, then leaving Ian would be . . . well, worse than fucking shitty. Way worse.

The unevenness of our situation agitates me. I don't feel comfortable at his warehouse. Stupidly, I wonder how many women have slept in his bed or made coffee in his kitchen. He's very tight-mouthed about that. He says he's not a playboy. In fact, his lip curled in disgust when I'd even implied it, as if I'd smeared his honor or something.

And I'll never be able to buy Ian the same kind of gifts he buys me. His closet is filled with clothes and shoes that cost more than several months' rent for many apartments. I'm left wondering how long he's going to be interested in a deadweight girlfriend who has a hard time remembering to smile these days.

"You're frowning," Jake comments, waking me from my reverie.

"Sorry, boss." Making a face, I turn to leave.

"You really dislike this job, don't you?"

Oh god, is he going to fire me?

"No, it's good. Great in fact," I lie, but prompted by his knowing gaze, I fess up. "It's not you or this job. It's being inside. I haven't worked indoors since my first job out of high school waiting tables. I'm used to being outside, and frankly, I miss the rush of my old job. The pressure, the challenge. Out there I felt like I was doing something. Here I feel like the only thing I'm accomplishing is a notepad full of errors."

"I'm not going to fire you," Jake chuckles. "So you can stop the gruesome expression that you're trying to pass off as a smile. I want to find a job that you do like."

"Why? It's not your responsibility to find me a job. Is it because of Ian?"

"No. It's because you're a tremendously hard worker. You've done a job you don't like without complaint for the last four weeks. That kind of work ethic is hard to find. With your attention to detail, good memory, and quick mind, you'd make a great field agent."

"But?"

He gives me a knowing look but not a sympathetic one. Jake has no interest in complainers. "You'd have to write reports, conduct background checks—basically, you'd have to read and write better. Think about it."

His last words are a dismissal, and I return to my desk. The rest of the morning I contemplate his advice. *Learn to read and write better.* I pretty much gave up on the whole reading thing in elementary school.

Once I'd been diagnosed as dyslexic, I'd been taught a lot of coping strategies, such as better visualization and memorization skills. I have a rocking good memory, which is why I'd been a good bike courier. I knew landmarks all over this city and could find an address easily. I paid attention in class, and if my notes looked more like hieroglyphs than words, it worked for me. That's what I used now—more pictures than words.

Jake is telling me I need to stretch myself. My mom always accepted the way I had compensated, and since I'd managed a job and a place to live, learning to read and write better never actually occurred to me. Plus, if there was anything I hated more than being viewed as weak and impaired, it was going to school. I make a face even though no one can see me.

At noon, I call to Jake, "I'm going to lunch."

"The office will be locked when you come back. I have a meeting with a tech firm to take a look at some security systems. Put the machine on."

"Will do."

Another reason I'm not lunching with Ian is because today I'm having lunch with Sarah Berkovich, an old high school friend. She'd called me a week ago saying she saw the notice in the *Observer* about my mom's funeral. It would never have been there if I hadn't been standing next to Ian. In fact, my name wasn't even mentioned below the picture of him standing behind me with his hand on the small of my back. The caption read *Ian Kerr, billionaire investor, attending the funeral of a friend, Sophie Corielli.*

Sarah and I are meeting at Telepan—a place I wouldn't have been able to eat at before Ian. Even though the prices are considered midrange, it still would have been too expensive when Mom and I had five-figure medical bills hovering over us and I struggled to make rent on a one-bedroom, fifth-floor walk-up on the far Upper East Side. There was some pleasure in being able to agree that Telepan was just fine when Sarah suggested it, instead of having to say I needed to bring a sandwich from home.

Sarah is already there when I arrive. Her dark brown hair is full of wiry curls, which are about the only distinctively Jewish thing about her other than her last name. She has a heart-shaped face and a sloped nose that curls up just slightly at the end, making her look pert and mischievous. As I enter, she stands and hurries to the door.

"Vic!" she cries, and pulls me against her five-feet-eight frame. Thankfully she's wearing flats instead of heels, so I don't feel like a complete shrimp next to her. My family—and Ian—call me Tiny. Everyone else has their own variation of Victoria. For Sarah, it's Vic. Her generous breasts squish against my smaller torso. As she leads me back to our table, every male head and some of the female ones turn to watch her.

"God, you haven't changed at all," she says as we sit down.

"Neither have you. You look amazing, as always."

She uses a hand to smooth some of her wild curls back. "I'm getting better at putting on makeup, I hope."

"Definitely," I laugh. We'd had a sleepover once with Sarah acting as the beautician. We were going for smoky eyes but ended up looking like frightened raccoons.

"Before we go any further, I have to apologize. I'm so sorry that we lost contact. I had no idea your mother was sick."

She looks sincere, but I hope she doesn't start crying. Sarah was a weeper in school, and if she tears up here, given my precarious emotional health, I'll join her, which will be an embarrassing mess.

"Thanks, but no apologies are necessary. We moved close to the hospital and kind of lost touch with everyone. Plus, you went to Pace and I didn't."

The waiter forestalls any more apologies. I haven't looked at my menu, but it's a pizza place. I figure they have cheese pizza. After he takes our order, Sarah asks, "Are you still messengering? That's what you did after high school, right?"

"No. I got in an accident and thought I would look into something else, so I'm dispatching for a security firm." I'd actually gotten beat up by a paranoid drug addict, and my inability to get right back up on the bike got me fired, but she doesn't need to know those kinds of details.

"Oh no. I didn't realize it was dangerous. You're okay now though?"

I nod. "Yes, all healed up. How about you?"

"I graduated two years ago with a BA in English, which netted me a publishing assistant job. If I didn't live at home, I wouldn't be able to go out at all."

"I hear you." I completely understood those kinds of money problems. Every dime I had went for food, rent, or paying down Mom's medical bills. I didn't have the time, energy, or—most of all—the money to go out to a bar or a club. Now I have Ian, who seems intent on seeing that everything I missed out on before is brought to me on a silver platter. It's nice but overwhelming.

"Hopefully I'll get a promotion one of these days into an editorial position, make a little more money, and then finally move out on my own. But I don't want to live so far outside the city that I'm taking a two-hour train ride to and from work."

"But do you like your job?"

"Love it. I'd do it for free if I had to. I get to read manuscripts all day, work with authors, give input on covers and stuff. I once wrote the back cover copy of a book that got published." She pumps her fist. "My boss, Diane, tells me that the dewy innocence in my eyes will dry out after I've read my share of crappy manuscripts or dealt with awful authors, but for now, I'm still full of youthful exuberance." She smiles back at me, every ounce of her joy visible on her face.

I can't help but return her grin.

"I forgot how cheerful you are all the time."

"Irritatingly so, according to Diane," she says, unperturbed. "I'm guessing by the lack of gushing that you aren't as in love with your job as I am with mine."

"Unfortunately, no. It's okay, but I can't see me doing it for the rest of my life."

"Do you even need to work?"

"Because I'm dating Ian?" I ask.

"My god, Vic, it's like winning the lottery and *The Bachelorette* at the same time."

"It's better," I admit. "Not gonna lie."

She slaps the table and hoots a little too loud, but I don't mind. The waiter delivers our food and in between bites of cheese pizza, we catch up, talking about people from high school, particularly her hated ex, Cameron O'Toole, who she'd discovered was cheating on her while she was at Pace University and he was at Columbia.

"Cam is just finishing his MBA. New York is sick with business school grads, and they're all insufferable. No offense to your boyfriend."

"He never went to college, so no offense taken," I say.

"No college? Wow, one of those dropouts like Jobs or Gates, huh?"

"Kind of."

"You guys have a lot in common, then," she observes.

I'm taken aback by this. "What do you mean?"

"Neither of you went to college. You both made your way success-fully in the world despite it. That's cool. I see why you fit." She reaches across the table and pats my hand. "You're surprised, but you shouldn't be. You've always had your shit together. Even though you had your reading disability, you still sat in class like it was no big deal. You never asked for accommodations and you went out and got a job before half the class was employed."

She's more right than she knows. Ian and I do have a lot in common. We both lost our mothers too young. We both love too fiercely. We're both a little lost without each other. I've got to stop letting insecurities get in the way of our relationship.

"So did you confront Cam?"

"I did one better. I re-recorded his voicemail to say 'You've reached Cameron aka Cheating Bastard O'Toole. I like to cheat and have sex without a condom. You may want to get a checkup to be sure I haven't passed around an STD. Leave a message.'"

"You didn't." I'm laughing so hard I have to press my napkin up to my mouth so I don't spray pizza all over the table.

"Scout's honor, I did. He deserved it. He's a technological idiot, so I went ahead and changed his passcode so he wasn't able to fix it. I think it was at least a week before he got some help and the message was changed. I heard through the grapevine that all his friends mercilessly mocked him about it, and that no one wanted to go out with him after that."

"That was genius."

"I know. It still makes me smile, even though it happened three years ago."

"I'd like to do something like that to a guy I know," I admit. "Embarrass him so much he's shunned by his friends."

"Public humiliation is hard. What'd this guy do to you?"

"Enough." I don't want to reveal that it's Ian who has a vendetta against Richard Howe. He wouldn't want me spreading his private business, and besides, what hurts Ian hurts me.

She looks thoughtfully at me but doesn't ask me to elaborate on what "enough" means. "Who is it?"

Looking around to see who is next to me, I lean in and gesture for Sarah to come close so I can avoid other people hearing. "Richard Howe."

"Ed Howe's son?" she hisses. "Ed Howe, the family-first mayoral candidate?"

"Yes," I hiss back.

"Come on. Let's go somewhere we can talk." She stands abruptly. The waiter comes over immediately. Sarah and I fight for the bill, but I tell her Ian is paying and she gives in. We walk a little ways down West Sixty-Ninth Street toward Amsterdam. I reveal a small portion of Howe's dislike for Ian and his desire to see Ian fail.

"Are you afraid that he's trying to break you and Ian up?" she asks finally.

I choose my words carefully, because I don't want to lie. "I think that he'd do anything to hurt us, Ian particularly. He's really jealous of Ian's success."

"I can see that. Who wouldn't be jealous of Ian? Rich, good-looking, has a hot girlfriend." She winks at me and I give her a weak smile. "Did he hurt you?"

"He's trying to," I say. It's as much as I feel comfortable saying, but it's the truth.

"What you really need is dirt on him. Like I got on Cam."

"I know," I say glumly.

"Look, I've got to go back to the office," she says when we reach Broadway. "The best thing I can say is to follow him around. Get on your bike and shadow him for a few days. See if there's anything you can find that would embarrass him. Once you find it, go to him and say that you'll release that information if he doesn't leave the two of you alone."

"But what kind of information?" When Ian and I first met, his goal was to use me to get information to blackmail Howe. I can't really tell Sarah that, and I know Ian would be furious if I engaged in any kind of flirtation with Howe. But following him around? Maybe there's something to Sarah's idea.

"You won't know until you follow him. Might be fun." A cab finally stops, and Sarah climbs in. "Let me know if you want help."

With that, she waves good-bye. Seconds after the cab pulls away, Steve pulls up.

"Does Ian know you're following me?" I ask. I get in because if I don't, he'll just follow me up the street.

Steve grunts once, which I take as a yes. On the ride back to Jake's office, my lunch conversation swirls around in my head. Sarah reminding me how Ian and I do fit together. Her suggestion that I follow Howe. Then there's Jake's idea that maybe I could do fieldwork. Again, it's a lot to take in but all in a good way.

♦ ♦ ♦

IAN

When I arrive at my office building downtown, Malcolm Hedder is waiting for me. He pushes away from the granite wall as I climb out of the car.

"You're a long way from Queens." He looks out of place down here in his dark wash jeans and white T-shirt, a modern day James Dean.

"Throw her back," he says without preamble.

"So she's a fish?"

"She doesn't belong with you."

"If you cared so much, you should have taken better care of her when you had the opportunity. She's mine now." Steve's turned off the vehicle and has stepped out of the car, his hand on the roof.

I shake my head in warning. I can handle this. "I'm fine," I tell Steve. "And you have better things to do."

He squints at me, making up his own mind. Having decided that I don't need him, he leaves. He needs to get up to Jake Tanner's office so that he can watch Tiny. Now more than any other time, we need to be vigilant about her safety: Malcolm is lurking outside my office, insisting on her return as if I'm holding her hostage; Howe still breathes; and now her long-lost stepfather is demanding a meeting.

"You don't know my circumstances," Malcolm protests.

He's pathetic. I advance on him. "I'd have abandoned my own mother if I had to choose between her and Tiny. But you know what? Tiny never would have made you choose. She would have helped you find a solution that worked for both of you. But you're either too stupid or selfish to realize that."

Malcolm scowls at me. "Here's what we both know: You'll get tired of her. And then where will she be?"

"Don't pretend like you know me, Hedder. I'm a choir boy compared to you." I look at my watch. "I've got other unhappy children to deal with today. Are we done here?"

"You're placing her in danger," he blurts out as I brush by him. This stops me, as he knew it would.

"From you or your father?"

"Your life is dangerous," he shoots back with narrowed eyes.

"Really? Because I'm not the one engaged in criminal activity. I believe it was the job *you* asked Tiny to do that got her beat up by a drugged-out, paranoid customer."

He has the grace to flush but persists. "She's an ordinary girl and won't have the first clue how to deal with your business dinners. How are you going to feel when she unintentionally insults someone or can't keep up with current events because she doesn't even fucking read? You'll ruin her."

"This is why you lost her, Hedder. You've never valued her highly enough. You cared more for your own problems than you cared about her. I don't care what anyone else thinks of Tiny because she's a goddamn revelation and anyone who doesn't recognize that can go fuck themselves. Have a good day," I say pleasantly and walk through the revolving doors.

CHAPTER 4

As predicted, Louis Durand is standing at my office door when I arrive. After dealing with Malcolm, my patience is in short supply. From the look of annoyance on my admin Rose's face, he's been there long enough to keep her from getting her own job done.

"Ian," Louis cries in greeting. He's trying to hide his impatience, but the rhythmic tapping of the prospectus in his hand gives his true feelings away.

"Good morning, Rose. Louis." I take the printout from Rose containing the meetings and phone conferences set for today along with any important messages. I flip through each of the pages quickly. "Tell the *Times* and *Wall Street Journal* 'no' and schedule a meeting for Friday with Keller. It can be a lunch meeting. Make it for Megu at the UN Plaza. He likes that place. Also, have we arranged everything with the Frick?"

She nods. "The tickets will be delivered to your home this week. The first gift amount has been sent, and there's a draft of the commemorative announcement in your inbox. I've marked it as important."

"Good."

"You haven't read your emails yet?" Louis yelps in dismay. "I've sent four this morning and seven last night. All of them are urgent!"

"All of your messages can't be urgent." I don't feel guilty about not looking at my inbox after leaving work early yesterday. Jake had called at five to tell me he was sending Tiny home, and I wanted to be there when she arrived. Reading Louis's emails was the furthest thing from my mind last night, and I told him so. "I had better things to do last night than read business emails. And, frankly, you should have too. All work, Louis."

He scoffs. "That's not the maxim you lived by three months ago. Ever since—" He stops, perhaps recognizing that I'll not tolerate any negativity about Tiny. "Look, since you're *finally* here, we can get started."

I'm halfway into my office when Louis finishes his sentence.

"I didn't realize I was on the clock," I said mildly. "Or that I answered to you."

He stammers out a response. "Of course not. I meant I was just eager to go over the reports with you. These deals aren't going to be around for long."

Quickly, I calculate the pros and cons of firing him on the spot for clear insubordination. I hired him because he was bright and hungry. His great weakness is his tendency to make emotion-based decisions. Investments should be done without sentiment. I've been trying to train that out of him. He needs to lead with his head more and not his hurt feelings.

Two years ago, he'd wanted to scuttle a deal with a small transport company. The owners were a few guys from the Midwest who liked to order their steaks well done. They were rough around the edges, and Louis had been affronted by nearly everything—from how they held their forks to the condition of the home office, which was really nothing more than a shed. He'd claimed that it was a sign of the immaturity of the company, but I'd invested over his objections. Since then it's been over-performing the paper estimates. They were more interested in pouring money back into the fleet and their employees than making sure the home office looked good. I approved. Louis did not.

That might have been the start of the growing rift between us, but the last three months spent with Tiny have driven a sharp wedge into the fissure.

Last year was the best year Kerr Inc. had seen in the decade of its existence. Before Tiny, my sole focus had been ensuring my place at the top of the heap of snarling animals that comprises the financial world.

I just didn't realize how lonely it was up there until she came along. Once you reach a certain level, it's not about how many things you can buy—how many properties, cars, priceless works of art—it's how far and hard can you push yourself. But Louis isn't there yet, either financially or mentally. I suspect he might be looking at shortcuts to the top, which means I'll have to let him go regardless.

His discomfort is evident, but I make no effort to dispel it. He should know that I'm unhappy with him.

"Let's get to work then."

He enters the office quickly, and we get down to business. I take two meetings in the morning and review a report my team of investment analysts had done. A tech firm in Seattle was working on wearable technology and another company was making advancements in light refracting clothes that can render one invisible to the naked eye. Unless I get prototypes, I'm not investing millions in either company.

"I think the military tech firm is more interesting only because it has more upside. Government contracts are great because they are constantly overpaying," Louis says as we sit in my office sifting through the morning presentations.

"So our entire investment strategy hinges on how good the company is at fleecing the US government out of its money?"

He shrugs. "Someone's going to benefit from that stupidity. Why not us?"

"Why not indeed?" I say dryly. "Both these companies can be outpaced tomorrow. There's a competing cloaking technology being developed as we speak, and we don't have enough information to make an educated guess as to which is going to prevail. I'm not willing to back either until I've got a good sense about which will be VHS and which will be Betamax."

"What about the wearable tech?" Louis urges. He's eager to make some sort of deal today, as if he can't wait to spend Kerr Inc. money regardless of whether the deal makes sense. I test an idea that I've been debating for the last month. Sophie Corielli's death has affected me strongly, but in a different way than it affected her daughter.

I no longer want to spend every day shut up in my office. I've done little traveling except for work. I've done little entertaining except for work. I've reached the pinnacle of the financial world at the relatively young age of thirty-two because all I've done since the age of thirteen is work. I'd wake up thinking about ways to make money and execute those ideas until I was too tired to stand. Then I'd dream about more ways to make money.

But now my dreams are full of Tiny and the life we could have together. I've made enough money. Now it's time to enjoy it.

"I'm thinking of winding down Kerr Inc."

"Winding it down?" Louis shoots out of his chair and leans his hands on my desk, a giant thing made of my favorite wood, walnut. Thankfully, there's enough space between the two of us that I avoid being drenched by his saliva-filled horror. "You can't wind this down. You love it. It's your life!"

I toss the prospectus for the military firm on the desk and wander over to the windows. From the thirty-fourth floor, I can see Staten Island and the ferries. I wonder if Tiny has ever visited the Statue of Liberty. I haven't. I can count on one hand the number of New York City monuments I've visited.

The Empire State Building—but only because a woman I was dating wanted to have sex up there. What was her name again? Bettina? I remember the initial thrill of the possibility of being caught, but Bettina kept pushing the envelope. A dark corner on the top of the observation deck after I'd slipped the security guard a Benjamin was fine for me. I hadn't balked at screwing her on a Sunday morning at the Standard overlooking the High Line. But when I figured out she enjoyed exhibitionism far more than she enjoyed my cock, I sent her a nice tennis bracelet from Tiffany's and told her that there was someone out there better than me.

Funny how the thrill of those illicit activities weren't even a tenth as exciting as just thinking about fucking Tiny.

"*Was* my life," I corrected him, not bothering to look back. "It's just money. You and I both have enough to enjoy every little luxury even if we never work again."

"Maybe you do, but I don't," Louis retorts.

This confession draws me away from the view of the harbor. He's red-faced and not a little anxious. He fiddles with his tie and doesn't look me in the eye.

"What is it?" I sigh. "Women? Drugs? Gambling?"

"None of them. I just haven't been at this as long as you have," he mumbles.

"Maybe I'd believe that if you'd look at me when you said that instead of talking to your tie tack."

"Sorry if my ambition is making you upset," he snarls. From chagrin to attack in less than a minute, Louis is leaking defensiveness all over the floor.

Disappointment sets in. The lure of *more* was going to take another man down. Although on that subject, I'm the last who should talk. I've been making money hand over fist because I'm good at it. It used to fill my days and my nights with something akin to gratification, but now I realize it was a false sense of happiness. *Things* are nothing compared to a person. Louis's downfall is as much my fault as his own. I'd hired him, and because I'd failed to be a good mentor, I was going to lose him. I decide to change the subject as much for Louis's sake as for mine.

"How about investing in a cycling company? Green measures are expanding and cycling is becoming more popular. Why don't you check it out?"

Louis doesn't respond immediately. A raised eyebrow finally jerks him to attention. "I'll get right on that."

"Good. I'll expect a report in the morning." Without waiting for a response, I pick up my landline to begin the eradication of the one black mark in my life. Tiny is right. I've allowed this to linger far too long. A little pressure on his wallet and he'd leave his family just to save his own skin.

"Howe speaking."

"Richard. It's Ian Kerr. How are you?"

"Good. I'm surprised you're calling. Surprised but pleased. What can I do for you?" His uneasiness is evident.

"I could bullshit you all day, Howe, but you should know that you are a—" How had Tiny put it? Oh yes. "A boil on the ass of humanity."

He starts to sputter. "Just because you have had a modicum of success does not mean you can speak to me—"

I cut him off. "Of course I can. Your family barely has two dimes to rub together. You probably don't look at your bills or your mail. No doubt you've hired someone you can't afford to do that for you. But if you had, you'd notice that all of your bills are sent from one company. IKK Asset Management."

I hear only his heavy breathing on the phone. This is fun. I should have done this years ago. "IKK stands for Ian Kincaid Kerr," I explain.

"B-b-but why?" he stutters.

My good humor is wiped away. "You know why. I'm going to give you an opportunity to do the decent thing. Divorce your wife, renounce your family. Leave the city. I don't care where you live, but do it quietly because if I hear even one whisper of your name, I'll end you. Start making arrangements. The longer it takes you to leave town, the more debt I will call in."

"Surely whatever harm you think I've done to you can be amelio-rated in some fashion. Ian, old boy, we should meet. In person," he yelps.

"I can barely stomach talking to you on the phone."

I hang up. Why I hadn't threatened Howe earlier I don't even know. Some misguided idea of chivalry; not wanting to do to Cecilia Howe what Richard had done to my mother. Foolish reasons in retrospect.

The conversation should have left me elated, but instead my stom-ach is churning. I need to see Tiny, but I don't know if I should confess after she'd admired my restraint this morning. I run a hand down my face. I've rarely been uncertain before, because I've lived life without fear.

Now I have her, and I'm fucking terrified I'll lose her, and then I'll be empty again.

She picks up on the fourth ring sounding harried.

"Ian, hi, can you hold for a minute?"

"Sure." *No. I want to see you immediately. I need to hold you.*

After a moment she returns. "Sorry. I don't think I'm made for dispatching. If you're calling for an afternoon break, I can't. I feel over-whelmed, and I don't want to leave the desk. And I'm afraid if I do wander out of the office, I'll never return. Also you need to eat lunch at a normal time like a normal person instead of at three in the after-noon." She lowers her voice to a whisper. "How can you stand to work inside all the time?"

"You get used to it." I push aside the disappointment. I'll see her tonight. It's soon enough.

"Blergh. I don't want to get used to it. I miss biking." Her voice sounds plaintive.

I don't bring up the topic of not working at all because I don't want to get into another argument, but the biking issue is one I can address. "I was thinking I should invest in a cycling company. What was the name of that bike you liked in the SoHo store?"

"You can do that? You can just decide, hey, I want to buy a com-pany because my girlfriend likes what they make?"

"Yes, I can do that." My lips curve into a smile. She's probably shaking her head right now.

"That's weird. Very weird. I've got to go. Don't buy any companies that I like."

"Why not?"

"Because! You can't go spending money like that just because I think they make cool stuff."

"That's exactly how people should invest, Tiny. You buy things that people around you like because that means that those companies are developing not only brand loyalty but producing a product that meets market desires. It's an important part of market research."

"Really? Well, I guess that's why you're making millions a day and I'm a bike courier."

"You're not a courier anymore."

Silence.

"Thanks for the reminder. Look, I've got to go."

With that, she disconnects.

Fuck. I screwed that up.

"By the glower on your face, I'm guessing you're having lunch with me today," Louis says with forced cheer. I can see he wants to put aside the morning's uncomfortableness.

"Your powers of observation are legendary." I drawl but willingly go along. There's no need to fight with Louis. I've come to a decision about him.

"It's part of why you pay me so much. Come on, I'll buy you lunch and you can explain why you're wearing that loud monstrosity of a suit." Louis stands at the office door and pushes it open.

Heaving to my feet, I finger the lapel. "Tiny picked it out."

He rolls his eyes. "She is overtaking your life."

"You say that like it's a bad thing." My phone dings and I see it's a text from Tiny. It's a small series of pictures. Tiny is dyslexic, so when she texts it's usually emojis. I refuse to feel weird about that, given it's the best way for us to communicate. The image of a bicycle, water, and sun next to a sandwich tell me that she wants to go the beach this weekend, bike around, and then eat. I look forward to it. Clicking on the emoji icon for my phone, I search for one that says yes. I settle for the thumbs up.

"You're worse than a preteen," Louis says impatiently.

"Louis, if I wanted your opinion, I'd ask for it." Sticking my phone into my breast pocket, I exit the office. Louis is on my heels. Pausing at Rose's desk, I say, "We're off to lunch, but we'll be back for the Sun-Corp presentation."

We cab it to Morimoto's for lunch since I've instructed Steve to sit outside Jake Tanner's office and make sure no one harms Tiny. I wonder if she's figured out that he's been reassigned to bodyguard duty. I'm guessing no because she hasn't said anything about him to me, and she's not the type to accept being followed without some discussion.

When she's not so raw from her mother's death, and she's more certain about what she wants to do with her future, we can talk about the safety measures I'd like her to take. For now, I want to keep the lifestyle changes from scaring her off, but if she's going to be with me she's going to have to accept that power and a lot of money attract a lot of desperate people.

Steve's doesn't like the subterfuge, but he's keeping quiet for now because discretion is part of his job description.

After ordering, my mind wanders to Tiny again. Steve should deliver her some lunch. Feeding that woman is my new obsession. Along with fucking her, of course. I text Jake.

Are you feeding my woman?

If I say yes, will you view it as an act of aggression and threaten to kill me?

Not today. I'm more concerned that she's eating. She wouldn't leave her desk.

I'm pretty sure she hates this job even though she's doing fine.

Is it her dyslexia?

No, it's that she has a desk. I have men like that. Hate desks. Can't work behind them.

Keep your men away from her.

Wait, is it your name on the door here? I thought it was mine. It's cute, you thinking you can order me around.

The only thing I'd like to order is lunch for Tiny. If it's too much of a burden for you, then I'll have Steve do it.

It pains me that you'd use a prime machine like Steve to run errands. She's already had lunch with her friend, but I can get your six-figure bodyguard to buy her a sandwich from 'wichcraft, so stop texting me and go buy some company and harass those employees rather than mine.

"In my fantasies you're currently texting Kaga, asking his advice on SunCorp," Louis interrupts.

I text Thanks to Jake and then slip my phone into my pocket.

"Your fantasy life sucks then." I take a sip of Perrier and pick up my chopsticks.

"Don't you feel like you've been drifting these past couple of months?"

Deliberately, I place my utensils back on the table and fold my hands together. Piercing Louis with a look, I ask, "Are you bored, Louis? Because if you're bored and don't like the pace of our acquisitions, I am happy to write out a letter of recommendation that you can use to shop for your next job."

My threat has its intended effect. He clears his throat after a minute. "So it's like that," he says with disappointment.

"It's like that," I say softly.

"Then no, I'm happy with whatever pace you set." He gives me a tight smile.

"Great. You and Anna should have dinner with us some night. Let me know when you're free."

"Thanks."

The rest of lunch is spent in silence, but I do text Kaga on the cab ride back, not to pacify Louis but because the chase has always excited me.

The meeting with SunCorp goes long, and it's not until six that we manage to shunt everyone out of the office. Kaga had left a message with Rose halfway through that he'd heard good things about SunCorp and that the management team was enlightened. I did like them and thought that the investment might make sense, which was why our meeting ran over.

In the washroom attached to my office, I quickly wipe off the residue of the day. I don't have the time to take a shower even though the attached bathroom contains one. Having a bathroom wasn't a luxury but a necessity. There were weeks that I would sleep in the office, trying to establish myself, trying to absorb reams of data so I could best decide which investment was the best one.

I've been overclocking my engine for years, and Louis has been with me for the past five. It wasn't unusual for us to work on deals for seventy-two hours at a time, only allowing a few power naps to make sure we weren't so tired that we'd miss something important. And then there were the week-long regulatory meetings when we actually were in the process of acquiring, not just investing. I shouldn't have been so hard on him. Ever since I met Tiny, my entire schedule has been off. Acquisitions aren't as exciting as they once were.

I hunger for something different now, more physical, more personal. The more time I spend away from her, the more I realize how none of this is very important. Not whether SunCorp can accelerate the harnessing of solar energy and increase stored wattage power and definitely not whether that military tech firm can create an invisible cloak. None of it compares to her.

I'd probably enjoy myself more if I was sitting in the corner of Jake's front office watching her than enduring any of these meetings. Although I'm not sure how long I'd last before I'd have her bent over the desk.

The mere thought of her ass-up, her thighs wet with arousal, and her tits pressed against the wood desk, makes my pants uncomfortably tight. I decide not to relieve myself. I'll be home soon.

CHAPTER 5

Tiny looks exhausted when I arrive home. We eat in near silence, and she doesn't begin talking until we're in the living room enjoying a little after-dinner wine.

"I feel like a fool complaining about how tired I am when my ass was stuck in a chair the whole day," she says. I set my glass on the table and gesture for her to turn around so I can rub her tense shoulder muscles.

"Exerting a lot of energy is exhausting. Doesn't matter if it is physical, mental, or emotional."

"I used to bike sixty miles a day, and I never felt like this." Groaning, she dips her head forward in a wordless gesture for me to continue.

Giving her a gentle push forward, I help her into a prone position on the long sectional cushions in the living room. "Let me help you."

She lies there while I unfasten her pants and remove her shirt.

"I don't think being Jake's dispatcher is the right thing for me. I'm making so many errors taking messages and my notes are filled with pictures because it takes me more time to write out a word, but it's like forcing everyone to play Pictionary with me. I feel stupid. I hate that feeling."

I avoid the topic of her previous job as a bike courier. "Give it some time. You've only been there a few weeks."

She grunts her disgust into the cushion but allows me to unhook her bra, a lemon-yellow confection of lace and silk. My hands smooth over the curve of her shoulders and down over the blades into the hollow of her spine. She has a few dark freckles on her back and a mole halfway down on the right side.

I follow the line of her ribs from the back around to her side and try to rub away her tension with light pressure. Gradually she begins to relax, her limbs loosening and her breathing evening out. I remove her panties so that I can rub her ass better.

"Sorry for complaining," she mumbles.

"I hear no complaints." I lean over and press a kiss against a bare shoulder. "Just my woman sharing her day with me."

Besides, I think, *how can I fix what's wrong if she doesn't tell me her troubles?*

"Do you plan on doing anything else now that I'm all naked and relaxed?"

My lips curve against her skin. "I have many plans for you."

I allow my fingers to brush the roundness of her breasts and sweep over the apples of her ass cheeks in feather-light strokes until she's squirming beneath me, trying to turn over. But my weight pins her down.

"I'd like you to execute those plans now," she says, and this time, her breathing isn't as even or as deep.

I slide my fingers between her legs. "Let's see if you're ready." Liquid heat greets me, and we both moan as I slide two fingers inside her. Her ass rises to allow me greater access, and the tight rosette of her asshole peeks at me from between her round cheeks.

I drag my thumb down the crevice to her pucker and circle it. "Someday, bunny, I'm going to take you here."

"I don't know," she begins, lowering her hips as if to hide from me, but I lift her back up as I stroke her tight cunt.

"You'll like it." My thumb dips inside the little hole, and I feel her walls close around me, sucking me instinctively.

Slowly I begin to fuck her with my fingers, lightly in the ass and more forcefully inside her. "Touch yourself, bunny," I order.

Her hand dips between her legs to work her clit and it takes almost no time before her orgasm is upon her.

"Oh, fuckkkk," she moans as we stroke together toward her finish. Her walls are like a vise on my fingers, making me use more force to plunge in and out of her. She barely notices that my thumb is knuckle-deep in her ass. I am hard and aching behind the wool and cotton barrier of my clothes.

"Come on, bunny. Let it go." I curl my thumb downward and she explodes like a rocket.

"God, oh *god*!" she shouts. Her ass pushes hard against my hand and then I'm drenched with her come.

I pull her into my lap, wiping my hands on my abandoned suit coat. Three-thousand-dollar suit serving as a post-coitus serviette? Sounds about right.

"Shh, bunny," I croon, rocking her a bit as she shakes and shudders in post-orgasmic delight. "Liked that, did you?"

"I don't know. Maybe it was the pre-fingering massage that did it," she snarks back, gulping in air.

"Maybe," I say. "Let's go upstairs now. My cock may break in half if it doesn't get some attention."

"We can't have that."

I take special care not to overwork her that evening so that I can start the next day off right. This time we share a shower in the morning, and my smug smile sits on my face until I arrive at the office.

◆ ◆ ◆

"You have an unscheduled visitor." Rose informs me when I arrive. She does not like unscheduled visitors. Her strict adherence to routine is what makes her a great assistant. "He said you'd want to see him."

She hands me a card. It isn't a business card but rather a calling card with the name MITCH HEDDER in a bold but old-fashioned font. Underneath his name, the lettering reads "purveyor of fine things."

What a fucking tool. "He's right," I answer. "I'll see him today, but from here on out, he'll need an appointment."

She smiles in satisfaction, and I leave the card on her desk to throw away. Rose has placed Mitch in the large conference room down the hall from my office. The table seats thirteen, six on either side, with my chair at the head. Unlike my office, this room is modern with a glass-topped steel table and white leather Herman Miller chairs. One side of the room is paneled in walnut and the other is a bay of windows over-looking the Hudson.

Body language is as important as any words being voiced, and the glass-topped conference table prevents my guests from hiding their reactions under a layer of wood. With the clear table surface, I can view every leg twitch and hand wring.

Mitch Hedder must realize this, because he's not sitting. Instead, his hands are tucked into the pockets of his tan dress slacks and his back is turned. I can't read his expression or observe his hands, but I can see the determined set of his shoulders. He's tense and his legs are slightly braced apart. There's no question that he's looking at a reflection of the door, watching for me.

"Mr. Hedder," I say, entering. I pull out the seat at the head of the table and sit down. He can stand like a lackey or sit below me. Either way I'm in control, and as a bonus, I don't have to shake his hand. With a wave, I gesture for him to sit.

He hesitates, no doubt wondering if sitting or standing gives him an advantage. Neither, of course. He's had to come to me, and therefore he's already the supplicant. Finally recognizing the futility of standing, he rounds the table so he's seated with his back to the door but can still look out the windows.

Hedder is fit. His broad shoulders are encased in expensive and expertly tailored double-breasted blue wool. Stick a nautical cap on this guy and he'd look like he stepped off a yacht in Palm Beach. With a full head of multicolored blond hair, which he no doubt dyes regularly, I can see his appeal to a certain class of older women. Fifteen, twenty years ago, his allure would have been even more potent, and it's easy to imagine him charming Tiny's sweet mother off her feet.

"Beautiful view you have here."

"Thank you."

"Employ many people?" His question is casual, but I don't make the mistake of thinking anything he wants to know is just friendly interest.

"Not many. Around one hundred or so."

He shakes his head in mock disbelief. I don't for a minute believe that he doesn't know exactly how many people are employed here. "So few to run such a large enterprise, but I suppose it's the holding you refer to, rather than your varied and far-flung interests. Don't you even have business in the Far East?"

"The Far East? I didn't know that term was used anymore. But if you're referring to the continent of Asia, I don't know many who aren't interested in the Asian market, either for importing or exporting purposes."

He turns away from the window to face me, hands lying lightly in his lap. "A billion-dollar multinational company headed by a man under the age of thirty-five is unheard of if you aren't a tech genius. Yet here you are. A financial savant. A man known to have never stepped wrong. Whose investment savvy is the stuff of legend."

"I've had losses and mistakes. I suspect they don't fit with the current narrative," I respond. His flattery is the gradual build to some great crescendo that he expects will evoke a response. Either I erupt in anger or effusive pleasure. I don't think he's decided which way he'll play it. My nonchalance is making him rethink whatever scheme he's contrived.

Many people might underestimate Hedder, but this man is a predator. I know this because I am too, but my prey are companies and, well, a certain five-feet-four brunette with light green eyes. Lonely women are Hedder's targets, based on the research I've had done on him.

"Yes. Ian Kerr is a golden boy. Everyone wants to touch him, hoping that his brilliance will rub off on them. But no one becomes as successful as you in such a short time without having a few skeletons in his closet." With this opening salvo, he smiles as if to lessen the sting of his accusations. He is right, of course. I have many skeletons in my closet. The money I used to build my current empire has been washed clean, but it had unsavory origins. I don't really give a shit unless it bothers Tiny.

I don't think it would. She, of all people, would understand how desperation can drive one to take measures that could fall outside the laws of state and propriety. If you were starving and someone you love was hurting, you'd do anything. She gets that.

So does Mitch to some extent; he'd do anything to keep himself happy.

Because I don't care what Mitch thinks, I remain silent. We stare at each other—or at least I try to look him in the eye—but he can't maintain contact for more than a couple seconds before he drops his gaze.

"I know we have plans for dinner this Friday, but I wanted to come and take your measure. For Tiny's sake." His eyes flick over me. The dollar signs add up as he calculates the cost of my suit, my watch, and even my pocket square. The perusal ends as quickly as it starts and his attention moves back to the window. He watches himself smooth down the lapel of his jacket. As he stares at his reflection longer, I realize that he's more interested in looking at himself than watching others.

A narcissist to the core. But I should've known that by his history of nonstop pleasure seeking. He needs to be watched carefully because

Sophie Corielli, Tiny's mom, wouldn't have fallen for him unless he wielded some sort of magic. Sophie was too smart to be taken in by an ordinary man.

"I'm interested in everything to do with Tiny," I respond. Beyond the yachting gear, I note he's wearing a gold Rolex. Everything about him says money, from the carefully cut and dyed hair to the upscale clothes and his well-manicured hands. And it makes me want to leap over the table and throttle him.

"Then we have a mutual interest." He leans forward, tearing his eyes off his reflection and directing them toward me. His expression is set to earnest, but the only thing this man is earnest about is himself. "My son told me that Tiny was settling down, and with her mother gone—God rest her soul—it's my duty to take up the parental reins. Sophie would have wanted that."

There's no question in my mind that the very last thing Sophie would want is Mitch Hedder hanging around her precious daughter. I don't know why their four-year relationship ended, other than Sophie had gotten tired of Mitch's roving eye. I do know that Mitch has spent the last seven years completely devoid of contact with Tiny and Sophie.

While they were struggling to make ends meet, while they were crushed under crippling medical bills from Sophie's fight with mantle cell leukemia, while Tiny had to turn to delivering drugs for her step-brother to make sure that they could afford treatment when Sophie's cancer came out of remission, while all of that was happening, Mitch Hedder was accumulating enough wealth to deck himself out in designer threads and twenty-thousand-dollar watches. And not once in that time did he reach out to help them.

Strangling him with my own hands would probably be too good an end for him.

"It surprises me that you would say that, given your lack of attention and care toward the Corielli ladies in the last, oh, seven years or so." I find it a struggle to maintain an even tone, my anger toward him is so great.

He doesn't notice. With a careful hand, he smooths down the back of his hair. "I was under strict instruction by Sophie to never darken her doorstep. I wanted to honor that."

"Even when she had cancer?"

"There was little I could do." He gives a negligent shrug, one shoulder raised slightly to express . . . helplessness? Maybe that move works with the ladies down in Florida, but it just pisses me the hell off.

"Your watch could have paid off half their medical bills."

We both look at the gold-encrusted timepiece. He grimaces. "This old thing?" After a rueful shake of his head, he says, "No, this piece wouldn't have touched even a tenth of the debt. You should know. I heard you paid it all off and that you're planning on donating even more in memory of dear Soph."

My blood boils even hotter. "You knew exactly how much their debt was?"

"Malcolm kept me informed from time to time." He looks over his shoulder then, perhaps feeling my animosity creep down his spine. "I suppose it's too early for a whiskey. I'm parched."

"It's barely ten in the morning, Mr. Hedder."

"You know the old saying. It's five o'clock somewhere." His smile dies slowly at my stony glare.

"Not only is it barely ten in the morning, but you've wasted fifteen minutes of my day. That's fifteen minutes too many. You have five minutes to state your business, and then I'm walking out of here."

"Now wait a minute. I'm here to look out for Tiny. If you care about her, as you profess, then you won't mind my hanging around a bit. I've got some things of her mother's that Tiny might be interested in. Unless you've got something to hide, I can't imagine why I'd be a bother to you."

"Cut the bullshit, Hedder. I'll summarize your visit. You show up uninvited to my office. You suggest that I am of questionable character. You challenge my suitability to marry—yes, marry," I repeat at his look of surprise, "a woman you have ignored for the whole of her adult life, leaving her and her mother to struggle for every penny, to be worn down by worry, to be crushed under a mountain of debt while you act as the pretty appendage for some rich old socialite in Palm Beach or perhaps even San Tropez. You fail to show up for the funeral of this woman's mother, and yet you believe that we care about your opinion of us?"

I stand up and proceed toward the door, not even waiting to see if Mitch follows.

"For your sake, I hope you are correct and Tiny's longing for a parent doesn't overcome her newfound feelings for you," Mitch mutters.

It's a warning, but not an effective one. There are things I might lose Tiny to—her infernal sense of pride and need for independence is one—but a man who cheated on and abandoned her mother? Never.

I don't give him the satisfaction of a response other than allowing the door to close behind me. I stop at Rose's desk. "Our visitor is still in the conference room. If he isn't gone in the next five minutes, call security."

Before I can sit down at my desk Louis is at the door.

"What is it?" I ask impatiently. After enduring Mitch Hedder's presumptuousness, I find I have little patience to tolerate Louis's whining.

"I saw you taking a meeting." His tone is accusatory. "Should I have been in there?"

"If you should have been in the meeting, I would have invited you." My response is a dismissal, but this is a different Louis than the one I hired, one whose ability to take a hint, read nuance, and interpret a signal is suddenly nonexistent.

"Given that you're distracted by other things, I should be in these meetings. For the protection of Kerr Inc.," he says frostily.

He's overstepped and doesn't even realize it. "I *am* Kerr Inc. I shouldn't have to remind you of this." I reapply myself to the regulatory paperwork on SunCorp and dismiss him. He stands uncertainly at the doorway for a few moments. His suit pants make a whisking sound as he shifts his weight from foot to foot. He wants to retort, to say something, to take some power back, but I am Ian Kerr and Louis is a mere employee. He's feeling that insignificance and wants me to allay it. It's not going to happen. He's done here.

I continue to ignore him and he finally drifts away.

◆ ◆ ◆

TINY

I tell Jake I have to take a long lunch. It's the fourth long lunch I've taken this week. He merely nods and shoos me out. My guess is he thinks I'm having sex with Ian. I'm not, although that would be better than what I actually am doing, which is cabbing it down to Midtown and loitering around Richard Howe's office. So far I've followed Howe to four lunches with various clients and have taken several surreptitious pictures with my smartphone.

Howe enjoys eating fish. He orders it almost every time, and he tends to drink a lot. He also stares at the waitresses' asses nonstop. I report all of this to Sarah.

"Field work is pretty boring," I tell her.

"More boring than sitting inside at a desk and answering phones?"

"Good point."

"Who does he have lunch with?"

"No one interesting. A bunch of guys wearing blue suits. You know, the uniforms the private school kids wear on the Upper East Side? It's like these are the same kids wearing the same uniforms, only the kids are taller and the sizes are larger."

"It looks like that because they are the same kids," Sarah points out. "Any women in the group?"

"No. The only women they encounter are the waitresses. I'm not getting anything out of this."

"You've only followed him for one week and only at lunch. You have to vary it."

"What do I tell Ian? I'm sorry I can't be home tonight because I'm stalking this guy we both can't stand."

"Then you'll have to hope that something exciting happens during lunch."

"Sarah, have you been to the Aquarium?" I ask abruptly. An idea—probably a bad one—starts to formulate. Ian had once said that Howe is at the hottest clubs all the time, and right now there is no hotter club than Kaga's Aquarium.

"I've heard of it. That's the club with the pools on the VIP level and the giant shark tanks?"

"That's the one. Would you like to go?"

"God, I'd love to, but do you know how expensive it is? Even if I wanted to stand in line for two hours, which I don't, isn't the cheapest drink in there like twenty dollars? I'd have to suck on the same rum and Coke all night."

"Ian knows the owner," I murmur.

"Are you saying . . ." she trails off and then lets out a squeak of delight. "Is it crass for me to say yes, hallelujah, yes?"

"No, it's a pretty cool place." I hurriedly add, "Howe might be there."

"Ohh," she says. "Then yes, let's go. We can follow him around and record him doing stuff. Good call."

"He's leaving, gotta run. I'll let you know the details about the Aquarium."

I hang up before she responds. Howe looks across the street and for a moment, I wonder if he sees me, recognizes me. He steps toward the edge of the sidewalk, but a car passes and he's forced backward. I take the opportunity to turn and look in a window display, pretending to admire the dresses. In the glass, I can barely make out his form. He's standing motionless, still staring at me. My heart is beating extra loudly in my ears. Should I run? If he comes up to me, what will I say, other than *You're a piece of shit?* Actually, I'd like to say something to him. I half turn before I realize he's already gone.

Deflated, I walk up to the corner to hail a cab. When I get back to the office, Jake is gone. There's a white envelope taped on the door and inside is a note with words on it. I frown, because even though I know Jake wants me to read, he usually leaves me a voicemail. It takes me several minutes to read the two sentences, but when I do I realize it isn't from Jake at all.

"Don't poke a hornet's nest. You'll get stung."

I look around, an odd sense of dread gripping me. Nobody's staring at me. Everything looks normal, just another day at the office. I read the message again though and realize with a chill little feeling in my veins that someone is on to me. Someone knows I've been following Howe. Or . . . someone is following me.

Feeling uneasy, I tuck the message in the desk and try to brush it aside. That afternoon, the phone rings several times but no one ever says anything. I realize after the fifth one, hang-ups are fucking creepy.

CHAPTER 6

IAN

That evening I take Tiny to a rooftop restaurant in Brooklyn on an invitation from Kaga, who claimed he wanted to get to know Tiny better.

"I think he's lonely," I tell Tiny as Steve takes us across the river.

"Does he have any family here?"

"His sister visits from time to time, but he's largely a solitary creature, which is odd to say about someone whose business is entertaining thousands a night."

"Have you been friends a long time?"

"For many years. We met at one of his nightclubs, in fact. I believe he thought I was selling drugs, isn't that right, Steve?"

Steve grunts. We all understand that was a *yes* in Steve talk.

Tiny's lips curve up. "What were you doing?"

"Nothing so illegal as selling drugs but perhaps nothing exactly appropriate either," I admit. "I was meeting with a chemist who claimed to have inside knowledge on a shocking drug. It all turned out to be a bunch of nonsense which amused Kaga to no end. He brought me up to his office and proceeded to tell me that backroom deals belonged in dark alleys and dusty stockrooms and not in plush velvet club banquettes where bottle service was a grand an hour."

"So cheap," she said faintly indicating she thought it was anything but inexpensive.

"Exactly what I told Kaga. I gave him the tip to stay away from the pharmaceutical company. If anything, the chemist's willingness to spill secrets indicated a rather ill-run company. Others bought into the fake inside information and lost quite a bit of money."

"But you and Kaga came out smelling sweet," she concludes.

"We did. We've played cards together; sometimes jog together." *Engaged in sordid pursuit of easy women at one time or another.* "Over time, we have become friends."

"I've lost so many of mine," she admitted. "I'm glad Sarah called me. I can barely remember the names of everyone I graduated with, let alone keep track of their marriages, divorces, and jobs."

I worry that Sarah is using Tiny for Tiny's newfound connections, but I keep that to myself. No sense in tainting something she enjoys with my cynicism.

"Did I mention how lovely you look tonight?" Tiny's hair is stick-straight and her gorgeous breasts appear unbound again beneath a heavily sequined top in navy. She's wearing a matching navy satin skirt. On her feet are silver sandals.

"What color today?" I ask, sliding a hand over her knee. I'd left before she had dressed for the day. Every piece of lingerie she owns I've bought for her. Some of the items I purchased before we were even a couple, during the chase, when I wasn't sure exactly what I wanted from her other than sex. Others I've bought since. It's my favorite type of gift. Truly, it's not even a gift for her. It's a selfish present, one that I enjoy far more than she does.

Seeing the lace and silk and satin that I've bought on her golden skin is as pleasurable as anything I've ever done. The cloth that covers her sweet sex and the ties that bind her breasts are all chosen by me, hand-picked and purchased. When her arousal wets the fabric between her legs, that's fabric that I've bought. She belongs to me.

Soon everything she wears will be purchased by my money. It's a crass sense of ownership I'm seeking. Fleeting too. She could leave me and take everything with her or leave it all behind, but for now, it thrills me to know that every part of her intimate, secret body is touched by something I've paid for.

"Ian," she hisses, pushing my hand away and nodding toward Steve. She's prudish at times when it comes to sex in the car. She's determined to be modest in front of Steve.

"He doesn't care," I say. I pay him a lot of money not to care. Steve hits a button and the privacy screen goes up but not before I see his eyes roll. It's hard to say who he thinks is sillier—Tiny for being embarrassed or me for not being able to keep my hands to myself. "And now he can't see."

"But he knows," she protests weakly.

"Who cares?" I whisper in her ear. "Tell me what color."

"Mint green," she answers with a moan as my hand slips under the lace to stroke her soft skin.

"When you're sitting at your desk, thinking of me, do you get wet knowing that I picked these out for you?" I ask pinching her clit lightly.

She inhales sharply. "I get wet thinking about you," she finally whispers. Her legs shift restlessly. I know what she wants. She wants my tongue. My fingers. My cock. And she'll have it all.

"What do you do? Do you rub yourself under the desk? Do you go to the bathroom? Tell me." I push her panties aside and thrust two fingers inside her.

"Sometimes I'll press myself under my desk," she says. "Just to ease the ache."

"Does it work?" I pump slowly. Her left hand closes around my wrist, but not to tug me away; she draws me closer. I want to hear her talk. I need to hear it so that when I'm at work, I can visualize what she's doing during her day.

"No, not really." She bites the side of her lip. "I can't make myself feel as good as you can."

"Oh, bunny." At her words, my head and cock swell so large I feel like I will burst. "I'm always here for you. You need me during the day, just call me. My favorite thing in all the world is making you feel good."

Her cheeks pinken. "I can't call you in the middle of the day to come and screw me," she chastises.

"Why not?"

"Because it wouldn't be professional." She wrinkles her nose as if professional is a dirty word.

"Jake is running a security firm, not a bank."

"Still, I don't think it's right for me to ask you to drive all the way uptown for some afternoon delight."

I grin at her phrasing. "It'd be Steve who'd do the driving. And, bunny, there isn't anything I'd rather do than drive uptown to have sex with you."

Unbuckling my belt with my free hand, I unzip and shove my trousers down just far enough to release my very erect cock. When I grip it, she licks her lips. Jesus *fuck*. She is so hot.

"You need me, I'm there." I stroke myself, spreading my pre-cum all over. Her eyes hungrily follow my every move. "But since we're both here now, I guess it's an academic discussion. Do you want to ride me or shall I make that very important decision?"

Unfortunately Steve intones "five minutes" over the intercom. With regret, I pull my fingers out and wipe them on a handkerchief.

"I hate you," she whimpers. "I'm worked up. My panties are wet and we're about to get out of the car and have dinner with one of your closest friends."

"You look gorgeous and unmussed," I assure her. "No one would ever know. If you do feel particularly restless, I'm happy to address *any* issues in the bathroom."

"I need you to not touch me again until the ride home and then

I'll be the one to close the privacy screen and you'll be the one with wet underwear."

"Dinner will be very short," I vow.

Kaga is waiting for us on the rooftop, enjoying a drink at the bar. There were three women surrounding him.

"Miss Corielli, so nice to see you again." Kaga squeezes both her hands and leans down to kiss her cheek. We're seated in the corner of the rooftop, a small screen separating us from the rest of the dining area. Kaga prefers his privacy just as I do.

"How are you enjoying your new job?" Kaga asks.

She gives a self-deprecating little laugh, "I think Jake is a very kind person to give me this job."

"I don't believe Jake does anything out of kindness," Kaga says slightly bitterly. "If you're not competent you wouldn't be there."

"Maybe." She sounds unconvinced. "I know that Jake could have someone do my job ten times better than me. Plus, he knows I don't enjoy working there, which makes me feel bad," she finishes with a big sigh.

"Don't worry about Jake's feelings. He's a big boy," I say and Kaga nods his agreement.

I swiftly change the subject and we end up spending the rest of the evening arguing about the shitty city traffic. Tiny's solution is for all of us to ride bicycles, a suggestion Kaga greets with utter horror.

"It's good exercise," she insists.

"There are plenty of other ways to get one's blood pumping," Kaga replies, his eyes sparking with amusement.

I step in. "No one gets to make innuendos of those kind to Tiny but me."

He inclines his head. "I apologize, Ian. Of course. I would not like that either."

"You guys are cavemen," she shakes her head in reproof.

"Perhaps if she had a big shiny rock on her left hand, it would help to remind me of her status."

"I can see it will have to be large enough that blind men like you will be able to see it." I pick up Tiny's slim fingers and press a kiss against them. Her fingers do look bare. I'm anxious for us to marry so that we can both wear visible signs of our ownership.

On the way home, she snuggles into my side—full of good food and perhaps a little too many Moscow Mules. The promise to ravish me in the car is forgotten and as the car ride lulls her to sleep, my mind swings back to the frustrating day with Louis.

"Did you have a very bad day at work?" she asks, smoothing her bare hand over my chest. Now that Kaga has pointed it out, not having my ring on her finger bothers me. I need to give it to her, but I haven't found the right moment.

"I thought you were asleep, bunny," I say pulling her into my lap and dropping a kiss on her hair.

"No but I'm really full and feeling terribly relaxed. I'm sorry I'm not embarrassing you in front of Steve like I said I would."

"You'll have to make up for it later," I say.

"Will you tell me what's bothering you first?" she asks.

"I'm likely going to fire my vice president of operations," I say.

She pushes away and gives me a frown. "That sounds serious."

"It's not. It's probably been a long time coming. I told him that I'm thinking of winding down Kerr Inc. and he did not take that well."

"I hope you aren't doing that for me," she interjects with alarm. "I'm perfectly capable of entertaining myself. If you're thinking of slowing down, don't do it for me."

I pull her back, missing the weight and warmth of her body next to mine. "I've worked nonstop since the age of fifteen, even earlier. I went to school, did odd jobs hustling on the boardwalk in Atlantic City, playing poker games and leveraging those sums into higher stakes poker until I had enough money to buy my way into a small-time brokerage firm. I bought and sold everything I could get my hands on—legal and illegal. Kerr Inc. is a nice accomplishment, but I can't go anywhere from here."

"So you want to retire on top?"

"No," I shake my head. "I want something fulfilling in my life, and I know that the acquisition of more wealth, more status isn't it. The only reason that I want to have money now is so that our family never suffers. But the mere fact that I have so much makes us both targets. I don't like that. I want to live a quiet life with you. I want to drive our kids to school and chaperone them on school trips. I want to watch every softball pitch or soccer kick. None of those things can happen while I'm down on Hudson Street trying to figure out whether to invest twenty million in this new technology or that new technology."

"Oh." She leans back to stare at me as she digests this.

A moment of uncharacteristic uncertainty wafts over me. Does giving up Kerr Inc. diminish me in her eyes in some way? Was I not man enough without the billions backing me? "I'll still be filthy stinking rich," I say, unable to keep the sarcasm from leaking out.

"Lord, Ian." She rolls her eyes. "As if that even matters to me. I just had no idea you felt that way. I think it's awesome, actually. I wonder sometimes if I'm enough for you. Whether you'll lose interest because I'm not smart enough to figure out all the terms for buyouts and mergers and leverages and positions. Wanting to exit the fast lane doesn't make you smaller to me. Just smarter." She hesitates and then jokes, "Can we just run off to an island together and forget about the real world?"

I grab her hand and press a kiss against the back of her fingers. "Done. What island do you want me to buy? Something in the Baltic? Perhaps down by Greece? South America?"

A small smile appears while she pretends to contemplate her options. "Why not all of them? We can travel from island to island whenever we get bored."

"I can't think of anything better. Let's leave tomorrow."

"I wish." She laughs lightly.

"You don't need to wish," I answer. "It can be reality if you want it to be."

She tugs her hand away. "I think it's great that you want to do that, but I can't see us being happy on an island. For all your 'I'm getting out' talk, you'd be bored in five minutes."

She's right, but I don't like admitting that. "Perhaps, but there's a big difference between working nonstop and having a balanced life. And speaking of having a family, I'd like to stop using condoms," I tell her. "I've had a medical checkup and I'm perfectly healthy."

"You want to have children now?" she asks.

"When you're ready, but mostly I want to fuck you without protection," I say honestly.

Her eyes heat up and it's a good thing we arrive home or we'd have to employ the privacy screen again. As it is, we barely make it inside the door before I've ripped her panties down her legs and she has me out and inside of her.

"God, Ian, you feel amazing. I swear I can feel every vein."

I can't speak to her because I've no brain cells left. The lush feel of her bare sex against my unprotected length is too mind blowing. I can't form words. I can only grunt and thrust as the world spins around me. It's too fast and I'm losing control and I *need* for her to come with me.

I fasten my mouth against hers and the rough swiftness of our joining is blurring my vision and making me weak. Her hands grip my shoulders and then tangle in my hair as I push her skirt out of my way so I can find her perfect little clit. I press down with my thumb and she finds her release only seconds before mine comes shooting down my spine.

"That was . . ." she's at a loss for words.

"Fucking amazing," I finish for her. After a few more heartbeats, I carry her up the stairs until I find our bedroom and we start all over again.

CHAPTER 7

"I appreciate you doing this," Tiny says for the millionth time as she rushes around the bathroom trying to get ready. I don't recall ever seeing her this nervous before.

"It's not a chore." I slip my pearl cufflinks through a snowy-white dress shirt. Sitting on the bench, I pull on socks and loafers. This is my nightclub attire, as designated by Frank. Shirt, dark wash jeans, and a sport coat. Tiny picked the coat out for me, and it's currently lying on the end of the bed. Stretching out my legs, I enjoy the show she's putting on.

We're taking her friend to the Aquarium, and Tiny has put more effort and thought into what she'll wear and how she'll look for this evening than for any of the dates I've taken her on.

"Are you planning on sleeping with this chick tonight?" I ask. She pauses in zipping up her third outfit. No wait, maybe this is her fourth.

"Ha.Ha. Very funny, Ian. Help me." She turns her back to me and I slide the zipper up. This selection is a dress, which is probably a bad idea for a bar with a second floor made almost entirely of glass.

"Did you forget that people can look up your skirt at the bar?" I ask, sliding a finger up the inside of a creamy thigh. "Because I can see starting a lot of fights tonight if you intend to wear this, particularly with those panties on."

Her undergarments currently consist of a black lace thong that has one small panel in the front and is attached to a miniscule patch of fabric in the back with two rows of satin strings. In the dark light of the bar, it would likely appear as if she were wearing nothing. My palm covers her. "Did you forget that this is mine?"

"How about ours?" she winks, allowing my possessive gesture. "Unzip me, though, because I want to try another outfit."

With a sigh, I release her.

"I'm wondering if I should be offended that you've never worried this much about how you're going to look when we've gone out."

"I thought your preference was for me to be naked." Her fingers riffle through her clothes. Clearly she doesn't have enough.

"So it is."

"It's just that I haven't been out with Sarah for years and I feel so disconnected from everyone. It's like I woke up one day and every girlfriend I had had disappeared."

I refrain from pointing out that her five-year struggle with her mother's cancer might have had a lot to do with it. I didn't know Tiny and her mother when the cancer first appeared and then went into remission, so I don't know what the battle was like the first go-around, but I know that when Sophie Corielli's cancer came back a second time, Tiny worked extra jobs on top of taking care of her sick mother. She didn't have time to go out and party with her girlfriends.

I'm reserving judgment as to whether this friend of hers is worth Tiny's time. Where was she when Tiny was trying to hold the pieces of her life together? That's when Tiny could have used a friend. Now suddenly this Sarah turns up and asks if Tiny can get her into the exclusive nightclubs that she's seen mentioned in the gossip rags.

Tiny finally settles on a pair of leopard-print shorts with a low-cut black tank top covered in sequins. She pulls on a sexy black lace bra with scalloped edges. The shirt makes a slight musical sound as she moves and the light catches on the small silver disks, drawing the eye to the perfect swell of her breasts peeking out from the top of the tank. Before I can form a protest at how much of her will be on display, she throws an off-white jacket over the top and pushes up the sleeves.

When she straps on a pair of metal-studded stilettos, I know she's really trying to impress. She's a tennis shoes and flats kind of girl. I want to draw her into my arms and tell her that everything is going to be fine, but I wait until she's done fixing her pretty hair into a messy side braid. Strolling over to her, I tug on the braid.

"I like this. I can think of several things I want to do with this braid."

She gives me a coy look and purses her painted lips. "You can look but don't touch."

The coquettish attitude is tempting me to bend her over and show her how I can touch her a million different ways without messing her hair or makeup, but the downstairs bell rings, signaling the arrival of her friend.

Tiny pulls her hair from my hand and rushes downstairs. I grab my jacket and follow her.

"Be nice," she hisses over her shoulder as she opens the door.

"Vic!" A tall woman with dark curly hair appears in the entryway. Tiny rushes over and gives her a hug. "You look amazing. I love it. Shorts, how chic!"

"Thanks, you look great too. Come and meet Ian." Tiny tugs Sarah's hand and they walk over to me. I use the time to measure Sarah. She's about six inches taller than my girl and slender. The navy blue and white bandage dress accentuates her thinness and stops dangerously high on her thighs. Jesus, these women need to eat more.

"Nice to meet you." I shake her hand. It's firm and dry, which I take as a good sign.

"Great place you have here." She smiles at me but it's friendly appreciation only. There's no flirtation in her greeting. Just to make sure she knows that I'm firmly in the hands of Tiny, I draw her to my side.

"Tiny says you've never been to the Aquarium." The relatively new bar is owned by Kaga, heir to one of the largest beverage corporations in the world. About ten thousand Kaga beverages are consumed every second. His brand of entertainment is currently creating outrageous nightclubs and throwing parties. The Aquarium is so named because the interior is painted blue and filled with water—aquariums, hot tubs, pools. We're the fish, and we're all swimming around in Kaga's bowl.

"Nope. But Vic says it's amazing."

"It is," Tiny says. "But I thought I told you the floor was glass."

"Oh, you did," Sarah replies. Her lips curve up in what can only be described as a naughty smile. "And I can't wait."

Tiny laughs. "Okay then. Let's go."

◆ ◆ ◆

The last time I took Tiny here we entered through the back door and went straight to Kaga's private box. But I didn't want to bring an unknown person into his space. Kaga is a private man. Plus, I had no idea what or *who* he's doing in there. Instead, we enter at the front, bypassing the huge line. The doorman waves us in. Obviously Kaga's people are trained to recognize certain individuals and allow them access without IDs or checklists. The meticulous attention to detail is part of why his clubs are so popular.

I lead the two women straight to the VIP section and into a booth overlooking the first-floor dance floor. The VIP section is set on a balcony at the front of the bar. On the exact opposite wall, some hundred yards away, is Kaga's black glass one-way viewing box.

A light flashes several times in a rhythmic pattern. "Fucking Kaga," I snort.

"What is it?" Tiny whispers in my ear.

"Morse code. He says 'don't talk, just dance.' I think that message is for you."

"So you're one of those?" Sarah interjects.

"Those what?"

"Guys who refuse to dance?"

"I don't refuse. I just know the limits of my skill set, which doesn't include dancing."

"You move pretty good in other places," Tiny murmurs.

"If you want to have sex, I'm your man, bunny."

"And if I want to dance, do I find someone else?"

"No." I shake my head emphatically. "You dance right here, and I enjoy every minute of the show."

"Come on," Sarah pulls at Tiny's hand. "Let's go try out the dance floor."

Tiny allows herself to be dragged away. They head downstairs to the first level, where the dance floor surrounds a circular bar that has two twenty-foot-high aquariums filled with sharks and sting rays.

"I'm surprised you let her out of your sight. I heard you were pretty attached to her."

Richard Howe. With some effort, I manage not to clench my fingers into a fist and drive it into his face multiple times.

"I know a good woman when I find her," I say, refusing to look at him. "Are you here to tell me you're leaving? I didn't need a verbal announcement. A letter would have sufficed."

While the cushion is too well-made for me to actually feel him taking a seat at the end of the blue velvet banquette, I sense it. It's only due to years of rigid self-control that I'm able to remain seated. Across the way I see the light flash again. It's Kaga wanting to know if I need an intervention. Not yet.

"I'm not going anywhere," he says. "Cecilia says you're too much your father's son to hurt her, and sending me away would hurt her."

There's a tap on the table as he sets down his glass. A waiter stops by and sets a tumbler of amber liquid in front of me. "From Mr. Kaga," he says with a nod of his head.

"I'll take what he's having." Richard tips his empty glass toward the waiter who looks at me for approval. I shake my head. No way in hell Kaga would serve Richard a drop of the famed Kaga reserve. With another nod, the waiter walks off, leaving Richard fuming.

"This place won't stay in business longer than six months with that kind of fucking service."

"You should find someplace else, then." I take a sip, hoping the smooth liquor will ease the rage that I'm barely suppressing.

"Aquarium is the hottest nightclub in the city and we both know it." Richard starts tapping the bottom of his empty glass against the table.

"Shouldn't you be at home with the lovely wife?" I ask.

"Sissy's too busy puking her dinner up and washing her mouth out with Scotch. Besides, the old girl hasn't opened her legs since they invented the iPod."

Sissy's had to suffer nearly two decades of marriage to this worthless piece of trash, and yet she stays with him. I should just kill him. Take a gun to his head and blow out his brains. But then Tiny would be alone, and I'd be sitting in a prison cell. There are other ways to ruin a person's life. For Howe, a life sentence of living a hand-to-mouth existence would be worse than death. I'll apply more pressure. Maybe if Cecilia was on the brink of ruin, she would leave him. Because damn her, she's right. I don't want to hurt her. "She should divorce you."

"Can't. Daddy would have a fit. Speaking of my old man, how does it feel to be fellated by him publicly? 'Ian Kerr is an example of what New York can do for people and what I want to do for New York.'" Richard mocks his father's latest sound bite. "He keeps asking me why I'm not a success like Ian Kerr who didn't even go to business school."

"Why aren't you, Howe? Degrees from Yale and Columbia. Old family name. Connections. You should be rolling in it." I dig the knife in as hard as I can.

"Fuck you," he curses. "You've just been phenomenally lucky."

"Or smart."

"You invested in one technology early that set you up for life. Everything since your investment in SeeMe is just gravy. That's fucking luck. And everyone knows your money was dirty. You're no better than a goddamn mobster." He looks ready to throw the glass on the floor.

"There were plenty of people who were offered the chance to invest in that video sharing software. I believe I heard you were even approached."

"I could have had her, you know." He abruptly switches the subject. I glance over the dance floor at Tiny and Sarah who are busy shaking their hips and arms to the heavy bass of EDM being spun by the DJ. "If her mom hadn't died, she would have eventually succumbed."

Finally I turn to look at him, and he flinches from the murderous look in my eyes. "If it pleases you to delude yourself, go right ahead." Another sip. I concentrate on the liquid, savoring the cherry notes on top of the smoke and wood, but I don't take my eyes off of him.

"If you only knew the women I've had in the past." Richard's words are a tease and the closest he's ever come to admitting that he slept with my mother; that he took advantage of her at her lowest moment; that he drove her to suicide. I squeeze the tumbler so that the cut crystal of the base digs into my palm. I want him to admit it. To verbalize his deed so that I can take him down without feeling an ounce of remorse.

It takes a superhuman effort, but I'm able to respond without inflection. "I don't doubt your past is littered with stories. None of them are of any interest to me," I lied.

"Then let me tell you—"

"Mr. Howe, there's a phone call from your father." Kaga appears suddenly. "He says it's urgent that you present yourself at campaign headquarters immediately. Something about a young woman claiming to have personal information about you."

There are two burly bouncers standing behind Kaga who are clearly ready to drag Howe out of the VIP section, willing or not. He leans forward, so close I can smell the cheap booze and desperation. "You are nothing, Kerr. And whatever you've built can be ripped down in a moment. Without your money, you wouldn't be able to buy a whore in the city let alone sit here like a sultan purveying his harem."

"Your clock is ticking, Howe. I can bring you down with one phone call. And all of this—" I sweep my arm toward the bar "—will be out of your reach.

He looks behind him and curses. "I'm not the only one with plans. Keep your loved ones close, Kerr. Not everyone has the same principles as you."

"I'd take your threats more seriously if you weren't such a complete and utter failure at life, Howe. Maybe I'll give you more time. Your humiliation is entertaining." I flick my hand in dismissal. Kaga nods his head and the two bouncers grab hold of one arm each and pull Howe toward the exit. Shock paralyzes him, and I savor the spectacle until he gathers himself and jerks his arms out of their grip and trots hurriedly down the stairs.

"Call from his father?"

Kaga shrugs and sits down. A glass appears in front of him before his ass can hit the cushion. "His father should be keeping a closer eye on him. And you need to either pull the trigger on Howe or just let it go."

"I'm pulling the trigger, but I'm not going to sink to his level and ruin an entire family." I look into my tumbler. "At least not yet."

I swallow the rest of the glass and try to push thoughts of Richard and Cecilia aside. Below me, Tiny's sequins flash under the strobe lights as she twirls and shakes. I concentrate on her until the rage recedes and the tension eases. She's all I'll ever need.

"You really love her," Kaga says in wonderment.

"She makes my world turn."

◆ ◆ ◆

TINY

"This place is amazing," Sarah yells. It's the only way to be heard over the club music that's pouring out of every speaker. We're on the edge of the VIP dance floor, the one with the glass tiles. Some of the partygoers are just in their underwear, still wet from the plunge pools that circle the outer rim.

"It's a lot more fun this time around," I admit. I'm nervous though, looking for Howe in every corner.

"Do you see him?" she shouts again.

I shake my head. It's hard to see anything here. My idea was a good one in theory, not so great in practice. But at least Sarah is having a good time. I decide to allow myself to enjoy the music, my friend, and the hot gaze of my lover. A couple of guys try to insert themselves between us, but Sarah sidles closer, placing her hands on my hips so as to block them. When it's apparent they won't leave, Sarah and I exit the dance floor.

"Bathroom?" I ask. She nods and we head off toward the ladies' room. The nice thing about the VIP floor is the bathroom is super swank. There's an outer sitting area with a wall full of mirrors and two small sofas. Inside are six separate stalls with toilets that have more buttons than the remote for my television.

"I don't know who's hotter," she says as we're washing our hands. I'd pointed him out as he was crossing the dance floor. "Kaga or Ian. I'd do either or both. At the same time if I had to."

"Since I'm not sharing Ian, you'll have to make do with Kaga."

"Like that would be a tragedy. His cheekbones are so sharp I think I'd cut my tongue on them. I need to test it out to be sure. Is he single?"

"I don't know."

"He seems single," Sarah says, making use of the complimentary cosmetics at the counter. "Ian can't take his eyes off you, but Kaga's looking everywhere. Assessing things."

"He *is* the owner," I point out.

Sarah shakes her head. "It's different. When I look at Ian, he doesn't even see me. His eyes are locked on you and you alone. It's all he sees. Cam never looked at me like that. I don't think any guy has. It's amazing. And shit, that picture of him in the *Observer* does no justice to him. He and Kaga look like they should be on billboards wearing nothing but what God gave them. You need to make that happen for the rest of womankind."

"That'd cause a riot." I smile. "I've seen Ian Kerr naked and it's enough to stop traffic. There'd be women fainting in cars and men beating themselves up for not looking as good. It's for the good of all mankind that he keeps himself clothed in public. Trust me on this."

She whimpers. Or I thought she whimpered, but after a moment the whimpers turn to choked sobs. We stare at each other and then look into the sitting room. Someone is crying out there.

Grimacing slightly, I tiptoe over and sure enough, a woman is crying in the arms of a friend.

"Is she okay?" I ask, wondering if I should get Kaga. "Do you need anything?"

The friend, a raven-haired woman thin enough to be a model, frowns at me. "It's nothing. She'll be fine."

The crying woman pushes away and despite her tears, she's stunning. Two models, for sure. They both have prominent cheekbones and elegant bodies that look good in anything.

"Are you the one?" she asks, pointing to me.

"The one what?" I say.

"The one dating Ian Kerr. You said you saw him naked."

In the short time I've dated Ian, he's never mentioned another woman and we've never run into any of his girlfriends. My luck has run out.

"Yeah, she's dating Ian Kerr. What of it?" Sarah says, her chin jutting out aggressively.

Tears well up in the model's eyes, making her look luminous in the sparsely lit sitting room. "I'm Melinda." Her voice is hopeful, as if she's optimistic that Ian has mentioned her to me.

"I'm Victoria Corielli," I say instead, because I've never heard of her before. It doesn't seem right to say that—not with tears still running down her face.

"He went to your mother's funeral." It isn't a question. God, has *everyone* seen that *Observer* picture?

"Yes. My mom meant a lot to him."

"I'm sorry for your loss," she says sincerely.

"Thank you." This is so awkward. I want to leave, yet it seems rude to walk out on her. I look to Sarah for help, but she just grimaces as if to say she doesn't know what the appropriate thing to do is either.

"Come sit with me for a moment." Melinda pats the sofa cushion next to her.

"Melinda." Her friend says in warning but the woman shrugs her off.

"Please," Melinda pleads. What else can I do? I go and sit down, but I perch on the very edge.

"He's wonderful isn't he?" Her lips are trembling with the effort to keep her sobs in. I've never seen anyone look so amazing while crying. She looks like a kicked puppy.

"Yes." I find myself nodding to her. "He's truly wonderful."

"So thoughtful and tender." She sighs.

"Yes, very thoughtful and very tender." I hide my impatience. It's one thing for her to be sad that she's not seeing Ian anymore, but if she starts talking about their sex life I'm out of here. The friend gives me a pained look, clearly wishing to be anywhere but here.

"I remember—"

I hold up a hand because I don't want to reminisce with her. "I'm sorry that you're sad, but I hope you can appreciate that talking about what you did with my current boyfriend is really not cool. If you have something you want to say, then say it, but I'm not going to sit here and listen to you tell me about how much better you are for him than I am."

"Oh," she cries in surprise. "I wasn't going to say that at all. I just . . . I just miss him so much. I've never had a better boyfriend. He's ruined me for all other men."

I run an agitated hand over my forehead, searching for the right words so that I don't come off as an utter bitch. But Ian is mine and I'm keeping him, no matter how sad this chick is. "I'm sure you'll find someone perfect for you, but Ian Kerr is mine now. And since you know how wonderful he is, you also know that I'm going to fight to keep him. I'm not going to tell you to stay away because that's stupid. Just know that he's in love with me and we're going to get married and have a family." The marriage thing might be a slight exaggeration. He's mentioned it, but I don't have a ring on my finger.

A gasp sounds in the room as if everyone has drawn in a breath.

"You guys are getting married?" Sarah cries.

I bite the side of my lip. What did I just say? I nod because it's true. If I believe that Ian is sincere, and I do, then it's all true. "Yes."

"If he's said he wants to marry you, then he must," Melinda says with a wail. "Because he never lies. He's always completely honest with you."

Her friend pulls Melinda in for a comforting embrace and mouths, "I'm sorry."

I grab Sarah's hand and scoot out of the bathroom as fast as possible. "That was the single most awkward experience of my life."

"Hey, at least you know he's a good guy."

"One that ruins girls for all other men. Shit, if Ian ever left me, I'd be like that too." I press a hand to my racing heart.

"Given that he wants to marry you, I don't think he plans to leave."

"I'd seriously fight for him." I smooth back my hair. "Against anyone."

Sarah leans against the wall and looks at me with envy. "I want what you have."

"Let's get back. I have a pressing need to stamp my ownership all over him."

As we're walking through the crowd, someone bumps me hard, almost turning me around. Before I can see who it is and yell at them for being rude, I realize that the person pressed a crumpled up piece of paper in my hand.

"What is it?" Sarah asks, coming to look over my shoulder.

"A note, I think." I open the paper and hand it to Sarah to read. There's no way I'm going to make out any letters in this light. "Read it for me."

Do you really think a stupid bitch like you can hold Ian Kerr? Leave him or you'll be crying just like the brunette in the bathroom.

"Shit," Sarah says, stuffing the note back in my hand. "Those bitches. We're going after them."

"No," I put my hand on her arm. "That wasn't from them." I scan the crowd looking for my target, but I'm not sure who I'm looking for. A woman, I think. It's the same person who left me the message in Jake's office, I know it. It's the same type of wording. The same paper. I bet if I had it tested it would be the same ink and the same handwriting. This has to do with Richard Howe. I know it. I just know it.

CHAPTER 8

IAN

"Maybe you should just tag her," Kaga suggests as I watch Tiny and her friend thread their way through the crowd toward the bathrooms.

"Is that what you've done with Sabrina?" I don't take my eyes off Tiny's sexy ass. If she didn't have a friend with her, I'd meet her at the bathroom door and drag her into a stall. A skirt could be very convenient in a nightclub. I'd have to remember that in the future when we weren't patronizing bars with glass floors.

"Don't need to. She's at Columbia."

"Damn, Kaga. Even though I didn't go to college, I know that there are more temptations there than there are in this entire bar. You're insane if you think that she's completely untouched simply because you know her general whereabouts on a college campus."

He glares at me, his dark eyes narrowing. "What do you know?"

"Jake says she's having a *great* time. She's been spending a lot of time with a DJ. Plays at one of your clubs, in fact."

I shouldn't enjoy needling Kaga so much, but shit, if he plans to sit back and wait for his girl to ripen like a peach and fall into his waiting hands, he's more than insane. He's certifiable.

I'm about to launch into a sustained discourse on the futility of waiting when Tiny and Sarah appear at the table. Kaga and I both rise to allow the women to take a seat when I notice the tight expression on Tiny's face.

Before she can sit down, I cup her elbow and draw her toward me. As gently as possible, in direct contradiction to the fury that's generating inside me, I ask in a low voice, "Everything all right?"

Either I'm not quiet enough or Sarah can read my concern because she pipes up. "Just bathroom gossip. Nothing serious."

I give Sarah a nod but the only person I care to hear is Tiny.

"It's nothing, Ian, really." She slides into the booth next to Sarah. A server brings another round of drinks for the table, but Tiny doesn't reach for her Singapore Sling. Instead she picks up my whiskey and takes a deep gulp.

"Why don't I show you the owner's lounge," Kaga invites Sarah, trying to give Tiny and me some privacy.

Sarah scoots out immediately. "I'm yours." Before Kaga can take her away, though, she turns and leans across the table. "There were two women in the bathroom. One had dated you in the past. She started crying when she saw Tiny because apparently you were the best boyfriend she'd ever had. She's never been able to maintain a steady relationship with another guy since you broke up."

Tiny presses her lips together and nods her head in confirmation.

Sarah went on. "She wasn't mean or anything. Just really, really sad. We all felt bad for her. She wished Tiny luck and said to do what she could to hang on to you."

Kaga's face is impassive but I sense humor lurking behind his eyes. I'm going to get shit about this at the next poker game.

"Come along, my dear," Kaga murmurs, tucking the brunette's hand into the crook of his elbow. "The two lovebirds need a moment."

I lay my arm across the back of the banquette and curl my hand around her shoulder. "Is this something we should talk about?"

She tilts her head back and takes a deep breath. "I just felt bad for her. We all did. The entire bathroom started sniffling."

"I hope you didn't offer me up as appeasement," I joke lightly.

"How long did you date Melinda?"

Melinda? I roll her name around in my head but it doesn't ring any bells. "I can't remember," I say honestly.

"She's gorgeous. Looks like a model. Probably six inches taller than me. Long brown hair. She had it in a high pony." Tiny puts a fist on the top of her head to mimic the hair of this unknown girl.

"I don't know if this will make you feel better or worse, but I don't actually know who you're talking about." A few stray hairs have fallen forward on her face. I brush them back, dragging my thumb across her cheek.

"How can you not remember her? She said you were her best boy-friend." Tiny's frown is not soothed by a few tugs of my thumb.

Snatching up my drink, I down the contents before responding. "I didn't have girlfriends, bunny. I dated women. We enjoyed each other for some period of time and then we went our separate ways. At times, we simply used each other for pure, safe physical release."

"But you said you weren't a manwhore." She's puzzled because her paradigm consists of a steady relationship or a nonstop stream of hookups.

"I wasn't. I don't enjoy casual sex. It's better when you know the person, but knowing a person and sleeping with them doesn't a relation-ship make." I don't like the distance she's putting between us. I slide my hand around the curve of her waist and pull her to me. With a finger under her chin, I tip her head so she can look me in the eye. "I'm thirty-two, almost thirty-three, and I've had my share of encounters with the opposite sex and some have been more casual than others. But no one I've ever been with has been anything like you. I don't remember other women. I don't want to. Melinda obviously remembers me because she hasn't had anything better. That's on her.

"You're the best I've ever had, Tiny. In bed and out of it." I grin roguishly, memories of some of our activities outside the bed tripping through my mind. I can see by the flush in Tiny's cheeks she's sharing similar visions. "When I close my eyes, I think of you, and the only memories I have are those I've made with you."

"How?" she looks bewildered.

"Because I make it so."

She lets me capture her mouth for a long, drugging kiss. With steady pressure I affirm all the words I've just stated. She's the only one I want now and forever. Beneath me she softens, her lips part, and her body cants toward me. Under the table, I press my palm against her cloth-covered sex.

"If you'd let me wear a skirt, you could be touching me right now," she whispers naughtily against my mouth. Her words are like gasoline on a flame.

I grind the heel of my palm down and press my fingers tight against her. "I can make you come right here at the table."

Her thighs tighten around my hand. "Without taking my clothes off?"

Is she issuing me a dare? *Challenge fucking accepted.*

"I can make you come at least once, no penetrative touching. No under the clothes touching."

She laughs then, a low sultry sound that strikes me right in the groin.

"I know you can. This is why that girl is crying in the bathroom."

"Back to that?" I sigh and withdraw my hand. "If you aren't going to let me make you come here, then let's go home where you can scream without anyone but me hearing you."

"Can't." Her lips twist into a wry grimace. "Sarah."

"Kaga will take care of her. He'll make sure she gets home safe."

"You should leave with the one who brought you," she quips. I can tell I'm not moving her from this seat until we get some reassurance from her friend.

I pull out my cellphone and call Kaga. He answers at the first ring. "You need some pointers? Can't close the deal?"

"Tiny lives with me. I've already closed the deal." I wink at Tiny but she rolls her eyes at my comment. "Unlike you, whose girl is currently roaming the halls of an ivy-covered campus with feral frat boys chasing her down."

"I'm going to take so much money from you at the next poker game, you'll be in a fetal position begging for mercy after the first hour."

"If money is going to make you feel better about your inaction, I'll just leave some here on the table because I'm a good friend."

"Fuck you, Kerr. What is it you called about?"

"Tiny won't leave without knowing that Sarah is going to be okay, but if Tiny doesn't leave now then we're going to put on a show that will probably get your bar closed down for public indecency."

"Hold on," he sighs.

"Hello?" Sarah comes on the line. I hand the phone to Tiny who carries on a short conversation with her. After she hangs up, she gives me a nod.

As I help her out of the booth, she says, "You have some good lines, but it's still pretty bad you don't remember her."

"Are we back to Melinda? My guess is that she's sadder she lost her VIP access than anything else." I place my hand at the base of her spine, just under her blouse, enjoying the feel of her warm skin against my palm.

"That's cruel."

"Maybe, but more than likely the truth." I shrug. I'm not interested in discussing a random woman I slept with and have since forgotten. The only woman I care about is standing in front of me. I press a button on my phone to signal that Steve should bring the car around.

"Wait." Tiny gasps. "She's right there with *Howe*."

I follow her arm and spy a tall, thin brunette standing right next to Richard Howe, who apparently hasn't yet left the bar. He has a hand around her bare waist and she's dressed in a backless tank and a tiny mini. They're talking at the base of the VIP stairs. It's hard to say whether they're arguing or whether this is Richard's move to get her to have sex with him in one of the plunge pools or a banquette.

Her appearance sparks a vague memory. "I think I dated her for a period of a couple months—maybe three—several years ago." She looks generic to me. At one time, early on in my success, I slept with models and aspiring actresses and any other lady who turned my head. As I got older and needed something more than physical interaction, I started dating women in finance. Bankers, lawyers, and writers. The pillow talk was more interesting, as was dinner conversation. But still, none of them held my interest and I'd always moved on.

"What's she doing with the scumbag?" Tiny scowls, her forehead crinkling angrily. We watch as Richard's hand dips down over the model's ass and cups it. From our superior angle, it's easy to see his fingers disappear under the girl's skirt. She looks surprised and then resigned. Her fingers run up and down his lapel. Even if she doesn't want him, she's willing enough.

"He's a meal ticket. Modeling is a tough gig." I apply light pressure on Tiny's back to urge her forward. I don't really care what Howe is up to tonight. He can fuck a hundred models as long as he doesn't look Tiny's way.

But there's no way to avoid Howe as we exit, since he's standing at the base of the stairs. Both he and the model turn toward us, and Howe gives Tiny an appraising look that makes her shift slightly to use my frame as cover. I reach behind me and draw her to the opposite side, away from Howe.

"I see your taste in women still runs toward the trashy side," Howe says snidely.

Melinda gasps, but Tiny only squeezes my hand.

Kaga wouldn't care if I laid Howe out on the floor with a punch to the jaw, but I'm not going to give Howe ammunition for an assault charge. The one thing you learn when dealing with cops is to never throw the first punch.

"Your inability to judge quality when you see it is why you are a failure, Howe. In the future, it'd be good for your health to pretend Tiny and I do not exist. Remember what I said before. Your time here is limited."

I give a short nod to Melinda. She reaches out a hand toward me, but I shift away so that it merely brushes my sleeve.

"Someday you'll pay for all this," Howe says.

"That day is never going to happen." Kaga's place is too successful, and the packed crowd is preventing us from making a quick escape.

"He's not worth it." Tiny directs this to Melinda.

"Not all of us get Ian Kerr to take us home," she says sadly.

"You could do better." Tiny reaches out a hand. "Trust me. You're an amazing girl. Don't settle."

I stifle a laugh. Nothing could be more insulting than for two gorgeous women to be completely ignoring Howe. It's better than a punch in the face because it hits him where it really counts—his vanity.

Howe's face turns livid as the model allows herself to be drawn away. "You're right." She visibly straightens her shoulders. "You're so right."

Leaning forward, she gives Tiny a kiss on the cheek and sends me another sad smile before drifting into the crowd. I take Tiny's hand and push through to the exit. Howe is left behind us, completely alone.

CHAPTER 9

"Is seven too early?" Tiny asks.

"No, but if my meeting runs late, just start without me." I glance at my watch. "How do you want to run this meeting? You know that the likelihood that he has anything of your mother's is almost nil."

"I'll regret it if I don't at least go and hear him out."

"He wants something," I warn.

"I *know* that. I know he's not a good guy. I lived with him, remember?" she shoots back with asperity. "But wondering if he does have something of Mom's will bug me far more than if I let him bullshit us for a couple hours. You don't have to come."

"I'm coming." Reluctantly I agree, knowing she's right. "But I'm going to be late."

"We're going to be in a public place. There's nothing he can do that can hurt me. Words, Ian, can't hurt me. I don't care enough about Mitch to let his opinions about anything bother me. Go forth and be your bad investment self."

After telling her I love her, I hang up and hurry to the conference room. Today's meeting is with the wearables firm. They have ideas for everything from clothes that change colors depending on your mood to shoes that provide differing cushioning depending on the walking surface. The meeting runs longer than I anticipated but a few glances at my watch has them hurrying to wrap it up.

Because of the overlong meeting, I'm not able to head home to get ready. Instead I make my way to the en-suite bathroom attached to my office and pull out a dark suit appropriate to the stuffy Plaza environment.

Quickly, I finish dressing and call Steve.

"Mate," he answers.

"Where are you?"

"Idling outside 14011".

That's the address to my home in the Meatpacking District. "I'll call for a car to take me up to The Plaza. Can you keep Tiny in the car until I get there?"

He laughs at me and hangs up. Right, as if Tiny would stay put until I arrived.

I call for a car and they promise one will be delivered in the next ten minutes. I check my watch. It's 6:35, and I'm going to be late. As I take the elevator down, I give Tiny a call.

"Hey," she sounds rushed. "I'm glad you called. I'm going to be late. I haven't left yet. Are you there?"

"No, bunny, I'm running late too."

She laughs. "It was just crazy today. A client's husband came storming in saying that it was against the law for us to be following him and taking pictures of him cheating on his wife. It was all very dramatic. I'll tell you about it at dinner. No, after dinner," she revises.

"When we're by ourselves," I suggest.

"Yes." She blows out a big breath. "This meeting is so uncomfortable for me, that even if you hadn't made me promise to bring you along, I would have forced you to go anyway."

"We're a team now. I'm there for you in whatever capacity you need," I assure her, walking out onto the sidewalk. "Stay in the car until

I get there. I can call ahead and let them know that whatever he orders can be put on my tab."

"I'm not going to cower in your car," she says, annoyed. "Ian, stop worrying."

"I can't. I love you. You are the most important person in the world to me and he knows it. He's a user."

"Will you trust me?" she says impatiently.

"I do trust you." I look for the car. It's still not here. I won't be using that firm again. "It's him that I'm worried about."

"Just get here soon and we won't have a problem."

"The damn car isn't here. I'll be there as soon as I can," I promise. Because I don't want her going in pissed at me, I change the subject. "By the way, the next time the tailor comes to New York, I'm going to have to ask for looser-fitting pants."

"Why's that?"

"Because I kept getting hard thinking about you today and it was very uncomfortable."

She laughs delightedly. "You should have rubbed one out in the bathroom."

"What makes you think I didn't?"

I'm getting hard just talking about it. Fuck. The effect she has on me is unreal.

"I hope you have some energy for me tonight," she teases.

"I promise that there isn't a dirty thought you can have that I can't fulfill after drinks."

"I can't wait," she says throatily.

"I'm going to hang up on you now before I get arrested for public indecency."

She's laughing when we disconnect which puts a smile on my face, and that's why I'm taken off guard when the first fist strikes my face.

CHAPTER 10

The punch caught me unawares and snapped my chin to the right. A lefty then. Most people lead with their dominant hand. I take another to the gut before I bring my own fist straight under his chin. The force snaps his head back, but another punch hits me from the right. Then I realize there are two people. The tight cut of my suit might have looked nice in the boardroom, but it was preventing real movement, and with the next punch I throw, I hear a corresponding rip in my jacket sleeve.

Fighting two people in an alley near dusk in the city wasn't as easy as the movies made it out to be, but I grew up on the boulevards of Jersey, where the gamblers and mobsters and grifters spent their time. If you were a kid who didn't want to sell his body, you fought. Sometimes you fought for money, but most of the time you fought to keep what you had. And the more money I won at the tables, the more people wanted to meet me under the docks and behind the casinos to see if I was strong enough to keep it.

I haven't fought off two guys in a long time—at least not with my fists. I preferred to fight using paper and greenbacks. I've realized you can do a lot more harm with money than you can with your hands. But the time spent in the seedy parts of Atlantic City has never left me. And I am stronger now—lifting weights on a daily basis and sparring with friends in the gym has kept me sharp. The asphalt of the alleyway is steady under my feet, unlike the sand and mud I'd fought in years ago. Planting my left leg, I swing my heel into the side of the bruiser on my right. When he stumbles, I jam an elbow into his jaw and follow him to the ground to avoid the punch of his smaller friend. Another elbow into Big Guy's eye socket dazes him, and I use the opportunity to push upright.

Diving at Small Guy, I drive him into the wall of the alley, the small space serving as an aid rather than a hindrance. It's tight for two fighters and almost impossible for three. This time, my footing is uneven because I choose to use Big Guy as my floor, grinding the ball of my foot into his windpipe as I smash a fist into the nose of Small Guy. I hear it crack under my fist. I quicken the pace of my blows, wanting this to be over and cognizant of the time ticking by. Small Guy can't get his hands high enough to hit me in the face because I'm too close, so he punches me in the obliques and then my upper ribs.

I use my elbows and body as much as I can so that my hands won't look like raw meat when I get to Tiny. I stomp on the downed guy's nose and when his face lolls to the side, I bring a knee up to Small Guy's groin. When he cups his crotch, I take advantage of his dropped guard to drive an elbow into his chin and that's enough to knock him out.

"Sir?" I hear from the end of the alley. Breathing hard, I turn to face the driver of the car I called for. I glance at my watch. 6:50.

"You been there long?" I ask.

"Um, ten min—I mean, no, just got here," he lies. He looks all of fifteen.

Beneath me, I hear a groan. I make sure to step on both their faces as I walk out of the alley, straightening my suit coat and pretending that I hadn't just knocked two guys out. I need to take one of them with me, and I don't think this young man is going to be too helpful. I pull out a hundred dollar bill and slap it in his hand. "Drive up to The Plaza and then forget about me."

He nods wordlessly and gets in his car. As he speeds away, I call Steve.

He answers on the first ring. "Mate."

"Had a little altercation, and I'm going to need a pickup."

"I'm on my way."

"Where are you?"

"I was outside your place. Tiny hasn't come out yet."

"No, you have to stay with her." I'm sharper with him than usual, but I need Tiny to be protected.

"Mate." It's only one word, but I've known Steve a long time and can read all that he's trying to say. Which is essentially that I'm acting like a goddamn fool because I can't just call anyone to come and help me clean up this mess.

Pinching the bridge of my nose, I pace. "Call Jake and get him to send over a driver for Tiny. A female one," I add.

"I'll get the most female male he's got on staff," Steve says sarcastically and hangs up.

Walking back into the alley, Big Guy is starting to sit up. Small Guy is still out cold. I crouch down next to Big Guy. In the dusky light, I catalog their clothes, appearance, and possible origin.

Both are wearing bad suits, which makes sense because the Financial District is thick with suits from those warehouse stores, but the average mugger doesn't sport even the meanest suit. They are both white with sharp noses, heavy eyebrows, and shaggy hair. The light's too low to see more; their skin could be anywhere from pasty white to deeply tanned.

Big Guy was big, broad-shouldered and slow. His friend was quicker but lacked power in his punch. Low-rent thugs without real skill, although maybe against someone who had no fighting experience they'd be terrifying. I'm only irritated. Malcolm Hedder? Mitch Hedder? Richard Howe? One of them likely is behind this. "I've got dinner plans, so this needs to go quickly. How much money do you need to sell out the guy who hired you?"

Big Guy looks away, the blood flowing from his broken nose mingling with the blood leaking out the side of his mouth. "I'll give you all the cash in my pocket for a name." I wave the thick wad of cash toward him. "There's fifteen hundred right here."

Hesitantly he reaches toward it, but Small Guy has roused and raises himself on his elbows. "Don't do it. You know what they said." He turns and spits out a mouthful of blood and maybe a tooth or two. The words are tinged with a slight accent. Bosnian is my guess.

"I don't have time for this. It's either money now or one of you goes with me and my friends to get questioned for free."

Big Guy looks back at the downed guy who shakes his head, the brows on his face beetling together to emphasize that he is adamant about being quiet. Big Guy gives my money a regretful look and then tries to punch me again. I block him with my arm and then spring forward with both fists flying. He's caught off guard and stumbles backward over his friend. I'm up on the balls of my feet, ready for them, when Big Guy lumbers to a standing position and slowly pulls out a knife.

"You should've taken the money," I say and then gesture for him to come forward.

"You started the party without me," I hear behind me.

"Just trying to make my dinner date," I quip.

Steve hands me a gun with a suppressor, and at the sight of the two of us with guns, Big Guy stands down. "Throw the knife to me," I order. Big Guy tosses the knife and it lands about five feet away. To Steve I say, "Take the guy on the ground. He's the one giving orders."

Steve brushes by me and toward the assailants. Big Guy doesn't even try to defend himself when Steve clocks him with the handgun. As the larger assailant crumples to the ground, his friend powers to his feet and runs toward the end of the alley, jumps on a Dumpster conveniently located under a fire escape stairs, and runs off. Steve and I watch him go.

"I guess we're bringing this guy home. Think Tiny will like the present?" Steve asks.

"He's going to Kaga's," I order. "Drive me to The Plaza and then take him. I'll deal with him later."

"You need a little cleaning up," Steve remarks, giving me a once over. He's dragging Big Guy behind him, so I go over and pick up the deadweight's other arm. We haul him out of the alley to the waiting Bentley.

"Shit, I'm going to need a new car after this," I say.

"Pretty much."

I get into the front with Steve and flip down the visor. I've got a cut over my eye and a faint bruise on my cheek. In the tiny mirror, I can see that my collar is speckled with blood and spit. "And I'm going to need a shower."

The car's clock says it's 7:00. "How late will Tiny be?" I ask.

"Car's picking her up now, so maybe a half hour?"

"Call the driver and tell her to delay as much as possible, and take me to Kaga's. We'll dump this guy in the basement. Kaga should have something for me to wear."

Kaga isn't afraid to get his hands dirty. Aquarium would be the perfect place to lock up a criminal.

"Aye," Steve answered.

"Tiny's driver *is* a woman, right?"

"It's a guy, but I told him to pretend like he didn't have a dick because if he touched Tiny or looked at her wrong, you would cut it off."

"You're a good man, Steve."

"Just watching your back."

◆ ◆ ◆

Kaga meets us in the alley behind the bar. "I've got a better place than the bar for this type of delivery," Kaga observes, peering into the backseat.

"I don't have time to go over to the docks. I'm supposed to meet Tiny at The Plaza at 7:00."

"You need a new watch then, because it's 7:20 right now."

"Are you done busting my chops?"

He looks at me. "Looks like someone already did that for me."

"Is it that bad?"

"In the light of The Plaza dining room, you'll still look like you took a header to the face, but come in. I'll have Priya apply some makeup to you. At least you can get through dinner without too many questions. What you tell Tiny after is something you can work on during dinner."

"Thanks," I grouse. Big Guy is conscious but steps out of the car meekly. I guess the three of us here have subdued him.

"Did you have other babysitting duties tonight?" Kaga asks Steve as we escort the assailant down into the basement of Kaga's nightclub.

"Yeah, told him he needed another bodyguard, but he didn't listen."

"You fight with one hand, you will be defeated," Kaga intones.

"Jesus Christ," I complain. "You pull that Zen shit out to mock me? It's a wonder Buddha doesn't smite you."

"I pull out the Zen shit to mock everyone, not just you. I can't fathom why you think you're special like that," Kaga replies.

He stops at a large door with a bar across it. He pulls the heavy sucker open and gestures for our prisoner to step inside. There's a chair, a water spigot, and a bucket in the corner. The floor is damp, as if it's been freshly washed. The assailant balks at first, but as we stand around him, arms folded, he walks in. Kaga secures the door behind him.

"Do I even want to know why you have this room?"

Kaga shakes his head. "Not really. Let's get you a different jacket."

"And pants," Steve interjects.

My pants look fine. I turn to tell Steve so, but then notice a rip down the side. "And pants."

Upstairs in Kaga's office, Priya has a suit over a chair and a table full of makeup. I stick my finger in some sticky shit and grimace.

"Do I really need this?"

Priya looks at Kaga, who's leaning against his desk. "What will you tell Tiny?" he asks.

"I fell at the office?"

"She's going to think you're cheating on her."

"How so?"

"Because no one falls at his office," Kaga replies drolly. "If you make up a story she'll automatically assume you're cheating on her. It's either you got in a fight or you're cheating. I guess you'll decide which one she'll forgive faster."

"Kaga, if you don't shut up, I'm going to stick my boot up your ass."

He shrugs and opens his mouth to deliver another platitude while Steve snickers in the background. Sighing, I give in. "Make me beautiful, Priya."

"I'm only skilled enough to minimize your bruises. I can't work miracles."

Her snarky comment leads everyone to laugh. Even me.

After Priya works her magic, she leaves the three of us alone.

"I feel like a goddamn clown." I pat my face lightly.

"You look scary enough to be a clown," Kaga observes.

I give him the finger, while busily looking up the number to the Champagne Bar. "Who's the manager of the Champagne Bar at The Plaza?"

Kaga knows every important bar manager in the city. "DeWight Jones."

"Champagne Bar, how can I help you?" a pleasant voice intones.

"Ian Kerr. I'd like to speak to DeWight Jones."

"Certainly. Please hold."

Muting the volume on my end, I ask Kaga, "What are you stocking over there?"

"Ordering something to appease the old man?"

I nod.

"The twelve-year Kashikoi."

"Mr. Kerr, so kind of you to call us. What can I do for you?" DeWight Jones has a baritone that would rival Barry White's.

"Mr. Jones. Tadashubi Kaga conveys his regards. Thank you for taking my call. I'm in need of your assistance. My fiancée Victoria is there, and she and her companion are waiting for me to arrive. I'm running very late. I wondered if you could deliver food to the table, as well as a bottle of the twelve-year Kashikoi for the gentleman and a Singapore Sling for my lady. She's got light brown hair and wears it very straight. Likely she is the only female under thirty in your establishment wearing pants."

"I see them. They're sitting by a window and appear to be thirsty. I will remedy that immediately."

"Fantastic. I'll be there shortly. Please start a tab and I'll cover it."

"Certainly, Mr. Kerr. Please tell Mr. Kaga that it would be a pleasure to serve him soon."

"He'll be in within the week," I promise recklessly. Kaga glares at me, but I've committed him now and he's far too honorable to back out.

"We'll be delighted to see him." DeWight sounds downright giddy. "And you, of course," he tacks on.

"I'll be there in thirty minutes."

"They'll be treated as our most important guests," he says. "They won't even realize the time is passing."

"Thank you." I end the call.

"Why is it we're friends again?" Kaga is annoyed.

"Because I'm one of the few people who can afford to sit down at the poker table with you," I say, stripping out of my ruined suit pants.

"True." Kaga hands me the replacement pair and Steve sits impassively, watching the bar floor start to fill up. "What do you want to do with our guest?"

The suit pants are slightly short and the shirt is a bit too billowy for my taste, but after I shrug on the jacket, I decide that it's better than showing up looking like I'd been in a bar fight over in Queens. "No torturing without me," I instruct.

I signal Steve that I'm ready and we head out. Kaga follows behind. "It's called *Chinese* torture. I'm Japanese, or did you forget?"

"Your people have been oppressing the East for centuries. I think you know plenty of good torture techniques."

"Only a couple. And Genghis Khan was the one who oppressed the East for centuries. We only did it for a couple of them. Khan was Chinese. Or Mongolian, if you want to get technical."

"By all means," I reply dryly while climbing into the car. "Let's be precise and accurate. I'll be over in the morning. Treat him well. Maybe a good night's sleep and a full belly will loosen his lips."

CHAPTER 11

Steve breaks a half-dozen traffic laws to get me to The Plaza by 8:15. I'm over an hour late and starving. Hopefully DeWight has brought over a lot of food. It's a good thing Big Guy didn't take my money because I'm going to need the bills for tipping. DeWight, as any high-end manager would, recognizes me when I walk in. These guys live and breathe the society pages because they don't want to make the mistake of offending someone who might be powerful enough to get them fired.

"Mr. Kerr, your table is right over here." DeWight directs me to three club chairs situated by the window overlooking Fifth Avenue.

I slip him a hundred dollar bill. "I need a steak, medium-rare, and another glass for the whiskey."

"Of course," he says and smoothly secretes the money into his pocket.

"Sorry I'm late," I say as I reach the table. Leaning down, I inhale the lemon scent of Tiny and all the shit of the day drifts away. She has that perfect calming effect on me. Everything is going to be fine so long as we're together.

"Hey, I missed you," she says and raises her sweet face for a kiss. I want to linger. Hell, I want to drag her off and fuck her blind, working off the adrenaline that the attack had spiked, but now isn't the time. Not while her stepfather looks on with avidity. I press against her lips for a quick, hard kiss, so she knows that I missed the hell out of her too.

"Hedder." I give him a short nod and avoid his hand as I sit down. As unobtrusively as possible, I examine Hedder for any hint that he knew of the attack. His glib face shows no signs of satisfaction or dismay. My inspection is inconclusive.

I draw Tiny as close as the bulky club chairs allow, placing her hand on my thigh and covering it with my own. Her hand is slightly cold. Whether that's from her drink or Hedder remains to be seen.

"I'm sorry for dropping in on you like this. When Malcolm shared that Sophie had died, I was a wreck. After I'd picked myself up off the ground, I decided that I had to come and see you, Tiny," Mitch says.

Hedder sounds sincere, but this whole speech would have been better if he'd delivered it near the funeral instead of four weeks later. There's no way he spent four weeks wallowing in grief, and it pisses me off that he's trying to connect to Tiny through some idea of shared loss.

A waiter arrives with my steak and an extra glass. I pour myself a hefty serving of the twelve-year Kashikoi and allow the smooth tones of oak and fruit to roll over my tongue. "Kaga's whiskey," I point out to Tiny. "Want a sip?"

She demurs and turns back to Hedder.

"I wouldn't have turned you away," Tiny says softly. "Mom wouldn't have wanted that."

"She was such a good woman." Hedder sighs. "I miss her, and I kick myself for screwing up so badly with her. And worse, you were left all alone without anyone to help when she suffered through both bouts of cancer." He reaches across the table and takes her free hand. She flinches, almost imperceptibly. No one but me would likely even notice, but my entire body is attuned to hers.

I switch hands, placing my right over hers and using my left arm to draw her close to me. It will look as if I'm embracing her, not just moving her out of touching distance from Hedder. "Tiny isn't alone anymore. She has me."

"That's right." An inquisitive look sweeps through his eyes and then is replaced by fake fatherly outrage. "Unfortunately, the things that are said about you publicly don't suggest you'll be a good partner for Tiny. How long have you known each other?"

Tiny stiffens. "Mitch, I told you earlier that my relationship with Ian is none of your business. I'm sorry, but you haven't been my stepfather for almost a decade."

"And I'm sorry for that, Tiny. Sincerely, absolutely heartbroken about it. I've wanted to come back and make amends, but I was too ashamed. I'm here now, though, and I want to make up for lost time. That includes sticking around to make sure this guy," he nods toward me, "doesn't take advantage of you."

She gives a snort of disbelief. "I'm sure if there's any advantage-taking in this relationship, it's me taking advantage of Ian."

Keeping her in my embrace, I lean forward slightly. "Tiny and I are equals. We do not measure each other's worth by the size of our bank accounts."

Hedder eyes me speculatively and then his eyes drop to Tiny's ringless left hand. "I see you haven't asked her to marry you yet. Is she good enough to take to bed but not good enough to marry? I marry the women I love."

If I wasn't holding Tiny's hand, I would have laid him out. Before I can answer, though, Tiny shoots back. "It's nice that you're here and that you want to pay your respects to my mom, but I'll tell you for the last time, Ian is none of your business."

Her glare could freeze any man, and Hedder is about as low as they come. He gives her a weak smile and holds up both his hands in an innocent gesture. "I'm just trying to look out for you, just as Sophie would want."

"My mom adored Ian. She told me before she died that she was so glad he had come into my life. She said he reminded her of my dad." Tiny lifts her chin in a proud gesture. I had never heard this before, and I send her a questioning glance. With a slight nod she affirms that the story is true and not one she made up for Hedder's sake. The words that Sophie told Tiny give me great pleasure. And suddenly, I want to be anywhere but here. No, scratch that. I want to be home, holding Tiny, and making love to her, not sitting here listening to some con artist try to tug on Tiny's heartstrings. Her heart is tender and in need of special care. She does not need her absentee stepfather crumpling it like an elephant in a china shop.

"The Plaza is a quality hotel," I observe. "But pricey. You must be well set. Do you want to contribute to the outstanding burial costs?"

I'm bluffing because I paid all of the funeral costs. It's about the only money I spent on Tiny that she didn't object to. She's not good at accepting things from me without argument. Time will change that. Time and a ring of my own on her finger.

As expected, the mention of parting with any kind of money makes Hedder blanch. "Sophie was adamant that she didn't want any help when she asked me to leave."

"And you never thought to check in with them? As you pointed out, Tiny was without help for years. She and Sophie shouldered the burden alone. If you have money, and I assume you do since you are staying at a place that costs a cool grand a night, why weren't you helping them out?" I want to see what lies Hedder will spin in front of Tiny.

Hedder sputters. "I had no idea that they were struggling. They should have reached out to me. Tiny, you should have contacted me."

"I had no idea where you were." She shakes her head in disbelief.

"I've been down in Palm Beach," he declares.

"Since I was sixteen?" she asks incredulously.

Giving a nonchalant shrug of his shoulders, Hedder replies, "I was going through a stupid midlife crisis. Someone lured me down there, and I stayed for a while. Got caught up in the lifestyle. Made some friends. It's home now. Not like the city, of course. Nothing can replace the city, but for my old bones, the warm weather is good for me."

"Have you been in touch with Malcolm, then?" she asks.

"Oh, off and on."

Tiny looks at me, and we both wonder if Hedder knows Malcolm's business. I can see she's reluctant to bring it up, and frankly it's a topic I'd like to avoid for the night.

"Malcolm told you Sophie died?"

Hedder fidgets with his napkin a bit, which lies folded on the table. There's no evidence that he has eaten anything, and there are no plates in front of him. Tiny's had something, but she looks longingly at my steak. I cut off a few pieces and place them on her empty plate. The bottle of whiskey is half gone. In the dark light, I can make out a faint redness around Hedder's nose and cheeks, as well as spidering veins in the neck—all classic signs of a heavy, if not alcoholic, drinker.

After closer inspection, it becomes apparent that Hedder is wearing some kind of cover-up to diminish the signs of his facial discoloration, no doubt caused by years of alcohol abuse. I missed that the other day when he was in my office. Of course he's not eating. He's got a bottle of one of the finest whiskies in all the land in front of him. He has no desire to sully that with actual food, no matter how badly he needs it. I'm curious how a drunken Mitch Hedder acts and whether his behavior will push Tiny far enough away.

I signal for DeWight, and he appears seconds later. "Another bottle of the Kashikoi, please."

Hedder's eyes flicker with uncomfortable greed at the mention of another bottle. Liquor is an obvious weakness. What others does he have?

"Certainly. The twelve-year?"

"Yes, and another steak please."

"Of course. Right away." DeWight backs away and corrals an underling to do his bidding.

"How come you get steak in here when I could only order little tiny things like the ceviche that came on a spoon? It was literally one bite," Tiny complains. "Are there no restaurants here?"

"There's the Food Hall, but no, The Plaza has no intimate dining space. They likely think you'll eat elsewhere."

The Champagne Bar served mostly tapas, finger foods. Steak is an accommodation being made for me, perhaps because DeWight wants something from Kaga, like another position at a different bar or restaurant or hotel. Kaga once told me he'd been accosted at one of his nightclubs, not because the person wanted to sleep with him—although that might be true—but because the individual was desperate for reassignment to one of the resorts Kaga's family owned.

"Thank you for the red meat. I was dying here."

"We can't have that. You need your energy tonight." She gives me a wan smile but the heat in her eyes is genuine.

"It was Malcolm's mother, Connie, who told me," Hedder interrupts.

I send him a killing look. Not only do I find his presence near me offensive but that he's interrupting my time with Tiny makes me even more irritated.

"Connie?" Tiny voices her surprise. "You still keep in contact with her?"

"Of course. I spoke to her on the phone a couple of weeks ago. She said she attended Sophie's funeral. I asked about you, of course, worried that you'd be alone, but she mentioned you had a friend with you." He nods toward me. "And another friend of mine saw a reference to Sophie's funeral in the *Post*."

"The *Post*?" Tiny looks at me inquiringly.

"I forgot you can't read," Hedder says with condescension in his voice. Tiny stiffens and the urge to impose some physical judgment on Hedder grips me again. "Yes, it mentioned that billionaire philanthropist Ian Kerr was attending the funeral of Sophie Corielli."

"I must have missed that entry," I say.

She shrugs, but a little hint of red shows at base of her neck. I could kill Hedder for making her feel embarrassed. "I only saw the one in the *Observer*."

"I needed to come up and make sure that everything was going well for you, dear." Hedder reaches forward to pat Tiny on the arm, but I stop him with a glare. I don't want him touching her. DeWight interrupts our glaring contest with another steak and another bottle.

"I'm fine," she says, and while I'd like that to be true, I don't think she is. She will be, but it's only been a few weeks since her mother's death, and I'd never been around someone who loved her mother as much as Tiny did.

"I'll be here for a few weeks," Hedder declares. "We should spend time together."

"Malcolm said that you had something of Mom's. What is it?"

"I don't have it with me. Besides, I'd like to visit the grave. We should do that together."

She presses her lips together and slides me a disbelieving look. We're not getting anything out of Hedder tonight.

I raise my glass in his direction. I don't understand his game yet. Breaking us up wouldn't be in his best interest, but he wants something. I won't underestimate him. A snake in the garden is still a snake, and there's no way that Hedder can afford to set up residence at The Plaza without having fleeced his share of lambs.

Even though she said she was hungry, the second steak isn't appealing to Tiny. She merely picks at it. I'm tired and my body is very sore and I'm sick of wearing this pancake makeup. Standing up, I toss a few smaller bills on the table to serve as a tip. "I'm ready to call it a night. Is that all right with you, Tiny?" I don't like that he uses her nickname. He shouldn't be allowed even that small intimacy with the woman he abandoned.

"Yes, I'm ready." She wipes her mouth and then sets her napkin on the table. "It was nice to see you again, Mitch, but I don't foresee needing you to vet my friends. It's been a long time since I needed that. And you aren't my father."

With that sharp admonition, Tiny turns to go, but Hedder grabs her arm. "Think about my request. I think Sophie would want it."

She doesn't shake off his hand immediately and gives him a small nod. "I'll think about it."

"You know where to find me." He waves a hand toward the lobby.

At the manager's stand, I hand my black AmEx to DeWight. "Take the rest of the Kashikoi and enjoy it tonight. Compliments of Mr. Kaga and me."

"And the gentleman?"

"He's had enough to drink."

"Very good, sir."

Within moments, DeWight is back with a leather-padded folio. Inside, I scrawl my name under the charges. Ten grand per bottle. I shake my head. Kaga is probably laughing his ass off somewhere. No wonder DeWight is so obsequious.

I alert Steve that we're ready. Tucking Tiny's hand in my arm, I take her out into the lobby. I finally get to see her fully. She's wearing black, wide-legged tuxedo pants paired with a black lace cropped top. A minute amount of skin flashes below the hem. The small glimpses of flesh only serve to heighten my awareness of her lithe body.

"Did I see that receipt right?" she asks in astonishment.

"If you saw that Kaga is charging a kidney for his cheap twelve-year reserve whiskey, then yes, you saw it right."

"That's his *cheap* whiskey?" Her eyebrows are at the top of her head.

"There's a thirty-year reserve. I think it runs around one hundred grand per bottle."

"I couldn't even drink it, knowing it cost that much."

"How much it costs sometimes directly influences how much you like it. Or so says Kaga. But in truth, there's a big difference in the age of the whiskey. The older it is, the smoother, deeper, and richer the flavors. It's an experience. I have a couple. Gifts from Kaga. We'll have a tasting contest at home some night."

"Oh no." She laughs. I see Steve pull up in front of the hotel.

As I'm leading her down the exterior stairs to the street, I whisper,

"I'm going to pour it onto your breasts and lick it off drop by drop, and then I'll drench your pussy in it and suck you until I'm full of you and rich whiskey."

She shivers and nearly stumbles as we climb into the backseat. I hit the button for the privacy screen and I'm on her before it's even halfway up, before the door is even closed, because I can't wait for one more minute. Pressing her against the door, I kiss her ravenously, wanting to erase the sourness of the night with the sweet sounds of our love. We tug at each other's clothes. My hands sweep under her shirt and hers are busy at my waistband and then they are folding around my ever increasing shaft.

We're so lost in each other that it takes a few moments to register that the car has been halted for longer than thirty seconds and I realize we must be home.

"Thanks, Steve," I say, helping Tiny out of the car. She ducks her head, still embarrassed by the fact that Steve knows we have sex.

"Thanks," she mumbles and then hurries into the warehouse.

He shakes his head. "Nothing like Barbara," he mutters referring to the exhibitionist. Steve had been the recipient of her attentions a while back as well.

"Barbara? I thought her name was Bettina."

"Nah, pretty sure it was Barbara."

We stare at each other in shared memory, and Steve even manages to crack a smile, which for him is equal to a belly laugh.

"No, nothing like Barbara," I admit softly, watching the lights turn on as Tiny makes her way upstairs. Slapping a hand on his back, I tell him, "Tomorrow morning we'll take care of the trash."

"Good idea."

"Not too early, though," I instruct, my eyes still on the lights in my home. Before I had Tiny, when I arrived at the warehouse the place would be dark. She was turning my residence into a real home. Steve senses my preoccupation, climbs into the car, and drives off without another word.

I take my time following Tiny inside, tracing her footsteps and wondering what parts of the walls and floor she's touched. I want her stamp on every part of my life—no area is too unimportant or miniscule.

There are lights on in the kitchen and one in the living room. Her path leads me up the stairs and into our bedroom. On the billowy comforter rests her purse, and the dim light of the bathroom pulls me forward. In the dressing room, I find her removing her lace shirt and carefully hanging it in the closet. Her pants come off next, and she tosses those in the hamper.

There's nothing left but a tiny navy-blue thong. Her back to me, she hooks two fingers into the sides and then slowly drags the material down over the apple-round curve of her ass and her strong thighs. She bends as she pulls the fabric down, so that her ass is prominently displayed and I catch a glimpse of her swollen sex.

Bending almost in half, she finally steps out of the thong, leaving it to lie on the carpet of the dressing room as she stands up, dragging her hands up her legs and then her outer thighs. This display is all for me, and it's working well.

"Come over and feel what you've made hard." I crook my finger toward her. She saunters over to me, her feet still encased in high wedges with navy ribbons around her ankles. There are other places I'd like to see ribbons wrapped. Her thighs. Her wrists. Her neck.

There are so many fantasies I have, and only one lifetime to get them all in.

"You look like a fucking goddess."

I don't move from the door, wanting to see how far her boldness extends. As she walks toward me I can see small reflections of light glinting off the arousal painted on her thighs. My breath quickens, and my cock feels like it grows another inch.

"I'm horny," she proclaims accusingly. "The looks you were giving me at The Plaza. The way you touched me in the car. You've worked me up."

"Bunny, I'm going to take care of you."

She stops in front of me and unhurriedly drops to her knees, dragging her hands down my legs. My hands go to my waistband, but she bats them away. "I'm going to get you worked up now. See how you like it. Hands up."

Widening my stance, I lean against the doorjamb, not caring that it's an uncomfortable position and the wood trim is digging into my back. I lift my hands behind my head in a gesture of surrender. "I'm ready to take my punishment."

"Good. You don't get to come until I tell you." Her smile is naughty. Whatever game she wants to play tonight, I'm in. I'm so fucking in.

"I'm your humble servant." And that's the God's honest truth. I'd do anything for her, including keeping my hands to myself and my orgasm at bay.

She unfastens my pants and drags down the fabric just enough that my cock springs free. With a soft hand, she cups my balls and pulls them above the constraining fabric. It's like wearing too-tight clothes, but the extra tension is only making me harder.

Her hand smooths down my hard length. "How big are you?"

"Big enough," I grunt as she pets the top of my circumcised head and then runs her finger under the bulbous tip.

"You're bigger than the span of my fingers." She stretches her hand out to display the deficit. Her pinky and thumb can't reach the base and tip at the same time, falling a few inches short. "And you're wide. It's hard to get my mouth around you."

She dips her head and sucks in the very tip of my cock. My hands clench behind my head in restraint. I want to reach for her head and shove my dick into her mouth and down her tight throat. We've done it once. She's taken me so deep that her voice was raspy afterward. This is her show, I remind myself. With some effort, I force myself to relax as much as possible.

"It takes a lot of licking to get your whole dick wet." Her little tongue laps at me, licking the edges and spending extra time laving the veins that stand prominently under the sensitive skin of my cock. "I'm going to have to use both my hands, it's so big."

Jesus. Can I die of a hard-on? Can I get so erect and so hard that I actually drop dead? Because I feel close to dying as she interlocks her two hands and starts squeezing her palms up and down my swollen member.

"Your body is a perfect fit for mine," I tell her.

"I don't know." Her voice is tremulous, and I can't tell whether that's part of the act or whether it's from her arousal. Maybe a bit of both. "It's just so huge I worry that it won't fit inside me. Maybe if I suck on it, it will get smaller."

I release a strangled laugh. "Yes, let's try that."

"But you have so much come. Sometimes I can't swallow it all. Sometimes it spills out the side of my mouth and dribbles onto my chin."

The filthy, erotic picture she's painting is making my entire frame shake with want. I switch my hands from cupping my head to gripping the wood trim, uncaring that the hard edges are biting into my skin. I need the pain to keep me upright. To keep me from throwing her onto her back and plunging into her like a fucking animal. Sides heaving, I manage to choke out an answer. "That's okay. You can just wipe it off with your fingers."

"Then should I lick my fingers?"

"Yes," I groan. "You should lick it all up. It's good for you. Lots of antibodies."

"If you're sure?" she says breathily. And then her mouth is on me. She takes me shallowly at first, humming a little so I feel the vibrations of sound rumble against my length. Her hands work my base in rhythm with her mouth in a steady, thrusting motion. My thighs tremble with the effort of standing upright. I need her to be with me. This gift of pleasure won't feel as good if she isn't going crazy also.

"Does it taste good, bunny? Did you miss having my fat cock in your mouth today? Did you think about me at your desk, laying you down and shoving my cock down your throat?"

She nods and moans around me, but doesn't stop the pace.

"I thought of you today, all day. My pants were so tight. I thought about your hot little body wrapped around mine. I fantasized about your mouth sucking me down. I nearly passed out at the memory of your throat bulging with my dick and the raspy notes of want you voiced after I'd fucked your mouth and throat so hard. I wanted you to come to my office so I could hoist you onto the desk and pull down your panties. I imagine you, slick and ready for me. Your little lips swollen with need. Your moans fill my office as I devour you. While you're still coming from your first orgasm, I slide my fingers inside and stroke you until you soak my hand as well."

One hand abandons my cock to dip between her legs. Christ, that's hot. I keep talking because I'm not supposed to touch her.

"What do you feel between your legs? Are you slippery? Do you feel empty? I can see your thighs clenching. Your body wants me to fill it up, doesn't it?"

She takes me deeper, and whether it's to shut me up or turn me on even more, I don't know and I don't care. At the first entrance into her throat, I'm speechless. Then she swallows and the muscles tighten all around me. I shout out a warning to her, "Goddammit, I'm coming." She only sucks harder, and I come, barely keeping upright as my entire focus centers around my groin. Pumping almost helplessly against her, she holds my hips in her soft hands to keep me from choking her. And when she's drunk it all down, my softened cock slips out of her mouth.

I loosen my grip on the wall to tuck one hand under her chin and tangle my other in her long brown strands. Tipping her head back, I search for visible affirmation that this is what she wanted. Her face glows in satisfaction, and in her eyes I see pride and power and confidence. Sinking to my knees, I take her mouth with mine as gently as possible. "You undo me," I whisper against her lips and then kiss her even more tenderly, tasting myself on her tongue.

"I wanted that," she croaks, the abrasion of her throat altering her tone. Impossibly, I harden again at the sound, as the memory of her swallowing me whole threatens to overwhelm me. With effort, I rise and pull her into my arms, carrying her into the bedroom.

As the high of the orgasm wears off, I feel an ache in my chest, thighs, and face from the earlier beating. I keep the lights low so she can't see any developing bruises. Pulling back the sheets with one hand as I hold her against my chest with the other, I lay her gently onto the bed and cover her with the comforter.

"Stay here," I order. In the bathroom, I quickly wash my face, throwing the washrag in the trash after I see that makeup has soiled it. It takes a hard scrubbing to get it all off, and it's almost more painful to remove the makeup from my bruises then it was to get the lacerations in the first place. Tomorrow I'll have to ask Tiny exactly how women do it. Or maybe I'll just watch her and discover it for myself. The clothes I borrowed from Kaga are tossed in the same bin.

Making sure most of the lights are out, I return to her. The disarray of the sheets reveals her restlessness. Kneeling by the side of the bed, I draw the covers back so her body is exposed. "Does my bunny ache?" I ask her, drawing my fingers down the center of her cunt.

"Yes," she admits, her voice still hoarse.

"You're going to have to make do with my mouth for now."

"Bring it." She gives a low, almost painful laugh.

I take my time, though, nuzzling her thighs and enjoying her spicy scent. Her arousal dampens my cheeks and nose as I re-acquaint myself with her treasure. With measured strokes of my tongue, I lap at her juices. This time I'm not a hungry bear marauding a buffet. I'm taking my time. This is a leisurely exploration of all the pleasure points that exist between her legs. And there are a lot.

Her little clit is stiff. I suck on it, flicking it with my tongue and enjoying the panting cries the action elicits. Her lips are engorged with blood, and though it is dark, I remember how they look: dusky and plump. I French those lips, sucking each between my lips and tickling the sensitive center with my tongue.

Two fingers slip into her, their passage made easy by her abundant arousal. Inside, I feel her hot and tight against my digits. Palm up, I stroke her with long, even caresses while I work the rest of her with my mouth. Every inch gets licked. Her inner thighs are the recipients of love bites, followed by soothing licks of my tongue, and finished by tender kisses. I might not mark her neck, but I'm going to leave signs of my invasion all over her legs. My beard growth gently abrades her, adding an extra layer of sensation.

Her hands alternate between pulling at my hair and pushing at the headboard for leverage. She moans and sighs and cries, a symphony of fucking accompanied by the juicy sounds of her cunt and my own groans as I feast on the delight before me.

All too soon she's coming. Her thighs shake and tremble, and her cries are more frantic. "Ian, Ian, *Ian*," she wails. Her chants of worship make me feel like a god. The blood is rushing from my head and hardening in my cock.

"Are you ready for me?"

"Yes, please," she begs. "I *need* you."

CHAPTER 12

Her legs fall open, and even in the dark of night I can see her glistening between her legs. My saliva and her come have mixed to form an erotic decoration of her body.

"Why are you stopping?" she whispers as I hesitate.

"I don't know. I see you here, and I just want to worship you." I run my hands down her sides, shaping her form. "You're so beautiful."

When her softness embraces the broad head of my cock, I close my eyes and savor the moment, knowing I should pull out right then and sheathe myself. But I don't want to. She mindlessly urges me forward, her hands grasping at my ass cheeks and her thighs pulling at me. I slip an inch farther inside. It's fucking heaven, and I don't want to leave.

Her back arches and her head tips back, her entire body urging me to take her hard. I plunge inside her with one long stroke, enjoying the naked feeling of her ridged channel sliding against my bare flesh. She cries out. I bite my own lip to suppress a shout. Her heat surrounds me from crest to base. I still for a moment so that I can feel the small pulses as her sex stretches to accommodate me. A squeeze of her hand on my hip signals me that she's ready.

I look down between us and wish there was more light so I could see in detail the way her folds part as I drag my cock slowly in and out of her. My shaft is slicked with her arousal, and the wet sounds of her slick passage are matched by breathless panting from both of us.

Leaning over her, I brace an elbow by her side so I can kiss all of the tender places I've stroked with my hand.

The cords of her neck stand proud as she arches into me. The tenseness of her body, the flush of her face, and the urgent way she claws at my back all tell me she is ready to come. I slip my free hand between us. Her clit is swollen and sensitive. When I press my thumb against it, she screams my name. The sound ricochets inside the bedroom and inside my head.

I work her steadily through her orgasm. Even when she whimpers "no more," I don't let up. There's more inside her. "Ride it out, bunny," I croon in her ear. She's entering that pleasure/pain stage where every touch is electrifying, and she's not sure whether it's good or bad. On the other side is another more intense orgasm, and I want her to reach it.

Sitting up, I pull her legs together and clasp her around her thighs with one arm while I work her clit with my other hand. Her nails rake the back of my hand and my forearm, and she thrashes wildly on the mattress. "Come for me, bunny. Come," I order. And then I feel her shatter beneath me. Her sheath squeezes my cock so tightly as she climaxes a third time that I nearly fall backward in ecstasy. She's shaking, almost crying, as she comes down off the high.

I slip out of her and, with three harsh jerks, start to ejaculate, long spurts of come spilling over the tops of her thighs, between her legs, and onto the sheet. With a groan, I pump myself harder, until there's nothing left inside me, and I collapse on the mattress beside her.

The sheets are torn loose from the bed corners, and beneath my legs I can feel the scratchy surface of the mattress cover. We are a sticky, sweaty mess, and I want nothing more than to lie there with her in my arms while she tries to absorb the power of the climax that just ripped through both of us.

"I don't understand how it gets better each time," she says finally, licking a bit of sweat off my chest.

"Because you're like good whiskey, bunny. Each minute that ticks by makes you taste better."

"Like twelve-year reserve?" she giggles.

"No, more like a one-hundred-and-twelve-year reserve. You taste any better and I'm not going to be able to spend even one minute without my face between your legs."

"You say that like it's a bad thing."

"It can be an absolute fucking reality," I tell her. Realizing that she might be uncomfortable, even if I'm not, I force myself out of the bed. With the adrenaline of the night having worn off completely, the aches and pains of the fight are making themselves known. Before I can prevent it, a slight moan escapes me.

"What's wrong?" Tiny sits up. Her hair is tangled in a thousand knots. She's never looked sexier.

"Nothing," I reply before leaning over to kiss her, but she pushes me back before my lips can find their target.

"Is that a cut over your eye? Did I scratch you?" She sounds horrified.

"You did, but not there." I present my back to her so she can see the evidence of her mindless excitement. They're marks I'll wear proudly. There are scratches on my forearms, ass, and thighs. I hope they burn when I shower.

"Then what?"

I realize I'm going to have to tell her something, and I don't want to lie to her. She doesn't deserve that. "Give me a minute."

She nods, but I feel her gaze tracking me—and not in a sexual way. In the bathroom, I find a washrag and wipe away the sticky residue of my come and maybe even a little of hers. I toss the cloth on the floor and wet a second one for Tiny.

She's still sitting on the edge of the ruined bed when I approach. I gesture for her to lie back while I clean her up. "After I hung up with you earlier, I was attacked."

Her hand grips my wrist, preventing me from using the cloth. A droplet of water splashes on her stomach, but she barely notices. "Where? Who did it? Did you call the police?"

"I don't know who they are, and no, I didn't call the police." Gently, I move her hand and commence my task of wiping her clean.

"Why didn't you call the police?" she nearly yells.

"Because I don't think either you or I need the eyes of the law turned toward us, given what's going on with Howe and Hedder."

She falls silent and then, more subdued, asks, "What will you do?"

"Tomorrow Steve and I will discuss the matter. See what we can come up with." While I'm not interested in lying to her, neither am I ready to confess that I've apprehended one of my assailants and currently have him locked in a windowless cell in Kaga's basement. I don't know what I'm going to do with him yet, and I'm not prepared to divulge that information to Tiny until I do. I don't want him on her conscience. She has enough to deal with.

"Is that why you were late?"

"Yes, I had to change. Steve took me to Kaga's, and his assistant applied some makeup to my face. I don't know how you women stand it. I felt like a clown." Finished with her, I toss the rag to the side. "Now I don't know about you, but I'm not going to be able to sleep in this mess . . . however, I don't know that I can make the bed," I admit with not a little chagrin.

She rises and then pushes me away. "I'll get the sheets."

She marches me toward the bathroom, throwing on all the lights. I understand. She wants to see the evidence of the brawl. I'd want the same, so I swallow any impatience as she turns and inspects me. The light reveals what the darkness—and I—have hidden. The cut above my eye is beginning to swell and turn yellow and purple. Tomorrow it will be black and blue. The bruise above my cheekbone is light and looks only slightly darker than if I were flushed.

My torso took the most abuse. I've got darkening bruises on my ribs and upper thighs. Tiny looks anguished. "How could you make love to me while you were all beat up?"

"Truthfully, I couldn't feel it. The urge to be inside you overrode any other sensory input."

She shakes her head in disbelief. "You should never have touched me. Why didn't you tell me?"

"Because if I had, you wouldn't have let me touch you," I answer with a touch of frustration.

Throwing up her hands, she turns and rummages around in the closet until she finds a spare set of sheets. I follow her meekly into the bedroom. "You could have mentioned something when you arrived for dinner."

"I didn't see a moment when I could interject 'Hey, got mugged down on Hudson Street' into the conversation."

"Down by your office?" She pauses in the act of shaking out the bottom sheet.

"In the alley next to my building."

"This is my fault, isn't it?"

In two quick strides, I'm around the bed and have her in my arms. "How could this possibly be your fault?"

"I don't know."

"Shit, Tiny. Maybe Richard Howe figured out I'm trying to ruin him. If anything, I should be sorry for bringing *you* into this mess."

At the mention of Howe's name, her body stiffens. "I hate that man."

"Me too, but it's late and we both have shit to do tomorrow. Let's make this damn bed because we've had a long day. I don't know about you, but I'm exhausted." I nip at her neck.

"Fine," she says grumpily. "When should we go to see Mom?"

"With Hedder? Never."

"But Ian, he asked. I know he's bad news, but I don't think a grave-side visit is going to do much harm. You're overreacting."

I bite down on my tongue and swallow my first harsh response, which is that she's being far too benevolent.

"Your beloved mother died just a few weeks ago. It's difficult to make rational decisions right now. I know. I've been there." I run my hand through her hair, smoothing the strands along my chest. "You want to be with people who cared for her, who'll bring her alive for you. I made a lot of terrible choices after my mom died. I wish someone had been there for me."

She thinks about this. "Malcolm will go with us. Or at least that's what Mitch said."

My patience snaps. "Oh, great. Your drug dealing, pimp stepbrother will go with your con artist stepfather. That's not a disaster in the making."

"Let's not forget how we met," she replies tartly.

"We met on the street between Seventh and Fifty-Second."

"Not the second time."

"Right, he sent you to me," I point out.

"He didn't know what you needed," she argues.

I want to shake her. Is she being deliberately obtuse? "I went to him because he runs a high-class escort service, and he sent you to me. He tried to fucking sell you." I'm outraged on her behalf. Just the thought of Malcolm treating her like a whore makes me want to drive to Queens so I can break him in half. My hold on her turns rigid in an effort not to hurt her while I fantasize about pounding Malcolm until his face is bloody and unrecognizable.

"Then I should be just as afraid of you," she retorts.

"I turned you down," I shoot back. "I asked you to dinner. I wanted to date you, not buy you."

"What's all of this, then? My clothes? This home? The driver?" She waves her arms around, trying to gesture at everything.

"It's me *loving* you," I roar.

Her chest is heaving. I collapse on the pillows behind me, my arms spread in complete surrender. "Bunny, I fucking love you. I don't want to see you hurt."

"Do you really think they'd hurt me?" She scuttles up against the headboard and folds her knees under her chin. I hear the pain in her voice, the loneliness that I can't chase away—not even with all the money in the world. It makes me feel helpless and angry, but I know she doesn't need that now or ever. I shouldn't ever raise my voice to her. I lay my palm next to her thigh, hoping she'll touch it and give me a sign of forgiveness.

"Not intentionally." She doesn't want to believe what little family she has left would be so cruel to her, but these are not good men. One tried to prostitute her without her knowing, and the other returned to try to profit from her mother's death.

"You can't wrap me up in Bubble Wrap. I'm not going to sit here in the warehouse and eat chocolates all day."

"I've never asked you to do that." But I'm going to protect her with everything in me, even if it pisses her off.

"Hmmph," she snorts. "I'm capable of taking care of myself. I was doing it fine before you came along."

Is her implication that she would also be fine if I left? Because that isn't happening.

"I don't doubt it, but you don't have to do it alone anymore," I say, gathering the weak reins of my self-control.

Her hand drifts down and lightly touches my hand. I remain motionless, allowing her to sort through her feelings. Her index finger traces the lines of my palm, an erotic feeling if there ever was one. I shift slightly as the blood starts collecting in my groin. She can crank my engine with a feather-light touch. Doesn't she realize how much power she has in her smallest finger? I'd crawl across glass to make her happy, and I'd endure a thousand nights of cold shoulders and a sexless bed if it would keep her safe.

"I know that they aren't concerned with my best interests like you are. And I know Mitch wants something." She stretches out her fingers and interlaces them with mine. I close my hand around hers. It's reassuring to hear her acknowledge Hedder's bad intent. "I can't deny him the trip, though. Mom wouldn't want that. Be vigilant but kind, she would say."

"That sounds like Sophie, wise and generous." My thumb rubs along hers. "Will you let me come, then? Just as an escort. I'll stay in the car. You won't even know I'm there." *But I'll be out of the car in a flash should anyone cause you to stumble. Before they blink, I'll be on them.*

"If I say no?" she asks.

"I'll follow you anyway," I admit.

"At least you're honest," she sighs. A twinge of guilt causes me to tighten my grip. It doesn't pass unnoticed by Tiny. "What?" she asks with challenge.

"I might have left out a small bit of information about my earlier altercation."

"A small bit," she says sarcastically.

"Infinitesimal." I roll over on my side to face her, still holding her hand.

"So small you didn't think it was important to divulge, right?"

"More like, so small I didn't want to worry you."

"But you're going to tell me now, right? Because you're honest with me?" Her eyebrow is cocked, and I can tell this is a test.

With a sigh, I give in. "I have one of the attackers stashed in Kaga's basement."

"*Ian Kerr.* Why didn't you tell me this before?" She tugs to get loose of my grip, but I won't let her.

"Listen now. I didn't tell you because I didn't want to worry you. He might not tell me anything. I promise that he's been fed and treated properly. Tomorrow we'll let him go if he doesn't cough up any information. Now come here and tend to my wounds, woman."

I tug on her hand. She resists for a moment and then slides down next to me.

"You have to make sure I get a good night's rest before I confront Big Guy tomorrow." I settle her into our sleeping position: her head on my shoulder; my arm curled around her back; her leg on top of my thighs.

"Big Guy?"

"They haven't divulged their names. I dubbed them Big Guy and Small Guy."

She snorts and all is right in the world. We made love, fought, and now we're entangled together once again.

CHAPTER 13

Kaga's holding room doesn't look much better in the morning. Down below the Aquarium club, there was little to distinguish between night and day. Big Guy had been provided a candle; its wick was nearly burned out when we opened the door. He didn't have the look of a hungry man, and less than twenty-four hours had passed. We had done nothing physical to him, but isolation and darkness can be its own punishment.

I lean against the door frame, with Kaga holding the heavy door open behind me. "Ready to talk?"

His face looks uncertain but a glance at the nearly burned out candle prompts a response. "What?" The question is pure frightened belligerence.

"How about we start with your name?"

He relaxes slightly and shakes his head. "You can't keep me here forever."

"You're wrong." Kaga remains silent. This is my show. "Not only can I keep you here forever, but no one would even know. Except perhaps your brother?" I make an educated guess based on the likeness of their features. He starts, eyes darting around as if worried that we have his sibling locked up in a neighboring cell. "How will he explain this to the police? He can't very well claim that the two of you were involved in a botched assault that led to your disappearance."

"Might as well let me go. Not talking," he says mulishly. He recognizes that if we haven't called the police by now, we aren't going to. Yet he's not smart enough to appreciate what kind of danger he's in.

"You should have come at me with the knife first. Why pull that out as backup instead of leading with your strong hand?" I ask. That part has puzzled me all night.

There's no immediate verbal response, but I watch his body carefully. His shoulders slump, and the look on his face is one of worry rather than fear. Kaga and I wait him out. Finally he says, "Didn't want to kill you. We're not into that. Just rough you up."

"No point in giving me a beating if you don't attach it to a verbal warning. Otherwise it's just a random attack with no deterrent. So what's my warning?"

His eyes jerk to mine with surprise, as if he just realized he had missed the most important part of this whole charade. "You got so many enemies you don't know which one is hiring out a beating?"

Kaga bursts out laughing. He continues to howl so hard he doubles over and the door slips from his grip. I have to catch the metal slab before it slams shut. Straightening, I walk out. This guy needs more time to think—this time without the candle. I start to close the door.

"Wait," he says with alarm. "This is kidnapping."

"I prefer to think of it as having a guest, but you can use a different term if you like." I shut the door before he can say anything else. Turning to Kaga, I resist the urge to shove my knee into his face. He manages to gain control and stands up, hands on his hips. "Thanks, asshole."

"You have to admit, that's kind of funny. This guy doesn't have a message for you because whoever hired him thought you would know who it was."

"What kind of message is an assault?" I complain. "I'm not some random gambler who can't pay my debts. Hitting me isn't going to do anything but make me angry. Frankly, this is the kind of show of force that bookies and drug dealers like to carry out. So while my first thought was Howe, I don't think the Hedders can be scratched off the list. Anyone else is going to come at me in the boardroom or on the trading floor with cash and liquidated assets, not with fists and knives."

Kaga nods in agreement. "You'll figure it out. What do you want me to do with our friend?"

"Let him stew for a few more hours and then let him go. It's a crying shame when you can't buy people off. I didn't know loyalty existed."

"It's probably fear-based silence," he observes.

I agree. "Then it's probably Howe, because he got those three women to clam up tighter than a duck's ass." The three women I'd tried to convince to come forward and ruin Howe had all resisted the money I threw at them. That was when I turned to Malcolm Hedder in the hopes of hiring someone who would get me sufficient texts, pictures, or video of Howe to cause his wife to leave him and his family to disown him.

If Cecilia ever filed for divorce, I'd bring the full power of Kerr Inc. down on top of him. I held the majority of his debts, quietly buying them up through different shell corporations. It would be easy enough to tip him into bankruptcy.

Except I fell for Tiny and couldn't bring myself to use her in that fashion, which left me without a way to separate Howe from his family. At least, for now.

"Speaking of Howe, what's Tiny doing this morning?" Kaga asks.

We head upstairs to Kaga's office. Even on the main floor, it's hard to know the time of day because of the lack of windows. The only way to mark time inside the Aquarium is by the number of people that are present. The bar is eerily silent as the only inhabitants this morning are Kaga and me. Priya doesn't come in until the afternoon.

"Steve took her to Jake's."

"How does she enjoy her new job?"

"Seems like she hates it," I admit.

"Rough."

"Yup."

"You having Steve follow her everywhere?"

I nod. "Until I can talk her into getting a bodyguard. It's just a smart precaution. Kidnapping for ransom seems more popular these days. That's one of the few upsides to the paparazzi. Hard to steal someone who's followed by cameras every time she steps foot from the house." We both look downstairs. "Not to mention the random hate-related muggings."

I can handle myself but Tiny? She's tough, but she'd never survive a beating from those thugs.

"Maybe you ought to ease up," Kaga suggests. We pause outside his office door.

I scoff. "This advice from the man who's monitoring a certain Columbia student's every interaction with the opposite sex?"

Kaga's impenetrable facade eases for a moment, and then he concedes my point with a slight dip of his head. "I have overstepped."

His stiff formality bothers me far more than his ribbing. Kaga's honor is what prevents him from pursuing the woman he desires. "We're both concerned about those for whom we care deeply."

The clasp of his hand against my shoulder is his signal that all is forgiven. He pushes open his office door, and inside I find Jake, Gabriel Allen, and Steve playing cards.

I look from Gabe to Steve and back again. Neither should be here.

"What are you doing here?" I ask Steve. He should be with Tiny.

"She's fine."

I'm already moving toward the exit when Jake chimes in. "I've posted someone outside the door across the street, and there's another guy, former black ops, inside reviewing some investigative tape. No one is getting to her."

"And you?" I turn to Gabe.

"Making sure you don't break any laws," he says, not looking up from his cards.

"Am I paying you hourly as you lose money to Jake and Steve?" Gabe is my lawyer. He's Jake and Kaga's lawyer too. Hell, he could represent Steve for all I know.

"Yes."

Shaking my head, I walk over to Kaga's well-stocked bar and pour myself an orange juice with a splash of vodka. Breakfast of champions.

"You'll be pleased to hear that I didn't touch him."

"He tell you anything?"

"No. I did find out that he assumed I'd know who sent him."

"I'm going with Howe, then," Gabe answers, throwing down his cards and striding over to the one-way mirror that allows Kaga to survey the entire club. "Cards should never be played while the sun is up. We're toying with the natural order of things, which is why my hand is so bad."

"We're going to let the guy go this afternoon. Jake can send a man to shadow him. No harm, no foul. You can continue to represent me without any ethical conflicts." I slide into Gabe's abandoned chair and pick up his cards. No matches and no face cards. I wince. That is a shit hand. Turning to more pressing business, I tell Jake, "I need a full-time bodyguard for Tiny. Preferably female."

"We call them 'personal protection service providers' in the business, and she's not going to like that," he says absently, his attention on the pot—which looks to be about a couple grand. Low stakes. He glances at Steve, who doesn't look up from his hand. "See your five and raise you five."

Steve matches with his own chips. "Call."

"It's just a precaution," I repeat the excuse I gave Kaga earlier.

"Can I be there when you explain this to her? Because I can't wait to see how you finesse this. She'll eat you alive." Jake lays down his hand. It's a straight, with a queen high. Steve fans out his cards. Four of a kind, ten high.

"Motherfucker." Jake curses and pushes away from the table. "Ten grand in three hands. How do you do it, Steve?"

Steve has unholy luck at the card table. It's unexplainable, and if I didn't know him, I'd argue he cheats. It's one thing to have the cards fall in your favor for one round, but with Steve, it's such a common occurrence that no one really wants to play with him anymore. Except for Jake, who views it as a challenge, and Gabe, because he thinks he can win at everything. He usually does but not against Steve.

Steve just shrugs and pulls in the chips.

"When are you going to ask Tiny to marry you?" Jake asks. "You are going to, right?"

"Tiny works for you for a few weeks and already you think you have the right to ask me about my intentions toward her?" I say incredulously.

"She's a woman alone," Jake shoots back. I can see his white knight complex is fully engaged, and he'll be like a dog guarding his bone if I don't give him what he wants. He's fiercely protective of all the women in his circle. His little sister gets the brunt of it. I doubt she's even had one date since Jake got back from the Middle East.

"I haven't asked because her mother died, and I didn't want her looking back later thinking I'd proposed because she was in a bad state emotionally. And before. . ." I stretch out my legs, "before she was busy resisting my obvious charms and would have said no just to spite me."

"Sounds like you two have a healthy relationship," Gabe observes.

"Given that all you assholes are single except for Steve, you haven't the first clue what a healthy relationship is."

"Oh, we know. We're just incapable of being in one," Jake retorts.

"Speak for yourself," Kaga interjects.

He and Jake stare at each other for a long time before Jake says softly, "Sorry, old man, but I know you too well. We've shared too many experiences. You're a good man, but you're not for her."

Kaga tightens his fists and takes a step toward Jake. We all tense, preparing for a fight. It's a showdown that's been a long time coming, but with visible effort, he loosens his fists and dips his head slightly. "If you say so, Jake." With that, Kaga turns and leaves, abandoning us in his own office. The tension is thick enough to choke on.

"Ready?" I ask Steve. He nods. As we exit, I turn back to Jake. "You're going to regret keeping them apart for so long. There's no one more decent than Kaga. He'd do right by your sister."

Jake's mouth tightens, but he says nothing.

"Where to?" Steve asks as we climb into the Bentley.

"Office. I'll change there."

"What will you do about Howe?"

"It's time to ratchet up the pressure, not just in his social life."

Despite the appearance of Mitch Hedder, the attack was most likely orchestrated by Richard in response to the first round of pressure. If he was behind the assault, though, it meant direct and swift action must be taken. Not just for my sake but for Tiny's.

In the office, changed and prepared for a full day of analyst reviews and meetings, I call Tiny to give her the rundown on what happened this morning.

"He wouldn't talk. We're letting him stew for a few more hours and then releasing him. Jake's got a guy who'll follow him for a couple of days."

"You didn't hit him or anything?"

"No, Tiny, I did not. You'll be happy to hear my lawyer was there, so I was extra circumspect."

She sighs with relief. "I just don't want you hurt. Your eye looked terrible this morning. What will you tell people?"

"That I didn't duck quickly enough at the gym during a sparring session."

"You spar?"

"A little, although not as much as I have in the past. I had my share of fighting when I was young and dumb. I prefer to fight in a suit with a lot of cash. It's less painful and a lot more rewarding. Plus, if you get beat up, it's hard to make love to your girlfriend."

"Really? Because you had no problems last night," she said.

"Keep talking like that and we're going to have lunch early."

"Speaking of lunch, I'm going to cancel on you. Sarah called."

I shouldn't begrudge the time she spends trying to repair past relationships. I shouldn't, but I do. I take a moment so my next words to her show no evidence of my true feelings. "That's fine. I'll see you at home tonight."

"Love you, Ian," she says. And then I hear a door slam. "Hi, Jake." A grunt of a response and then another door slam.

"Wow, he's a bear this morning."

Undoubtedly. "Take an early lunch today. Stay out of his hair."

"What's this about?" she asks suspiciously.

"Nothing to do with you or me. He and Kaga had an argument this morning."

"Okay. Love you," she repeats.

"Love you too."

My next call is to Jake. "We're letting him out at eleven."

"I'll have a man over there fifteen minutes prior."

"Just have him observe and deliver the usual. Name, occupation, associates. We should be able to figure out who his brother is."

"You think it's Howe?" he asks.

"I do. I called him a few days ago and told him that it was time for him to go."

"You did?" He sounds surprised but pleased. "It's a good time. Out with the garbage before you start something new. Of course, you had to enjoy knowing you could crush him at any time. I can see why you've waited. I'll report back on the details of our friend."

He hangs up, but I'm left staring at the phone. *You had to enjoy knowing you could crush him at any time.*

Shoving away from my desk, I walk to the plate-glass windows overlooking the downtown harbor. Had I let Richard go all this time because I liked the idea that his continued existence could be snuffed out at any time with a mere phone call? Perhaps. Perhaps knowing I could make him suffer was perversely satisfying in its own way, and I used Cecilia to justify it.

Did I really care about Cecilia and her purported good deeds? Not particularly. I did enjoy knowing that I controlled Richard's future, though.

But now I want him gone. Tiny is the most important thing in my world. More important than revenge and retribution. Those things will only hold me back—or worse, they'll endanger the fragile future Tiny and I are building together.

Meeting Tiny, falling in love with her, I've realized that I'd rather look forward than backward. I'd rather live for tomorrow than wallow in the regret and pain of yesterday. It's the mantra I've been preaching to her regularly. Her mother would want her to be happy. Her mother would want her to move on. If I expect Tiny to look ahead, then I need to as well.

It's hard. Very hard. But I'm no longer alone.

CHAPTER 14

Jake returns later that day with information on my assailants. The Ludwiczak brothers were small-time criminals with rap sheets as long as my forearm. They'd been involved in everything from burglary to assaults. Both brothers had served time, but they'd been out for a couple of years. It appeared that they were offering their services as paid muscle, which Jake said could move them back into the Hedder column, but Richard is the mostly likely candidate.

The following day we take the Hedders to the gravesite in Flushing. Tiny's father had originally been buried on the west side, but there wasn't any space for her mother and father to be laid to rest together. With Tiny's consent, I had her father moved to a new plot, where Sophie and Sandro Corielli would rest side by side.

I hire a car to transport the Hedders, and Tiny and I follow in the Bentley.

The last trip we made out to the cemetery was not together. Tiny had gotten on her bike and ridden for miles, faster and faster until her feet were nearly bloody. She'd finally collapsed on the grass at the cemetery, drained of energy.

Fear had struck me hard that day. I'd followed her as best I could in the car, but she took turns that I couldn't and often I guessed wrong, having to backtrack and then reroute.

I thought maybe I'd lose her in those first weeks after her mother's death. She was emotionally gone.

It was a risk, but I took her out to the Long Island estate and told her that I loved her and wanted to spend every one of my future days with her.

She came back to me that day, but I still feel like she's unsure about her place in my life. And I'm helpless to fix it.

The tension in the car thickens with each passing block.

"You think I'm weak, don't you," she says.

The color in her face is washed away, and her lips are pressed thin and tight. I don't know if she's angry or sad. Likely both.

"Never. Not once," I answer.

"Then you think I'm stupid to come here with Mitch. I know he's scum. You think I shouldn't give in to him, pay him any attention."

She's trying to pick a fight with me. I press the privacy console. Steve doesn't need to hear this.

"I don't think you're stupid. I think you're too generous with your forgiveness and affection. I'm afraid that he's going to take advantage of that."

"I'm just trying to do what I think Mom would want." Her voice is aggressive, and her chin juts out in challenge. "I can't do what you think I should do all the time. It makes me feel like a toy. I hate feeling like I'm an Ian Kerr accessory piece. Maybe not one that Frank would have picked out, but a knockoff that you'd find on Canal Street."

I stare with incredulous disappointment, not sure where her insecurity is coming from.

Tiny leans her head against the window and sighs heavily. "I'm sorry. I just miss her."

Compassion eats away at anger. "I know you do."

Leaning across the expanse of leather, I run my hand over her shoulder and down her arm, trying to impart some comfort and love. Her whole world changed recently, I remind myself. The adjustment might take some time. I need to be patient.

"Will I ever stop missing her?"

I think back to the near knee-buckling grief I felt after my parents died. "No," I admit softly. "But it's less painful every day, every year."

She peels away from the window and crawls into my lap. The wound from the loss of her mother is stark in her eyes.

If I could, I'd suck all her pain out like poison from a wound. I tuck her head under my chin and hold her, hoping my embrace conveys what I'm not always good at expressing verbally. That I love her. That she's my everything. That we can endure anything so long as we're together.

We walk to the grave together. Mitch is already there, pretending to weep, blowing loudly into a handkerchief. Malcolm is rocking back on his heels, his hands shoved into his pants pockets. His suit must have been retrieved from the floor of his closet, given its rumpled state.

Beside me, Tiny's hands clench and unclench as she stares at the headstone, but it's Malcolm who looks as if he's the most uncomfortable person present. I stare at him from behind my sunglasses but his attention is fixed on Tiny—and for a small moment, a naked longing is revealed. The look is intense and anguished and so swift that if I hadn't been staring, I never would have caught it.

I glance at Tiny to see if she sees his very nonfraternal feelings toward her, but her eyes are fastened on the headstone. Her jaw is tight as she tries not to lose it in front of the Hedders. Her unspoken desire to remain calm is what keeps me from reaching for her.

Malcolm's feelings for Tiny put another wrinkle in the situation. He definitely could be the one behind my assault, if for no other reason than the reality that I'm the one making love to Tiny every night. It must be killing him. Before me, Tiny had had one boyfriend and a few hookups, as she'd described them. None of them were serious enough to have prompted a reaction from Malcolm. From what she told me, her one dating relationship had ended because her ex liked to sleep around.

After Mitch places a few flowers on the headstone, he comes over to embrace Tiny. She flinches at the touch, and I place my hand on her elbow to reassure her. She braces herself and pats Mitch gingerly on his back. Malcolm's gaze tracks Tiny's every movement. It's unnerving.

At least my presence is a sufficient deterrent to keep both Hedders from enacting some kind of con at the gravesite.

"Thank you so much for bringing me, Tiny," Mitch says. I grit my teeth at hearing her nickname come out of his mouth. It was her mother's name for her, and it doesn't sit right with me that he's using it.

"You can thank me by telling me what you have of Sophie's." Her voice cracks at her mother's name, but her stare at Mitch is unwavering.

"Let's go back to The Plaza. We can sit down and—"

"No," Tiny interrupts. "I want to know what you have of hers. I had dinner with you. I brought you here to pay your respects, and now you tell me what you have of my mother's."

"Your mother would have wanted us to be friends," Mitch replies.

"Bullshit." Tiny responds. I stifle a laugh at Mitch's shocked expression. "Bull-fucking-shit. You don't have the first clue what Sophie wanted—not when you were married and not now. I'm going to assume that this is some long con you're running to get money out of Ian, and you don't have shit of my mother's. You're a snake, Mitch Hedder—a disgusting vile snake to use my mom's death to make a play for cash or whatever it is you think you can get out of me or Ian. I'm done."

She grabs my hand and tugs me toward Steve and our idling car. Behind me I can hear Mitch scrambling to follow us.

"You have it all wrong, Tiny. Your mother left me. I still loved her."

If steam could come out of a person's ears, I would be seeing it right now. Tiny's face is a thundercloud of anger. She whirls and advances on Mitch. He takes a step backward and loses his footing. We all watch as his arms pinwheel futilely in the air to gain balance. He fails and falls backward, nearly striking his head on a granite headstone.

"Go, just go," Malcolm waves us off. With resignation, he helps his father off the ground. "He won't bother you. If he has something of Sophie's, I'll get it for you."

"Thank you," Tiny says.

As she turns away, Malcolm calls out, "If you need anything, I'm here for you."

She looks over her shoulder with a bemused look, probably remembering exactly why Malcolm sent her my way in the first place. She had fond feelings for him at one time. I suspect that they've cooled dramatically. "I have Ian now."

Those words make me want to pick her up and howl at the moon with satisfaction. I content myself with simply holding her hand.

"Should we go home?" I ask once we're in the car.

"I'd like to go back to work," she admits. "If I go home, I'm afraid I'll brood. I'm in one of those moods where I want to put on melodramatic music and cry for hours." At my wince, she laughs. "Even you don't want that."

"I feel like I could distract you."

"I don't doubt it, but you should save up your energy for tonight. I'll be ready then." She leans forward and gives me a quick kiss.

When I get to my office, Louis is waiting for me.

"Kaga OK'd the SunCorp management. Let's do some more due diligence about margins and ROI, and we'll make a decision next week." He nearly claps with glee.

At my desk, I flick through my contacts, pausing at the interior decorator that worked with me on the warehouse remodel. After a short hesitation, I delete her card. I slept with her during that remodel, and I don't want Tiny to be the subject of any snide commentary if the decorator is miffed she's not invited to stay the night.

Frank can give me a referral. I need to call him anyway to have his assistant pick out a dress for Tiny for a fundraising event at the Frick in a couple of weeks.

"Ian Kerr!" Frank sounds unusually upbeat. "How are all the clothes for your new friend working out?"

"I hope no one from your office is in touch with the *Observer*."

Frank gasps. "We'd never break a confidence!"

"I hope not. I wouldn't want to stop working with you."

"As if you could," Frank chides. "I've dressed you for over a decade."

"Longer, I think. I'm actually calling about two things. First, I need a recommendation for an interior decorator. The exterior is Northern European, but the interior can be anything other than modern. Tiny complained to me that the warehouse is soulless."

"I have just the person. She's worked all over the Hamptons."

"I'm not looking for beachy, Frank."

"No, no," he reassures me. "She's definitely classy."

"Make sure you tell her that I'm happily attached to the woman who will be directing her efforts. If she can't operate under that premise, I'll work with someone else."

Frank pauses and says hesitantly, "I've never had a problem with her."

"You're gay. Why would you?"

"I'm still hot. The ladies still want me and mourn constantly that I play for the other team. I'd be swimming in pussy if I were straight, I tell you."

"Fair enough. Straight men all over the city rejoice that you are kind enough to vacate the field for them."

"I'm a very generous person. What's the other thing?"

"Get me samples of some bolder fabric patterns for suits. Order a yard of each." Tiny has been gravitating toward the more fashion forward suits in my closet. I haven't decided whether she thinks it's a dare or whether she really likes them, but hell, if it's a game she enjoys playing then I figure she needs the pieces for the board. I don't care if

I walk up Fifth Avenue in my underwear if that's what Tiny wants. A loud plaid suit? Maybe we'd start a new trend.

"He hates doing big swatches," Frank warns. "He" is the Savile Row tailor who makes all my suits.

"I fucking hate those tiny swatches. They're so small that I can't get a sense of what anything is going to look like."

"He thinks it's a waste."

"Tell him to sew some dolls and sell them on eBay. Also, I'm taking Tiny to the Frick Ball in a couple of weeks. It's her favorite museum. She'll need a dress."

"*A couple of weeks?*" he shouts.

I pull the phone away from my ear as he sputters loudly for a minute about how women plan for months for this event, maybe even years, and how I'm a cretin with a bigger wallet than my fashion sense. "You have two weeks, Frank," I state firmly and then hang up the phone.

The Frick Gentlemen's Ball is an annual charity event that benefits the museum's art reference library. Tiny's mother loved The Frick Collection, and they went there together frequently. It was, in fact, the last outing they shared before Sophie passed away. I hadn't told Tiny about the event yet—it had been a busy few weeks—but I'd tell her tonight that I'd made a sizable donation in Sophie's name.

As I think about charitable contributions, it occurs to me that there is another thing that Tiny might be interested in sponsoring. I walk down the hall and knock on Louis's door.

"Change your mind about SunCorp?" he says, looking up in surprise.

"No, I want us to look into a charity for dyslexia."

"Really?" He looks pained.

"It's a good tax write-off."

"You're still paying 60 percent of it," he counters.

"We can spare 60 percent of something. Have you always been against giving money away?" I quirk an eyebrow at him.

"When you hired me, your exact words were 'your rapacious desire for success set you apart from the other applicants.'"

Those words sound vaguely familiar. At one time, I had a win-at-all-costs mentality. It's the only mindset one can have when you're poor, orphaned, and desperate. "We're going to give more this year," I say decidedly. "Get me a list of five potential charities. They don't have to be the biggest or best, but make sure the organization is spending the money wisely." I turn to leave but then remember my plans for the weekend. "And I'm taking Friday off. Tiny and I are going to Long Island. Pretend I'm vacationing in the Maldives and can't be reached."

Behind me I can hear Louis cursing. He yells, "They have phones there. And Wi-Fi!"

"Not where I'm going, they don't."

CHAPTER 15

Tiny looks worn out when I pick her up at Jake's.

"He's still in his office," she says. "I swear he sleeps here."

"It takes time to build a new business," I observe mildly. "Should we eat out tonight or order in?"

"Let's make something," she suggests.

"I don't know how to cook and no offense, sweetheart, but do you?"

"My cooking rolodex contains about three recipes. Pot pie, shrimp with noodles, and a beef pot roast cooked in a crockpot—which you don't have."

Her mouth turns down a little, probably remembering all the wonderful things her mother made.

I try to cheer her up. "You do realize we live in a place where even fast food can be delivered, right? Not to mention that there are a dozen restaurants within walking distance."

"I know, but I think it would be fun."

Leaning forward, I tell Steve to drop us at the Chelsea Market. "Let's cook then."

Inside I can't help pointing out all the food stalls with prepared items we could take home. "We could get seafood," I say looking at the lobster advertised at the Lobster Place. "Or apparently enough bread to feed an entire city."

Tiny shakes her head and drags me down the corridors to stop at a vegetable stand. She shakes out a plastic bag and hands it to me to hold while she fills it with a bunch of greenery labeled "spring onions."

"Is this where you get food?"

"Yes, dear, it's where mortals eat. Actually that's not true, this is like a rich person's grocery."

I ignore the sarcasm. "Where would you shop for your mom?"

"About two blocks over was a market that had good fruit. We were trying to eat healthy, but it was so expensive." She squeezes her lips together.

Leaning forward I palm the back of her head and pull her close. "Love you so much, bunny."

She allows me to comfort her all of a second and then pushes away to grab another bag which she fills with an herb that even I can correctly identify as cilantro.

"What are we making?"

"Pasta and shrimp cooked in lemon and white wine sauce. Why don't you go over and get some bread? Maybe sourdough rolls, and I'll meet you at the seafood place." She points down a ways.

I kiss her again and leave to do her bidding. Inside the bakery, I find dozens of different loaves of bread and rolls. On the advice of a helpful clerk, I buy something called a Tuscan log sourdough, which is shaped like a log roll with short, stubby branches. I figure what we don't eat, we can use to feed the ducks this weekend in Long Island. Although I don't know that we have ducks up there. I might have to buy some.

When I catch up with her at the seafood counter, there's a man— make that an asshole—chatting her up. He has an arm braced against the glass case, and his eyes are taking off her clothes piece by piece.

"Hey, Ian," she says when I approach.

"Hi, bunny." I put my hand on her neck and kiss her on the forehead. I need to get a ring on this woman right away. "Are you having problems deciding which fish to buy?"

He smirks. "Just making conversation."

I run my tongue over my teeth wondering how mad Tiny would be if I punched this guy out. Pretty mad, I guess, so I lean down and kiss her again—only this time on the lips. Hard.

She rolls her eyes. "I'm waiting for our shrimp."

The guy still doesn't leave. He hovers, like a stupid dumb cow, on my right, as if Tiny is just going to peel away from me and give him her number.

"Check out is over there," I gesture toward the registers.

"I'm not ready," he says, confused.

"Oh, you are." I stare at him steadily, and he's not as dumb as I thought because he finally walks away.

"A pound of prawns." A tatted, bald-headed man offers Tiny a white parchment-wrapped package. "Where's the guy who wanted the scallops?" He looks around.

"We'll take those too," Tiny says hastily.

We pay, and she waits until we're in the hallway before questioning me.

"You looked like you were going to punch that guy out."

"Nah," I lie.

"Then why is the bread loaf crushed in your hand?"

I look down and the Tuscan log is indeed bent in half as if a sharp wind has sheared off part of the limb. "Looked like it was too soft. Just testing out the wheat-to-oat ratio."

"Seriously? That is what you are going with?" She laughs. "You know you sound like a caveman. Again."

"That's advanced evolution. I thought for sure I wasn't much past the Neanderthal stage."

"Ape," she teases.

"Knuckle dragging when it comes to you, bunny." I wrap an arm around her waist and usher her into the bakery to buy a new loaf of bread.

"Even if I didn't completely and totally adore you, I would never have been attracted to that guy."

"Why's that?"

"He's not you."

"Keep that up and we're going to have a really late dinner because words like that make me horny as hell."

I manage to act like a normal human being and keep my dick in my pants until after dinner.

Tiny makes me dry the dishes with a dish towel I didn't even realize I owned.

"We do have someone who comes and cleans."

"Once a week, and she won't be here until Friday. That's two days away. The dishes would be disgusting by then."

"Can't we put these in the dishwasher? Isn't that what it's for? The washing of dishes?"

"You're very spoiled, Ian Kerr."

"I'm very hard," I tell her. "Watching you move around the kitchen is surprisingly erotic. I think it was all the bending over and waving your ass in the air."

"Did you drop the scallops on the floor on purpose? So I would have to bend over and pick them up?"

"We couldn't eat that asshole's scallops, Tiny. Besides, they fell off the counter."

"You are so full of shit." She shakes her head and laughs.

"And I'd like for you to be full of me." Throwing down the towel, I pick her up and toss her over my shoulder.

She beats her fists against my back, laughing. "Let me go, you Neanderthal."

"I thought I was a caveman."

In the bedroom, I throw her on the bed and pounce on top before she can turn over. "You've been waving this ass at me all night."

She wiggles it provocatively against me. "What you going to do about it?"

A strap on her sundress falls from her shoulder to her arm. Slowly I push up the skirt to reveal a pair of white sheer briefs. "I'm still hungry, bunny." I press the base of my palm against her ass and rub my thumb against the wetness between her legs. "Very hungry."

She moans and pushes back against my hand. "That feels good, Ian."

Reaching around, I cup her fabric-covered breast. Her nipple juts into my hand, and I pinch it in approval. "And this? How does this feel?"

Her response is to grind her ass even harder.

"What I should have done in the market is slide my fingers up the back of your skirt."

"Is that right?" She pants lightly.

"I'd have put my fingers inside you." I push the silk right inside her.

A whimper tumbles from her lips, but I can only shallowly pump inside her as the fabric constricts my movements. Suddenly, I can't wait another minute. I rip the panties down her legs just far enough so I can plunge inside her. Her bare ass bounces in front of me like two glorious moons. Maybe I am a caveman, because I feel the need to claim my woman.

Keeping her legs tight, I push inside her, gasping at the initial snugness and then groaning as she softens and accepts me. The tight sensation, the sight of her ass, the sound of her moans send me into a frenzy. I start thrusting and can't stop. Reaching around, I pluck at her clit and pray she comes because after only a few thrusts, I'm coming.

"Goddammit," I grunt, still pumping my hips. "Sorry . . . I'll make it up to you."

"I'm good . . ." she sighs, sounding satisfied. Grateful she found her own pleasure while I was lost in mine, I pull out and drag her panties down the rest of the way and sit on the edge of the bed. When I lift her into my arms, bracing one of her legs on either side of my waist, the hot juice of her orgasm mixed with my seed seeps out of her and wets my groin. Impossibly, I harden again.

"Really?" She sounds amused, which is better than irritated or—worse—uninterested.

"I'm not sure. Let's go test him out. For science."

"You do seem unnaturally robust. It may be worth further study." She tugs at my hair playfully. The sundress is unzipped and tossed to the side.

"I agree." Pulling her head down I kiss her hungrily. The short interaction has only whetted my appetite. "We'll need to go through this routine several times so that we can account for variables like clothes, distance in the car, how many times we've kissed before entry, that sort of thing."

"Maybe I would have been a better student if this was one of my high school classes," she grins.

"No, this is an independent study that can only be conducted with one particular instructor." She busily unfastens my shirt, and I awkwardly shuck my pants, holding her with one arm and then the other so we aren't separated for even a moment while we dispose of all my unnecessary clothing. Turning over, I place her on her back.

Her body looks like an art piece against the dark comforter. There's only a little light as the skylights filter the colors of the darkening twilight into the bedroom. I've had other women lie on this bed, sprawled out and wanting my touch, but none have moved me like she does.

"I'm going to test you," she says and runs her hands along her inner thighs to her knees, spreading herself wide for me.

My knees buckle and I fall onto the bed between her legs. Despite having come not ten minutes ago, I can't wait to be inside her again.

I lock a hand around an ankle and expose her even more. "On what subjects will I be tested?"

"It's a hands-on exam. One where you show your, ah, aptitude through . . ."

Her attention wanders when I slide one finger inside her. She's swollen and very sensitive from her recent orgasm. I drag my finger slowly out and then push back in, this time with a second finger. She opens her mouth to speak, but when I use my thumb on her clit as I pump with my fingers, she's not able to form words.

"I'm very good with my hands." Resting on my haunches, I release her ankle to grasp her hip with one hand, holding her still as I stroke deep inside her with the other. "What kind of grade do you think you'll give me?"

A whimper rises from her throat. "A-a-average."

"Really?" I shove three fingers in her this time and use my pinky finger to brush against the tender ring of flesh that I've only lightly played with before. I want to be in there too. I want to fuck, conquer, claim every part of her body. "Your body is telling me something different. Your skin is flushed all over from your arousal. Your lips—both sets—are swollen and red. And you're *very* wet." I shake my head in mock dismay. "Listen to yourself." In the stillness, we both hear the decadent sounds her body is making as I stroke her. I increase the pace and slap my palm against her clit, using my entire hand to stimulate her.

"It's o-okay," she breathes. "But I still feel like I'm missing something."

"Is that a challenge, Tiny?"

She stretches her arms up toward the padded headboard and uses it as leverage to push back against my hand. "Always."

I can't help but laugh at this. Always challenging me. I love it. I love *her*.

"Is this what you want?" I release her hip, still palm deep in her pussy. Capturing my throbbing cock in my free hand, I stroke firmly, tugging on the head and squeezing pre-cum out onto the tip. I swipe a bit of the pearly fluid onto a finger and bring it to her mouth. "Do you want this inside you?"

"Always," she repeats, eyes glittering with want. Despite having finger-fucked her, she's still tight and it takes a moment for her to adjust to my size. And then I'm finally fully seated, surrounded by her slick flesh. A hushed sigh of relief and pleasure quavers in the air.

"My hand is drenched." I lift up the fingers that were inside her, clearly coated from fingertip to base with her wetness. With deliberate slowness, I swallow all three fingers, sucking hard so I don't miss even one tiny drop of her essence. "You taste fucking magnificent."

Her eyes are wide and glazed. At the sight of my erotic gesture, she tightens around me, and I feel familiar flutters signaling the start of an orgasm. "Not yet, bunny," I tell her and pull out until just the tip is inside her.

"Don't be mean." She scowls and tries to push down on me.

"I'm not." I lean over and tongue one hard nipple and then the other. "A little anticipation never hurt anyone."

She thumps a small fist against my shoulder, but I can't feel it. All sensation has pooled in my groin. I push forward slowly, in tiny measures, so that my cock can enjoy the slow burn that my fingers experienced. My thumbs massage her shoulders and her small muscled arms. I want to do this forever, simply working myself in and out of her tight, hot cunt until our breath has gone and our bodies turn to dust.

Only Tiny exists now.

When I close my eyes, it's her face I see. When my fingers curl, it's because they long to stroke her silky skin. When I breathe, it's her scent in my nose. There are no other women but her.

"I love you," I tell her, feathering kisses along her jawline and behind her ear. I palm the top of her ass cheeks to press her tight against me, to show her how I want her to meet my thrusts. She plants her small heels in the mattress and grinds up against me. My world is narrowed to her flesh meeting mine. "I *need* you."

"You're everything," she moans. I reach between us to press my thumb against her clit. As she arches into me, her hushed whimpers turn into louder gasps when I circle it repeatedly. The sounds she makes are like the spark from a flint, and it's setting us both ablaze. Trembling with desire, she writhes and pumps against me, seeking relief from the growing ache overtaking her body.

The erotic motion of her undulations combined with her breathless whimpers are my undoing.

"Come for me then," I command through gritted teeth. I press into her harder, the sounds of our bodies slapping together matching the moans from her mouth in symphonic pleasure.

Relentlessly, I pound against her, driving her farther and farther along the bed. With her hips canted upward and her heels digging into the backs of my thighs she has little leverage. All she can do is open herself to me and the never-ending assault of my cock into the sweet suck of her cunt. My orgasm is racing down my spine, the tension pooling at the base just waiting to surge forward and spill inside her. But not until she comes first.

"Tell me, bunny, how hot are you? How badly do you want to come right now?"

"So bad," she croaks.

"I want you to milk me, to squeeze me tight, and come all over my dick."

She's shaking below me, every inch of her is stretched taut. Behind me I can feel her feet curling inward, and below me her body tenses. She's so close, and I love how she reaches for her pleasure, strives toward it. With a grunt of male gratification, I take matters into my own hand and slap her lightly across the clit. The sting of the slap catches her off guard. She cries out, first in surprise and then in a long, heat-inducing wail. "Oh god, *Ian* . . ."

I can't hold back for another second. Roaring my own satisfaction, I let go. My rhythm turns to shit as the animal in me takes over. I lift her legs straight up into the air, holding them together. The position creates a tight channel of flesh, and I fuck her relentlessly until I'm nothing more than a mass of exposed nerves and flesh.

In her, I'm completely lost. There's no sense of time or space . . . just *her*. I drive into her again and again but it's never enough. I can't fuck her hard enough, long enough, deep enough to satisfy me. I'll return to her and only her, time and time again seeking the release that I know I'll only ever have from her body.

She makes me lose my mind and all my control, and I fucking love it. Her amazing body is the only one I'll ever want to touch, taste, fuck, fantasize about. She's everything to me. *Everything.*

Collapsing next to her, I soothe her post-climax shudders and allow her to do the same. A tangle of arms and legs, we kiss, savoring each other and telling each other how precious and important the other is.

"My heart," she says between kisses, "you're my heart."

"Mine too," I answer.

The night air cools the sweat on our skin, causing Tiny to shiver. Pulling a sheet over her, I drag my ass out of bed. In the bathroom, I grab a washcloth. Tiny moans in relief and appreciation when I press the cloth against her to clean her up. She pulls up the covers, and I climb in next to her.

She cuddles up to me, her leg slung over my thighs. "Ian . . ." she says. "I want to tell you something."

"Hmmm?" My mind is on other things. The need to bind her to me permanently rides me hard. "I want us to get married. Soon. Do you want a big wedding?"

"Married? I mean, I guess I thought you were serious, but I figured . . . I don't know." Her voice trails off.

"That my proposal of marriage was somehow insincere? I've never wanted anything more. I just didn't want to pressure you because of all the emotional upheaval you're experiencing now." Rolling over so she can see me and judge the sincerity for herself, I declare, "I want you to be my wife. The mother of any children we have. My partner in life. I want that to happen now so that I can introduce you as Mrs. Ian Kerr."

Her eyes close for a moment and silent tears leak out beneath the lids. Her words, though, are classic. "Maybe you should take my name. You can be Ian Corielli, and I'll introduce you as Mr. Victoria Corielli."

"As long as it means you're mine in the eyes of the world, I'll be Mr. John Smith."

She wraps her arms around my neck and clings to me. This time the shudders I'm soothing are from maybe, possibly, hopefully joy for our future. "I'm okay with Victoria Kerr," she chokes out. "You better give me a big rock and lots of flowers since you're proposing to me while we're naked."

"I proposed to you when I first took you to the house on Long Island Sound."

"You didn't propose. You said that you wanted me to be your wife and fill your big house with lots of little people."

"That's a proposal."

"It was a demand."

"It was a request couched as a demand."

Her body is shaking with laughter. "You've been in charge for too long. That was no request."

Pushing to my knees, I reach into the nightstand and retrieve the box I bought before Sophie died. Her eyes grow huge and her hands come up to cover her mouth. I flip the box lid open, pluck the ring out, and toss the box aside.

Lifting her shaking hand in mine, I slide the ring onto her finger.

"When I was fifteen, I made a hundred different stupid vows. I'd avenge my mother. I'd rise to the top of Wall Street and smite everyone down. I'd crush Richard Howe beneath the sole of my boot. I'd win at everything. But I never wished for happiness because I didn't know what it was until you came into my life. How could I want something I didn't know I was missing? Now, everything I've achieved pales in comparison to having you love me. When I say that you're my heart, my everything, those aren't just words. They are the only truth in my world. I'd give up money, revenge, success—anything, as long as I can lie down next to you at night and wake up with your face beside mine.

"There is no greater achievement in my life than having you fall in love with me, and I recognize on some mysterious level that that is pure luck. I need you to marry me and be my wife. I need you to be the mother of my children. I need you because without you I am nothing. I am a pile of bones and flesh filled with misery. You bring me to life. Love me, marry me, be with me in this life and all the ones we live from this point ever after."

"Well, since you put it like that, I guess I must." She rises and kisses me. Our mouths seal the promises we've made to one another.

"What was it that you wanted to tell me?" I ask.

"That I love you." She pulls me down to her, the thin but precious metal rubbing against my shoulder blade.

I make love to her again then, slowly. We barely move. I simply slide in and we rock together, allowing the strength of our emotions to carry us into the heavens.

CHAPTER 16

"Did something get delivered this morning?" Tiny asks as we get ready for our trip to Long Island Sound. The sound of the garage door lifting on the street floor had jarred her awake, and she'd jumped in the shower before I could convince her that we needed an early morning fuck to start the day off right.

"Yes, something for our trip," I say, rinsing off my blade. She's sitting on the edge of the vanity watching me shave, a towel wrapped around her wet hair. I'm surprised at how much I enjoy the domesticity of living with a woman, but a lot of that could be attributed to one particular female rather than the situation itself.

Before, if I brought a woman here—which was rare—I couldn't wait for her to leave. I actually stopped bringing women to the warehouse at all after one woman refused to get out. I got dressed and waited silently at the stairs until she got the message. I still see her occasionally out at charitable events—the city's social scene can be unbearably small at times. She'll glare at me, whisper something derogatory to a friend, and inevitably try to feel me up toward the end of the evening in an effort to prove I'd made the wrong choice. I don't miss the days of being single.

"I still don't know how you can use that without cutting yourself." Her gaze watches my every motion intently. Shaving fascinates her because I'm old school, using a straight-edge razor and badger bristle brush. There have been several mornings where I was late getting into my office because she took a very personal interest in my morning routine. Who knew the badger brush would feel so good on my cock?

"Practice." She hands me a damp towel, which I use to wipe off the residual soap. Leaning close, I rub my cheek against hers. "How's it feel?"

"Soft. Smooth." She strokes my other cheek a minute, and I close my eyes to enjoy the caress. No, I wouldn't ever kick Tiny out of my place. I want to keep her here forever.

"Want a little relief before we go?" I drop my hand between us and press against the damp cloth covering her legs.

"No," she mutters grumpily and pushes me away. "I don't want a quickie. I want that." She points to the thick erection poking out of my briefs.

"It's all yours, bunny." I spread my hands wide, giving her the choice. It's not like an hour delay is going to kill us.

With a wry look, she hops down and heads for the closet. "I'm tempted to say yes, but I do want to get out of the city this weekend, and I'm afraid if I take you up on your offer, we'll never leave."

She's right. I follow her into the closet and pull on a pair of old faded jeans, a white ribbed wifebeater, and a beige linen collarless shirt. I do a couple of buttons in the middle but let it hang open. Because I've dressed quickly, I'm able to sit on the padded bench in the dressing room and watch Tiny finish changing. I make a mental note to thank Frank for suggesting the bench. I can think of about a dozen things I'll be able to use it for when Tiny and I don't have plans that involve leaving the warehouse.

She has new panties on—light purple with a keyhole opening decorated with strings tied into a bow right above her ass crack. I wonder if I tug on the strings whether the panties will fall right off. I lick my lips in anticipation.

Her beautiful breasts swing lightly as she bends over to pull up a pair of denim shorts that have interesting rips in them. "I hope you don't wear those out in public." I can see the lower part of her ass cheek through one of the rips.

"These are my beach shorts. I usually wear them over a bathing suit."

Her explanation is given matter-of-factly, as if they weren't the most delectable, tantalizing pair of shorts ever. Golden skin peeks through from loose threads that are barely held together by the side seams whenever she moves. The hint of flesh is more erotic than a bare ass.

"I didn't read about any of the beaches around here closing because of riots."

"Ha. Ha." She mock laughs. "While I think it's great you're in love with my ass, no one else is."

"You're wrong, but I don't mind that you think there's only one man for you."

She slides her arms into a short-sleeved, red-checkered plaid shirt with pearl snaps. The western-style shirt is tailored and accentuates her narrow waist and round hips.

"Let's go," I say abruptly. We need to get on the road, or she'll be bent over the bench in about two seconds. There are only three small pieces of clothing separating me from her body. With a sigh and uncomfortably tight pants, I pick up our two carryalls and head down to the garage. Tiny's right behind me.

"My god, what is this?" she exclaims at the sight of the delivery.

"It's an Aston Martin Vanquish Volante." I place our luggage in the trunk, noting the picnic basket I'd asked for sitting neatly to the side. On the front seat I see a pair of Aviators, a wide-brimmed straw hat, and a scarf. Great service. I make a mental note to do business with the dealership again, even if this car doesn't suit.

Tiny trails her hands along the bright white paint above the door handle. "It's very shiny."

"It's not as fast as some coupes like the Ferrari 458, but it's more comfortable. Plus, it's an automatic." I pat the rear fender.

"You're saying this like it matters to me."

"It should. I bought it for you."

"But I don't drive." She's still circling the car. She might not drive, but I can see the car interests her. It's a two-door soft top convertible, which will be perfect for summer months on the Sound.

"Figured you could learn. When we're in Connecticut, it'll be harder to get around without a car, and I want you to be able to go places if I'm not around."

"I could bike."

"Sure. But you could also drive. You won't convince me you aren't even a little tempted." I glance pointedly at her hands, which are still running over the edge of the glossy white exterior. It's a loving gesture—a caress. And it signals what I rarely see in her for anything but me. A little desire. A little want. She asks me for so little, and I want to give her so much.

"You've already given me this." She waves her ring finger at me. "I'm convinced that I could buy a small country with it."

I shrug lightly. She isn't wrong. The five-carat emerald cut baguette diamond on a thin white-gold band did cost as much as a small country's gross domestic product, but that's information she doesn't need to know. If she did, she wouldn't wear the ring out of the house. "It's nonreturnable, so I guess we'll never know."

She rolls her eyes. She knows it's expensive, but by mutual agreement, we're not going to discuss the cost.

"How do I get in this thing?" she says after several moments of silent contemplation.

I press down on the LED buttons on the side, and the flush-mounted door handle swings out.

"Very fancy," she says, picking up the items left on the seat and climbing in. "I feel very . . . Thelma and Louise."

"A convertible, hat, and sunglasses make you feel like an outlaw on the run ready to drive off a cliff and die?" I ask incredulously. Slipping on my own Aviators, I slide into the driver's seat, hit a button, and watch the garage door roll up.

"Not the dying part but maybe a little outlaw." She plops the hat on and wrinkles her nose. "How is this going to stay on?"

"I think that's what the scarf is for."

With a push of a button, the engine revs to life and we roar into the street, the over five-hundred horsepower engine rumbling loudly on the pavement. She shoots me an elated grin. Yeah, she likes the car. I smile back at her before switching my attention to the street. Out of my periphery, I can see her arranging and rearranging her hat and scarf. The low speed of the city traffic makes it possible for us to talk.

"How come you aren't making Steve drive me around in Long Island?" she asks, fiddling with the various buttons and controls on the dash.

"Because I figured you'd like to be in charge of your transportation outside the city. I know I do."

"Why don't you drive yourself here if you like it so much?"

"It's easier to get things done if you have a driver. No waiting around. No trying to find a place to park. If I'm stuck in crosstown traffic for an hour, I can read three analysts' reports. It's not a waste. Outside the city, though, it's nice to be in charge."

She nods and sits back, a hand trailing outside the door. Tiny's had so much of her life torn away. Her mother died. She's had to move. I think she feels a little lost, and if giving her the ability to drive, the ability to move about on her own, can restore a little control in her life, it can only be a good thing.

As we merge onto the Connecticut Turnpike headed north toward the Sound, the traffic thins. It's Saturday morning. Tiny's getting quieter, and conversation grinds to a halt as she stares out the window. The windshield is helping to reduce drag, but her hair is whipping about like crazy. She looks gorgeous, but a little somber.

"Thinking about your mother?"

She gives me a rueful smile. "Yes, sorry."

"Don't be. I miss her too."

She sighs. "I was just thinking about how much she would like to have gone with us. Not to see the place but the trip. Getting out of the city. When she was sick, sometimes she couldn't leave the apartment because of the risk of infection. Even some random cough on the street compromised her health because of her lowered immune system. Then when she got better, we made this pact to go places . . ." She pauses and rubs a finger over the hand-stitched infinity rings in the leather. "But we were limited by our funds. We didn't have much."

My heart aches. When Tiny and I met, her fifth-floor walk-up had been dingy and small and impossible for her mother to navigate. It was desperate circumstances that allowed me to walk into her life and redirect the course of events. There was only one event I couldn't alter for Tiny: Sophie Corielli's death. All the money in the world can't stop a person from suffering loss. Tiny thinks the gulf between her having no money and me having so much of it is sometimes too large of a gap for us to maneuver, but money is nothing.

"I sometimes wonder if things would be different if Mom were still alive."

"Because of us?"

"I mean, I wouldn't be down there with you at the warehouse or driving in this two-seater." She turns and looks at the non-existent rear space covered by a wind blocker. It's only large enough for a bag or two. No, her mother wouldn't have been in this car with us.

"If your mother were here, we'd renovate the warehouse. Maybe turn the garage into an apartment. I could store the vehicles in the building next door. I own the block. Or there's a property I'm renovating on the Upper West Side. It's a double-wide townhome I bought that was foreclosed on. And Aston Martin has four-door sedans, or we'd drive the Maybach because I know she liked the footrests."

"You're saying we'd still be together?"

"Why wouldn't we be?"

"Maybe you felt sorry for me. Like, here's Tiny all alone. I want to make her stop crying."

"I'm not going to tie myself to you for the rest of my life because I feel sorry for you. I fucking love you." I try not to break the steering wheel.

"Marriages can be dissolved."

"Not ours." I'm growing angry. I can't believe she thinks my proposal was fake and that if her mother were still alive, I'd have dropped her by now.

"You only got involved with me because of Richard Howe, and now you won't even let me help you with that."

If we weren't on the interstate going 85 miles-per-hour, I would've slammed on the brakes and pulled over. "Don't say his name," I spit out through gritted teeth.

She lapses into silence, and we make the rest of the drive without uttering another word. I drive well over the speed limit and am lucky not to get a ticket. When we arrive at the gate to the property, she finally opens her mouth.

"Is this where we drive off the cliff? Because I'm sick enough over our argument to jump into a ravine." She touches my hand lightly, and my fury instantly drains away.

"We can jump in the Sound, but I'm guessing it's pretty cold," I joke. We drive down the paved driveway and around the house to the garage bay. Tiny calls the whole place a monstrosity because we could fit fifteen or more city apartments inside it. But it's the perfect place for a family.

"I'm sorry I brought up the Howe issue," she says, making no move to exit the car. Instead, she's got an elbow propped on the door and is staring out toward the water. "It's just that I feel like it's the one thing I can do for you. I feel so useless right now. When Mom was alive, everything fit. I had a job I was good at. We lived in a shitty apartment, but it was *our* shitty apartment. I didn't feel like I was stupid or had nothing to offer but now . . . now I feel real fucking inadequate." She furiously wipes tears away from her face. I fight back the urge to draw her over the console and into my lap. Somehow I know that's not the response she wants. She doesn't want me to feel sorry for her or to comfort her, and even though I'm dying to hold her, I resist.

Taking a moment, I choose my words carefully. "Before you, I had nothing. Yes, I have a few friends. They're great, but they don't love me and I don't love them. I've worked nearly every day with my right-hand man Louis for years without realizing that he's kind of a shitty human being. Worse, I was the same shitty human being. I cared about nothing but making money, and it didn't bother me if I stepped on a few toes or hands or faces to get to the top. There's no question that Richard Howe is a blight on humanity, but he's meaningless now because you're my future. Chasing down Howe doesn't bring my mother back, nor does it bring yours back. All it can do is stifle what you and I could make together. Tiny, if I didn't have any money, would you feel the same about me? Would you still love me?"

"Yes," she responds without even taking a moment to think.

"Then that's all that matters."

Her shoulders relax as some of the tension she's wound tight around her frame unspools. Taking a deep breath, I haul myself out of the seat and jog around to the passenger side so I can lift her out. "I thought we'd have lunch, but I'm going to need to make love to you first."

Her response is to twine her arms and legs around me. "I'm down with that plan."

Her stomach growls before I can take two steps toward the house.

"On second thought, how about we eat first?"

"Another good plan." She slides down, brushing her unfettered breasts against my chest. Groaning, I pull her in for a hot, hungry kiss—which is interrupted by another grumble.

"The spirit is willing, but the flesh is weak," she says with chagrin.

"Let's feed you, then. I think I can manage to keep my hands to myself for an hour."

"I hope not." She grins impishly and then swings around, purposely brushing her hip against my growing erection.

Awkwardly I maneuver toward the trunk. Inside is the picnic basket, and I unhook the blanket from the custom-made insert.

"So when did you buy the car?"

"I didn't buy it. We're test driving it." I transfer the basket and blanket to one hand and grab her with my other. The walk down to the shore is about a couple hundred yards. It's a beautiful June day with a light breeze blowing up from the sea.

"They let you test drive it?"

"Yes, for the weekend."

"That seems weird . . . and trusting. What if you run off with it?"

"You don't want to buy a car you haven't driven before. Didn't you test out your bike first?"

She shook her head. "No, I bought it used from another courier who was moving up. She bought a Vanmoof." Her voice sounds wistful, and I hide a grin, thinking of the packages that are sitting in one of the empty garage bays.

The sand on the beach is fairly coarse, but it's private. Tiny toes off her tennis shoes and wades into the water. "Oh shit," she yelps and jumps back out. "It's cold!"

I chuckle at her surprise. "I take it you never went swimming in the Sound?"

"Usually Brighton Beach in Brooklyn, or sometimes we'd hit Jacob Riis Park."

"Never been. Should we go together sometime?" I flick the blanket out and set the basket on one edge. Inside I find two plates, two glasses, and silverware along with salami, cheese, fruit, and antipasti.

With a nose wrinkle, she shakes her head. "No. Jacob Riis is pretty shabby, and Brighton's crowded."

"Then maybe we could go up to Vermont. Visit Ben & Jerrys," I suggest. It was something Tiny and her mother had planned to do before Sophie had fallen ill.

Tiny gives me a forlorn smile. "Maybe. I don't think I'm ready for that yet."

"Then come and eat and tell me where we should spend our summer. It can be anywhere."

I spread a pretzel cracker with goat cheese and a dab of jam. She wolfs it down with one bite. "Mmm. Can we take this picnic basket with us too?"

"Of course." With a raised eyebrow, I fend off her attempts to wrestle the knife from me. "Not today, bunny. Today you eat from my hand." I offer her another cracker. Her teeth are a shade sharper against my fingers than necessary, but I appreciate the pinch. Always challenging me in her own way. Once she asked me what I would do when the pursuit was over. My response was sincere at the time, but not entirely truthful. She will always confront me, fight me, and test me, therefore the chase is never ending. Even in this she looks a bit mutinous, and every bite from my hand bears a risk of deeper teeth marks being left behind.

The sad truth is, I'd like to feed her from my hand at every meal. The idea of her sustenance being totally in my control is dizzyingly erotic. But Tiny's far too independent to allow that to happen, so I'll take what I can get—like this meal and maybe a little bedroom play tonight. The new bed frame is made of solid mahogany with soaring posts at the four corners.

I've had quite a few fantasies about her being tied to those posts, spread eagle and helpless underneath me.

"What are you thinking about?" she asks suspiciously after swallowing down an herbed mozzarella pearl.

"You, of course." I palm my erection lightly. "He only gets up for you."

Her lashes sweep downward for a moment and then she glances up—almost shyly. "Is that true?"

It's a serious question, and one she's embarrassed to ask if her pink cheeks are anything to go by. Tiny's sudden bout of insecurity pains me because I know it has more to do with how unsure she feels about her place in my life than her own feelings of self-worth. I bring her hand to my mouth to press a kiss against the palm and then the wrist. "Don't ever doubt it."

Pensively, she bites her lip and looks out onto the sea. The water is nearly still, with only the slightest breeze to mar its glassy perfection. From here, the Sound looks blue and beautiful, but the glee with which Tiny had greeted the sea has been swallowed by a thoughtful melancholy. "When it was just Mom and me, the fact that I couldn't read was no big deal. I didn't realize until she was gone how much I depended on her to do stuff for me—like look up an address on the Internet or read the news to me in the morning as I was getting ready. She helped me set up my phone and filled out all the paperwork for our apartment."

To make it seem like the feelings she is sharing are not of too much or too little importance, I cut salami, plate cheese, and pour wine. She eats and drinks absently. "I'm just wondering if I would have made it if you hadn't come along."

"While I'd like to be a pompous ass and say, 'No, you wouldn't be able to survive without me,' I don't doubt you'd be fine." I take a swallow of the white wine myself before continuing. "You have a quick mind. You'd get a job delivering again. You'd get a roommate. You'd . . ." The words stick in my throat. The idea that she could meet and fall in love with someone else is not something I wish to contemplate or give voice to. "You'd have made it."

We finish the rest of the picnic, and Tiny insists on packing everything away carefully when she sees that I had intended to pick up the four corners of the blanket and dump the contents into the basket. "You might break the glasses," she protests as I gather up one side and then another.

"I doubt they cost more than a dollar to make," I note wryly.

"Still, we might want to use them again."

Standing back, I take the opportunity to watch her ass sway as she bends over to pick up one dish and then another. The shorts are riding high, and I can see not only her lower cheeks but the lace edges of her panties. When she reaches into the basket, the delicate crease where her inner leg joins her body winks in and then out of view. I can't resist any longer and kneel down behind her, sliding one large hand over the curve of her succulent ass and dipping in between her legs. The denim is so short and frayed, it's easy to slip two fingers underneath the fabric to rub against her honeyed warmth.

Her body stills under mine, and then I feel a slight pressure against my hand. Without any word of acknowledgment, she continues to pack the items away. The glass plates and silverware are followed by empty jars of jam and wrappers of cheese. I hold my hand rigidly in place, and the movement of her body as she packs and rearranges creates enough friction that she's soon lightly panting.

"Quite the workout," I observe mildly, all the while enjoying how my fingers are getting damper by the minute.

"Yes," she says, a tiny bit breathless. "All this cleanup is really taxing."

Her ass moves more forcefully, and in response to her silent demand, I slide one and then another finger inside her. She pushes back as far as the constraints of the denim and lace allow. Leaning forward, I brush the hair away from her neck and place a small bite against her shoulder. She shudders. "Can you come like this?" I pump slowly, only able to reach up to the second knuckle.

"Maybe," she moans and jerks against me.

"How about now?" I dip my other hand down the front of her shorts to press my fingers against her clit. The position draws the denim tight against my hand, as if we are bound together. "I can't wait to lick your honey off my fingers after you come."

She whimpers and while I can barely move either hand, she is able to work her hips and ass in minute movements, the tautness of the fabric and the steely restraint of my hands providing just enough sensation to bring her off.

The climax is small but powerful as she tenses beneath me and then throws her head back, releasing a small keening sound. Her nectar floods my palm, and I cup it to gather as much as I can. The suck of her channel against my fingers makes me groan in anticipation.

I ease her out of her shorts, and she collapses on the blanket, her sides heaving lightly as she tries to catch her breath. "I hope you're in good shape," I gently tease, "because I'm going to be fucking you on every acre of land and in every room this weekend."

"You're going to have to have a lot more in your picnic basket than cheese and wine then," she says, eyes closed.

I lick her juice off the palm of my hand. "I have plenty in my basket for you."

She chortles softly. "I can't tell if that's an innuendo or not, because right now everything sounds extremely dirty."

I manage to keep my hands off her long enough for us to make it back to the house. Dropping the basket off at the car, I tug her hand to lead her into the garage. Entering the code to raise the door, I watch her face as the bikes come into view.

"Oh my Lord," she breathes. "Is that a Vanmoof and a Cervelo?"

"The day I saw you in SoHo there were two bikes in the window. I couldn't figure out which one you wanted, so I bought both."

She ducks under the garage door before it's fully raised to see the bicycles up close. I can't tell the difference between them. The Cervelo is lighter and, per the salesperson, corners better because it has a stiffer suspension. The Vanmoof is more elegant and more technologically advanced, with its integrated battery providing extra power via a tiny motor attached to the front wheel.

Whatever delight Tiny had shown for the car has nothing on the pure joy she is exhibiting now. Clearly her love of bikes overcomes her dislike of me spending money on her. She claps her hands to her cheeks and then runs over to jump into my arms. "Oh shit, Ian. I can't even pretend to be mad about this. I love those freaking bikes. Thank you!" A hundred kisses are pressed all over my face. "Can we go for a ride?"

"Sure."

We strap on helmets, and Tiny and I explore historic Southport on our new bicycles. Tiny had to raise the seat for me, and even that small task made her smile broadly. Being self-sufficient is important to her. I need to remember that and respect it.

Our weekend is idyllic. After biking, we return home to find a meal waiting for us. The house came with a caretaker's lodge, along with an actual caretaker. I've continued to pay the salaries of Bruce and his daughter Venita for them to air out the house and carry out a few tasks like coordinating delivery of the bikes and bed and making sure the kitchen was stocked with food. They'd done well so far.

Tiny and I try out the new bed, christening it with her being tied to the four posters while I spend a long time testing the limits of her ability to orgasm. After three, she cries for me to bury my cock inside her, and after the fourth she starts cursing me.

I smile the whole drive home. It was a damned good time.

CHAPTER 17

"The reports you requested from Jake are on your desk. Are they related to the SunCorp acquisition?" Louis is like an excited puppy as he hovers close to the sealed envelope that contains an encrypted USB drive hand delivered by one of Jake's employees. Each of Jake's clients receives his reports in this fashion. No over-the-air transmissions that could be intercepted. No printed photos or reports that could be pilfered from an envelope.

Every client is assigned a passcode and an additional authentication code that gets texted the day of the delivery. These small extra steps were putting Jake's security business in high demand. His attention to detail was becoming renowned. It kept prying eyes—like Louis's—from seeing sensitive information.

"I don't know," I say. It's likely related to Howe and the Hedders, but it could be business.

"If you'd given me the key, I could have looked it over this weekend while you were upstate." Was that a slight hint of reprimand in his voice? I'll be glad when the paperwork is finally through HR so that I can fire Louis.

Jen Frederick

"I hope you didn't work all weekend. Not getting enough rest can make you overlook important details," I answer mildly. Gesturing for Louis to sit down across from my desk, I slice open the envelope and two USBs drop out. Curious. I plug the first one into my laptop. Then I check my phone and type in the passcode. The name on the top of the report is only slightly surprising, as are the details. Idly I wonder if I had shared some of my vendetta with Louis, whether things would have gone differently and he wouldn't have felt the need to align himself in direct opposition. It's all rhetorical now.

The information in the report is damning.

It merely shores up my position should any legal proceedings be initiated. I don't need to wait for HR with this information. The summary is succinct and to the point. Jake has never been one for gilding the lily.

As I watch Louis' fingers tap the arm of the chair, it strikes me that I simply have never trusted him with that kind of personal information, despite the two of us having worked together as an efficient moneymaking team for the last five years. My instincts haven't failed me yet.

"*Someone* needs to keep the lights on," Louis replies snippily.

"Someone needs to remember who signs the checks around here." Despite the evenness of my tone, not even Louis could mistake the steel in my eyes—if he had the balls to look at me.

He tugs on the cuff of his shirt, apparently obsessed with getting the correct cuff-to-sleeve ratio. "You aren't the only multinational holding company in town."

It's a weak threat, but a threat nonetheless. I require only one thing from the people in my inner circle: loyalty. "One pussy is as good as the next?" I ask.

He exhales in relief. "Right. I mean unless she's shitting out golden eggs, then there's no point in jeopardizing a deal over her. I was worried there that she'd swallowed you up or something. Nice to see you're coming to your senses." He laughs a bit self-consciously and tugs at his

170

cuff one more time before glancing up. His smile dies off at the hard look on my face.

Clasping my hands together on my desk, I lean toward Louis. In clear tones, so there is no mistaking my meaning or purpose, I tell him what I think. "You have fifteen minutes to get your personal effects together, turn in your company-issued equipment, and leave the building. There will be no severance pay."

I watch for a few seconds as he opens and closes his mouth like a beached whale and then switch USB drives. After a minute of no movement, I comment, "You've got fourteen minutes now."

The second USB is devoted to Malcolm and Mitch Hedder. As the summary of the Hedders's past ten years rolls by, I hear the office door close quietly.

Malcolm Hedder was busy running his small-time operation of high-end hookers and prescription drugs. Jake notes that Malcolm had acquired a new escort who was about the same height as Tiny and had similar features. Jake also points out that this was creepy. I agree. But it wasn't just Malcolm's possibly escalating obsession with Tiny that caused me a twinge of concern. Mitch Hedder's last Palm Beach sugar momma had been found dead under suspicious circumstances, and several pieces of her extensive jewelry collection were missing. Now he was here sniffing around Tiny.

No, she wouldn't like a bodyguard, but she damn well is going to have one. Jake recommends four different individuals—three men and one woman. No question which one I'd pick, but the decision will be Tiny's.

Picking up the phone, I alert Rose to the new development. "Louis is taking a new job. Please call building management and let them know."

"Certainly, Mr. Kerr." Rose's voice is filled with smug pleasure. She informed me how much she didn't like Louis when I gave her the news of his impending departure last week. Thirteen minutes later, I'm in the office lobby, still digesting the Hedder report. That bodyguard for Tiny needs to be hired immediately.

The receptionist is my assistant Rose's daughter, Fawn, in keeping with the outdoorsy theme, I guess. She's nineteen-going-on-thirty and enjoys testing her baby wiles on the older men in the company.

"I love your tie today," she coos as I wait for Louis to appear. He's always been punctual before, but now that I'm kicking him out, he's dawdling. Probably attempting to download as many analyst reports as possible. Information is power, and Louis will attempt to leverage my superior research team for a better position somewhere else.

"Thanks, my fiancée picked it out." Not really a white lie. She did suggest that the pale blue silk would look good against the black-checked suit coat.

"I didn't know you'd proposed!" she exclaims.

"This weekend." I love the word fiancée. There's a sense of ownership and belonging in that word.

"Congratulations!" She smiles, and it's genuine. At thirty-two, I might be interesting but I'm old. "She has good taste then," she says and then turns back to reviewing emails—office ones, I hope. A muffled clatter of wheels down the carpeted hallway signals Louis's approach. He's dragging a wheeled cart behind him. The indignity of it is probably crushing.

"Everything go smoothly?" I ask.

A muscle in his jaw is working overtime as he struggles with how much he'd like to tell me to go to hell, possibly while sucking on a donkey's dick on my way down. But he manages to hold back whatever profanity-laced diatribe he'd like to trot out and instead hisses, "You're going to regret this decision."

Fawn's eyes widen in anticipation of a potential scene.

"I doubt it. My priorities have changed." I walk toward the glass doors of the entrance and out of Fawn's hearing. "You'll enjoy yourself somewhere else."

"All this over some illiterate snatch? Fuck, man, you can do better than that."

My hand curls around the edge of the glass door. I'm tempted, for a strong and long moment, to take Louis's head in one hand and the glass door in the other and bash the two together until one or both of them break into little pieces. But physical violence is transitory. Louis will hurt more when I remove his status and moneymaking ability.

"There's a very important piece you are missing here, Louis." I pin him with a stare and this time he can't look away. I won't allow it. "To be a good investor, to make good decisions, you have to be both unemotional and observant. You've shown neither trait here." He opens his mouth to interrupt, but I continue. "Every attempt I've made to inform you that Victoria would be an integral part of my life has been met with either dismissal or disdain, which means you failed to notice both recent warnings and past signs. I stick up for people in my circle. You were once there."

He gives me a weak nod as we both probably recall his first management meeting, which took place at Colicchio & Sons. The target's outgoing CEO lightly mocked Louis's lack of a Harvard education. I reminded the CEO that at least Louis had a college degree and a business school education—unlike myself. He'd shut up after that, and Louis had worn a grateful look on his face for an embarrassingly long time.

But in the months that I've spent with Tiny, I have sensed Louis's impatience with me. He'd worried I'd take too long to make decisions, his attention had begun to wander, and—like a jilted mistress—he'd sought affirmation elsewhere. Jake's investigative report telling me that Louis had racked up large debts at high-end department stores, as well as overextended himself with other expensive toys, only confirmed what I'd begun to suspect. Louis wouldn't be happy working at Kerr Inc. much longer. I'd merely hastened his exit.

His latest purchase had been a yacht. A fucking yacht. What a fool. He had been meeting covertly with Howe's investment firm, likely passing on reports and insider information.

"If you'd just wake up, Ian. There's so much business out there for us, and we're letting it pass us by." His brows are furrowed and the handle on his briefcase is clutched so tightly that his knuckles are white.

As he rolls out, his face hardens and a shifty gleam appears in his eyes—a look that says he's going to pull one over on me. But he's too late. If he thought I was a vicious, money-hungry asshole before, he'll appreciate how a predator with a family to protect will act. And perhaps he'll learn a good lesson.

"There's always more business," I drawl.

Louis doesn't waste time. Likely he has some reporter in his pocket. We all do. In just a few hours, the stock for Kerr Inc. falls dramatically. The business television ticker hints at instability in Kerr Inc. upper management.

Tokyo won't be alive for another few hours. I shoot off an email to the legal counsel handling the SunCorp offering. I want to move forward on this now that I've dealt with Louis.

I'd hoped to have a late lunch with Tiny, but the chaos caused by Louis's departure prevents that. Just another checkmark in his "con" column.

"I wanted to take you out, bunny, but I have some business to attend to."

"Oh, okay." She's clearly disappointed.

"I'm sorry. I could break away for maybe thirty minutes if you can come down here." Thirty minutes is time I don't really have, but I hate the sound of her dismay.

"No, it's not a big deal, besides I've got something to work on—but can you be home early? Like six or so?" There's a weird thrum in her words. I can't make out the emotion, but it sounds vaguely like excitement.

"I'll be there," I promise. And I will, even if I have to burn the trading floor down to get a moment's respite.

Rose brings me lunch and a sheaf of papers. "What's this?" It's a stack of resumes, of younger investment analysts and recent business school graduates. "Just some replacement ideas for Louis," she says demurely.

"Thank you." My soft laughter follows her out.

I field a dozen or more calls from hedge fund managers wanting to know more about the Wall Street rumors about Kerr management's instability. I tell them the truth—that Louis Durand has left the company. Despite my evidence, I don't share that he's been stealing information. It would only make the company look weaker. When Gabe reaches me by midafternoon, I know the tipping point has been reached.

"Do I need to sue anyone on your behalf?"

Gabriel Allen has a voice he wields like a weapon. I've seen other lawyers nearly piss themselves at a glare and a sharp command. His sonorous tones are set to comfort at this moment.

"You can pack away your therapist persona. I'm perfectly fine."

"I'm watching your stock fall by 15 percent. The more it falls, the faster the pace of the selling."

"My ticker says the same thing yours does."

"You're playing some deeper game." It isn't a question.

"I built Nessie for just this purpose."

Gabe's silent for a moment. "You knew, then?"

"I suspected. Asked Jake to look into it, and he sent the confirmation this morning."

"When were the flags first raised?"

"About a month after I met Tiny. I'd been spending more time with her away from the office. I could tell he was getting restless. I'd hoped that I was imagining things, but . . ."

"Better safe than sorry," he finishes for me.

"Yes."

"When will you step in?"

"Tomorrow. Maybe Wednesday. If the price is going to drop, let's wait it out." Instinct, honed at a young age, tells me that now is not the time for action.

"Your nerves are made of steel." He compliments me.

I snort. "As if yours aren't? Besides, this is only dangerous if you care.

Kerr Inc. could die tomorrow and I'd still have enough funds to make sure that Tiny and I lived a good life. But thanks for the concern. I won't forget."

"I was elected to call you. Everyone was perturbed, but we didn't want to inundate you with calls if you were busy putting out fires."

"I'm watching the conflagration right now and enjoying the heat."

Louis has inadvertently timed his leak perfectly because the domestic stock market closes with Kerr stock at an all-time low. By the close of trading, Kerr Inc. stock had fallen by nearly a quarter, erasing nearly nineteen billion in market cap—a record drop-off by a holding company that had only seen growth since its inception over a decade ago. Some business talking heads called it a correction, saying that the market cap had been too high for too long. I see it as an opportunity.

Whatever cooked information Louis had shared with his reporter friend is leading this downturn, but as I'd reminded Gabriel, I have a separate, private holding company with an obscene amount of ready capital. When Kerr Inc. stock falls to 30 percent below opening trading, it will be the time to buy. My guess is that it will happen before noon tomorrow.

The rest of the late afternoon I spend handling phone calls from frantic board members. I assure them that all is fine. I don't know if any of them have been listening to Louis's whispers, so I don't share my plans with them.

Right before I leave, Rose alerts me to the director of The Frick Collection on the phone. "Mr. Kerr, I'm so sorry to bother you today. You must have a lot on your plate."

"No problem, Ross. What can I do for you?" I try not to sound impatient because the Frick event is one that must go smoothly. I need Ross Fairchild to ensure that.

"It's about your donation. I know we've received the first one but . . ." he trails off.

"In light of the impending financial news, you're worried my pledge may not be sound?" I finish for him.

"Of course not. Only, if we are to provide naming rights for such an important expansion, we want to ensure that the renovations encounter no barriers. I'm certain you would agree if you were me."

I tamp down my anger at his insinuation that I'd make a promise and not live up to it. "What will it take for the event to proceed as planned with the naming rights as we previously discussed?"

"The entire amount?" he suggests. At my stony silence, he relents. "Perhaps 60 percent?"

"The cashier's check will be on your desk first thing, Fairchild. The event better be fucking perfect."

"Of course, and thank you for your understanding."

Fuck you.

I slam the phone down and close my eyes. The amount of the Frick donation is sizeable, and while I have contingency funds, it isn't bottomless. I hadn't accounted for the entire five million to be called in like that.

Any other time and I would've told Fairchild to fuck himself, but then again, any other time and he wouldn't be asking.

The phone rings again, but I'm done for the day. I need to see Tiny.

CHAPTER 18

When I arrive home she's already there, vibrating with energy. The sight of her helps to drain away some of the tension of the day.

I drop my bag on the floor and enclose her slender waist in my arms. "I'm disappointed. When you told me to come home right away, I thought for sure you'd be wearing nothing but whipped cream."

"Not every night is your birthday," she teases.

"No, but we can pretend," I answer. "But before I ravish you, you appear to be bursting with news. What is it?" I bury my head in the side of her neck, growling and rubbing my afternoon scruff all over her tender skin. She squeals and pushes ineffectually at my hands.

"Stop. I seriously have something to tell you."

Drawing back but still keeping her within the circle of my arms, I say carefully, "Are you pregnant? And if so, do you want to be?"

"No! Come over and sit down though." She leads me into the living room and has me sit on the sofa. There's a cold beer, fresh from the cooler, waiting for me on the side table. Picking up the beer, I obediently take a long drink. She waits, hovering at the edge of the coffee table, as if she can barely contain herself.

"Lay it on me," I say, placing the beer on the table and leaning forward.

"I was thinking about Howe," she begins.

With a groan, I lean back and cover my eyes. "No, Tiny, you said you wouldn't."

"I haven't done anything." She pauses. "Much. I haven't done much of anything."

"I'm going to kick Jake's ass." I pick up my phone to start a verbal flaying.

"Wait. I never left the office. Okay, a few times, but I knew Steve was following me." When I set the phone down, she continues. "I asked Jake about the research he'd done on the other women rumored to be involved with Howe. He told me that you'd done background checks and had them followed, but they appeared to be ordinary women. There was one girl who was a student at Columbia. Another who was an intern for a councilman connected to his dad. The third, though, was a waitress. She worked at Table 57, a restaurant that Howe liked to go to without his wife."

"His wife didn't like going because it was too down-market." I finish for her. "I know this. I read the report when Jake put it together."

"Well, the waitress bothered me. The other two women came from money, so maybe it was easy to see why they would turn away yours. And maybe they didn't want to be in the eye of a scandal, particularly the intern, but the waitress was like me. She seemed to be barely scraping together enough to live on. Jake said she lived in Brooklyn and took a two-hour train ride to get to Table 57. You'd think she'd be OK with suffering through a few pictures in exchange for the hefty half-million you were willing to pony up."

"You'd think," I say.

"But then I thought about blackmail. Did you know that Malcolm wanted your signature in the hopes of blackmailing you in the future?"

"I thought that might be the case," I say, unconcerned. I never gave Malcolm my signature, and there wasn't anything that would tie me to him—except for Tiny, and she was worth any risk.

"I had Jake check the marriage records for her mother. They showed that her divorced mother remarried once, for like six months, to a guy who is currently in prison. But there was another kid who lived with them."

"I'm interested. Keep talking." I think I know where this is going, but I want to hear it all.

"The kid from the second marriage was in juvie, and he got out. Lauren, that's the waitress, was the one who picked him up upon his release, according to one of Jake's contacts."

"So she's related. A half brother. Maybe a stepbrother," I muse out loud. "He gets out conveniently around the time I start sniffing around."

"Yes," she claps her hands. "It's crazy, but maybe Howe's bought off a judge or something. The kid gets let out and Lauren is super grateful. Whatever he holds over their heads is more important than the money."

"Let's check it out."

"Both of us?" Her eyes are glowing.

"Would you let me leave you behind?"

"No."

"Then it's futile for me to insist on going alone. So you knew about Steve?"

"Yes, and you knew I was following Howe around?"

I nod. "Steve wasn't spying, but he did ask me if I knew you were watching Howe eat lunch several times a week."

She grimaces. "And you didn't say anything?"

Taking another swallow of the beer, I raise an eyebrow. "I was waiting for you."

"I guess we should start sharing things with each other." She studies her hands.

The room seems slightly chilled, and after a day like I've had, the last thing I want to do is fight. "We're both used to carrying our own burdens. This is a process." I pull her toward me for a quick kiss. "We're learning we can lean on someone else. That's new and it will take time."

She gives me a grateful smile and rises. From the kitchen she says, "Jake says I'm really good at this and that I'm wasted behind the desk."

"He does, does he?" I follow her. She's rummaging around the refrigerator looking for ingredients. Apparently she's excited enough to cook. I wait for direction on what to chop. "What exactly does he think you're good at?"

"Investigative work. He says I'm good at seeing puzzle pieces and putting together a bigger picture." She hands me an onion and two tomatoes and a few cloves of garlic. When we first met, Tiny informed me she had a limited mental recipe box. Since living together, we have both learned to cook new things. She dumps butter to melt in the pan while she starts dredging pieces of beef in flour. I start prepping.

"I've always felt you were quick."

"Jake says I could do fieldwork and more," she babbles on as if I hadn't spoken. "If, you know, my reading skills were better. I can't do any of the searches, like using the marital records database or looking up the criminal blotter."

I stay silent, and not just because I am tired of hearing "Jake says" come out of her mouth; I can sense that this is important. I consider and discard a dozen different responses before settling on one. "What do you want to do?"

"I think I'd like to try again. You'd have to hire me a tutor. One that specializes in helping dyslexics read," she says quietly. Her head is down, and I can't see her expression, but I think I hear something in her voice that sounds like hope.

I nod, painfully aware of how close to the surface my own emotions are. She's asked me for almost nothing. Clearing my throat, I say, "The best. I'll hire the very best. No matter where they are in the world. They'll come here and teach you what you need to know."

"Thank you," she says quietly. There's a sheen in her eyes, but I know that hugging her will look too close to pity. I simply give her a small kiss on her forehead and return to my sous chef tasks. Beside me I hear her sigh in pleasure.

"I don't know why I'm so emotional lately," she admits, firing up the pan.

"Maybe you *are* pregnant." I'm only half joking. I'd love it if she were pregnant.

She sucks in a breath and pats her belly. "I-I don't think so, but we haven't been careful."

"That's a bit of an understatement. I'll call around tomorrow for a recommendation for an OB." I pick up her hand, messy from the food, and kiss the ring. Her face glows with pleasure, and I want to shove everything aside and take her right there.

Instead, I pick up the onion and start chopping. Soon the pungent smell is serving its cock-deflating purpose.

The beef dish is a simple but tasty one, and after we've squeezed the last bit of lime into the sauce pan to join the butter basted meat, fresh tomatoes, and vegetables, dinner is ready to be plated. The wine that didn't make it into the sauce is poured into glasses.

"You seem to be getting the hang of the cooking thing," I say as I fork the tasty food into my mouth.

She shrugs. "I like cooking here. Plus, having Steve drive me around makes it easy. He parks illegally, and I run in to get groceries. I'm out before he can get a ticket. It's a perfect setup. I would have invited him in, but he said he had to get home and have dinner with his girlfriend."

I give her a disbelieving look. Steve is the opposite of loquacious. A mute person is more talkative than him. She sticks out her lower lip, just a tiny bit, and frowns. "Fine, he didn't say anything, but I'm learning his grunts and facial expressions."

"Steve always looks constipated to me whenever I bring up his girlfriend."

"See," she points out, "you know his body language too."

Later when we are drying dishes, I ask her to expound on her learning disability. "Can you tell me something about your dyslexia so I have a better idea of what kind of tutor we'll need?"

"Around the third grade, I was doing poorly in writing and reading—lagging behind. I had a good memory, and we were often placed together in groups. I'd just ask one of my partners to read part of the book out loud. I'd remember enough to get by but struggled, particularly with spelling. Like, I heard a word or a sound but couldn't apply it to paper. Finally, they put me through a bunch of tests and out popped the dyslexia diagnosis. So I can read, but just not well, and it takes me a long time to get through anything more than a couple sentences long."

I remember her struggle over reading my mother's last letter and feel guilty for asking her to make the attempt. She reads my thoughts with ease. "Stop. Please. I liked that you asked me. And that the issue of my poor reading never comes up because it isn't important to you."

"It isn't." I draw her down onto the sofa next to me and pull her legs over my lap. "It's the least important fact I know about you. You're smart, loyal, and brave. You like to call yourself pragmatic, but you're far more optimistic about everything than I am. I'd rather wake up next to you every morning than anyone else, reader or not."

"I wish I could read though." She rubs her cheek against the cloth of my T-shirt, and my heart begins to pump just a tad bit faster. Proximity to Tiny—oh hell, just thinking about her—accelerates my heart rate. She makes me feel alive, and that's worth more money than the world holds. "When you hired that volunteer to read to Mom in the hospital during the chemo days, I was jealous because I couldn't do that."

"She loved you more than there are grains of sand on the beach."

"I know." She sighs.

Her hair feels feather-soft under my hand, and I hate that I'm going to disrupt our quiet moment together. I delay the inevitable for just a few moments as we sit quietly embracing. The sun sinks lower and the amber rays give the warehouse a nostalgic Norman Rockwell patina. "I'm going to be getting up tomorrow around three a.m. I need to watch the opening of the Asian markets," I say, searching for the best way to explain this. "I fired a member of my management team, and he's unhappy."

She makes a move to sit up and swing her legs off my lap, but I hold them down. I want her to be in my arms when I tell her how her life will change. "Is there something wrong?"

"Nothing's wrong. Nothing that a little money and time won't take care of." I strive for calmness. "Louis was this brash kid out of business school with a huge chip on his shoulder. He's the middle son in a family of overachievers. His dad is a successful investment banker, managing partner at Witt and Durand, and his brother went into business with a few friends and started a hedge fund, first trading in oil futures and then expanding into all kinds of energy—solar, natural gas, and even coal. The little sister is a violin virtuoso and is touring in Europe.

"Louis started out at his father's firm but he didn't fit in well there, mostly because his father kept asking him why he wasn't more independent like his siblings. He came to me hungry, ambitious, and not a little bitter. I used all of that. I worked him like a dog, and we made money. I was well on my way to building Kerr Inc. into a multinational holding company to be reckoned with, but in the last four years, it's become huger, grander, and richer than perhaps I'd even imagined."

"Twenty-nine million dollars a day," she murmurs.

"Yes. Twenty-nine million a day in earnings was what the journalists parsed out from the increase in revenues for Kerr Inc. and the corresponding increase in the market cap—or the total amount the public shares are worth," I explain. "I'm completely and utterly to blame for both feeding Louis's appetite for wealth and not injecting enough balance into our lives. Before you, Tiny, I existed for one thing—and that was to make more money. Buy more companies, spearhead a larger push to invest globally in Brazil, India, and China. And I have to tell you that there is nothing less fulfilling than watching your stock price tick up and having no one around but the people you pay to be your companions.

"When I saw you on the sidewalk outside of that wig shop, I realized that my quest for more would never be satiated by adding more companies to my portfolio. I wanted what I didn't have—a family." I intentionally leave Richard Howe's name unsaid, but Tiny squeezes me, her small hand pressing harder into my chest, her legs curling around me, as if by holding me tighter she can eliminate decades of pain. What she doesn't realize is that just her presence in my life, the fact that I can call her mine, has made me able to look forward. Her hugging me tight is an awesome fucking bonus.

"But Louis didn't like this?"

"No, because his focus is singular: making more money. Nothing else matters." I settle into the cushions, lying down and draping Tiny over me like a blanket. "I was—still am—eyeing an investment in a Japanese company that's on the cusp of some revolutionary solar energy technology. Most solar panels are polycrystalline because monocrystalline silicon is too expensive to mass produce. SunCorp believes that it can produce high-quality monocrystalline silicon in greater quantities, which could impact not only solar energy but the entire semiconductor industry."

"I can tell you're excited about this company." She pats my chest. "You're so animated."

"Perhaps." I dip down to kiss the top of her head, the scent of lemon shampoo tickling my nostrils. I stir restively, thinking of a dozen things better we could be doing in a prone position than talking. Hurriedly, I continue. "There are dozens of competitors. Clean energy is one of the hottest markets right now, and everyone wants in—from the wind farmers to those who are trying to turn ice-trapped gas into a power source. Deciding which clean energy company to invest in is the challenge."

"But you like this one."

"I do. Their people are smart and multinational. It's not just a Japanese company. They're attracting bright minds from Switzerland, Brazil, and the US. Their management style is a great blend of Western ambition and Eastern honor. I had Kaga run a check on the people at the top, and he says he'd do business with them. But I haven't moved fast enough for Louis, and he prefers I swallow the company rather than just invest."

"Why is he so impatient?"

"Because he's worried I'm being *too* patient. I'm willing to wait, willing to lose it."

Maybe my tone changes, but something I've said causes her to push away and sit up so she can look at me. "Did you wait because of me? Because of my mom dying? Because I couldn't get out of bed for a week?"

"No," I say sharply. The last thing I want or need is for Tiny to believe that she somehow caused any of this. She'd internalize that guilt and hold it close until it corroded what is good and pure between us. "I'm willing to lose it because I trust my instincts, and it wasn't time to make a move. I'm not sure it's time still. Like I said, there are hundreds of clean energy tech companies to invest in, and SunCorp is just one. If I lose this one, it's because I let it go intentionally."

She searches my face, looking for signs of insincerity. Finding none, she allows herself to lie back down. I pull her tight against me again. "Louis jumped the gun, then?" she asks.

"Yes, because my focus isn't just on business anymore. I don't want it to be. There's no real purpose in making more money, other than I enjoy playing the game. But I don't want the game of acquisition to be the only thing in my life." It's important that Tiny understands that the changes occurring in my life are the product of my own desires—that her being in my life is paramount.

"What is it that he did?"

"He took analyst reports from me and told a business news journalist that the upper management of Kerr Inc. was going through a crisis. He ran with it."

"And the journalist could name Louis as his inside source. Did he also suggest that you were mentally unstable due to drugs or something?"

"The innuendo was heavy, but I think it was just alcohol."

"I assume you have a plan, because you're far too calm if you don't have one."

"For years, I've set aside ready capital with low returns like public sector bonds, gold, currencies, and treasury bills. It's sizable. I'm going to wait until the price of Kerr Inc. stock is low enough and use my private fund to buy it up. I named it the Nessie fund—the monster in the lake no-one has ever seen."

"Your purchase of the stock will signal you feel confident about the company and drive the price of the stock up. Will you sell then? Or will the financial police think you're doing something shady?"

She is picking financial insight just by being with me and doesn't even realize it.

"Financial police?" I can't keep in a huff of laughter. Tiny curls up and punches me lightly in the arm.

"I'm sorry. Not everyone goes to trading school."

I swallow back any hint of a smile. "The SEC. Yes, that could be Louis's goal. He might suspect that I have a contingency fund. But I doctored several reports that he stole from the company, including the SunCorp one. I believe he'll use that information to buy his way into another holding company, perhaps a hedge fund. When they use it to make, buy, or sell decisions based on his inaccurate information, Louis will be blackballed from Wall Street. He's not even notorious enough to be able to give inspirational speeches on how to sell shit; he's no Jordan Belfort. My guess is he'll have trouble getting a managerial position at a big box store in Jersey."

"Ouch. But I guess he deserves it. When did you do the doctoring?"

"Last week. I figured that if he was going to act it would be when I took the weekend to go to Long Island. This coming week will be busy. I'll be making sure that all my ducks are in a row when the SEC does come calling." I pull us both upright and rise to get the paperwork that I'd printed out. "Along with investigating Louis, I had Jake check up on the Hedders."

Tiny's face screws up like she's smelled something rotten. "What about them?"

"They're bad news, both of them," I say. I'm not going to reveal to her the creepy part about Malcolm hiring a new prostitute who looks like her, but I do relate the information Jake gathered about the elder Hedder. "The police don't have any new leads. Mitch is a suspect, but he has an alibi."

She looks at the print outs I'm holding. "I just can't see Mitch using physical violence against someone."

"It's not a violent crime. She took the wrong cocktail of prescription medications. It could have been a mistake, or someone could have mixed them purposely."

"Killing someone is a violent crime." She frowns. "It doesn't fit Mitch. He's an unfaithful jerk, but not a killer."

"He's someone you haven't seen since you were sixteen," I remind her gently. "People change. You don't know what Mitch Hedder has been up to for the last nine years. What we do know is that despite not being gainfully employed since he ran out on your mom, he has been able to amass enough money to enjoy an extended stay at The Plaza. Those rooms run close to a thousand bucks a night. Does that square with the Mitch you know?"

She shakes her head slowly. "No. He's never had that much money. I don't know where he got it, but killing? That's a huge deal, Ian."

"I'm telling you all of this for a reason." I pick up another sheet of paper. "I have Steve because a man with a lot of money can't be too careful. It's unlikely that I'd ever be in danger, but we know from the attack that someone out there doesn't like me much. I've had Steve drive you around because I want you to have the convenience of a driver but also because I need you to be safe."

"The bodyguard," she says with great distaste.

"I know you don't like this, but tomorrow I'm going to share the news of our engagement. While I'm not famous, this city loves to gossip, and for a short time, you're going to be of interest. I'm not going to have an ounce of serenity if you aren't protected, so it's either you have Steve with you all the time or you have your own hand-picked bodyguard."

With a sigh, she rises and walks over to the floor-to-ceiling windows overlooking the Hudson. "And I don't get a say?"

"You do in who follows you around."

"But not in being free."

"You won't even know the person is there."

"Every time I go out, someone is going to follow me around, and you're saying that I won't even know?"

"You don't seem to mind Steve." I say implacably.

She waves her hand. "He's like a friend. A silent, surly friend."

"You can hire another one like him."

"I knew this was coming," she sighs. "But I don't like this," she says.

"Noted."

"Who then?"

I read aloud from the profiles of the four different people Jake has suggested for her. Three are former military. Two Special Forces and a Marine. The fourth is a former policewoman who left her job after her partner was killed on a drug bust. She'd been accused of participating in under-the-table dealings, but Jake believed that these were false accusations from the actual dirty cops. I trusted Jake.

"I want Marcie, the woman," she decides.

"Good choice. That's who I would've picked." I set the papers on the table. "Now that we've done all the hard stuff, let's go upstairs. It's been far too long since I've been inside you, and I've a hankering for some dessert."

Later, after a long bout of lovemaking, Tiny asks. "Why would you have picked Marcie? Is she pretty?"

"I have no idea. I would've picked her because I'm a jealous mother-fucker and I don't want another man spending that much time with you."

"You never said anything."

"Because I'm not a stupid fucker. Just a jealous one. I know better than to tell you what to do."

"Is that right?" she says, shifting provocatively on top of me. "I distinctly remember you barking orders at me not thirty minutes ago."

"Except here in the bedroom." My dormant cock is rising between us. "Get on your knees and grab the headboard."

"Or else?"

"Or else your ass is going to get spanked."

"I thought punishment was supposed to be something you didn't like." She rolls over and wiggles her ass in my face.

If that isn't a challenge, I'm not sure what is.

♦ ♦ ♦

I get out of bed just as Tiny is nodding off and prepare for the day. The Tokyo exchange will close in an hour and the Hong Kong exchange directly after. Stock in the larger energy companies in East Asia has been stable all day. Louis hasn't made any moves . . . yet. Any serious moves to either take over SunCorp or invest heavily would have moved the needle.

If Louis bases his offer on the pilfered documents, it will be too low. They'll be offended and shut the door to him, making them more amenable to my own offer. It's damn manipulative, but I didn't get to this position without turning every opportunity to my advantage.

As I'm sitting at my desk, the red light above the monitor on the wall that displays the security feed blinks on and my phone rings.

"Kerr here."

"Mr. Kerr, this is Carson Dunlap from Tanner Security. An alarm has been tripped at your residence. Do you need assistance?"

I watch a black-masked, slim-built figure jiggle the back lock on the video monitor. I press a button and the lock gives, allowing the uninvited guest to slip inside. "No, we're just fine."

Dunlap hesitates. "Sir, I saw the intruder gain access to your residence. I can have the NYPD outside your residence in under ten."

"Really?" I tap another button and the feed switches to the living room. The assailant's head peers around the corner. Seeing no one, the intruder creeps in and heads directly to the stairs. "Jake must pay them quite a bit if they're so responsive."

I get no immediate response. "I can send someone from Tanner Security to provide backup should you need it. They'll be there in five."

"That's fine," I say absently. From my bottom desk drawer, I pull out a biometric handprint safe. Deactivating the lock, I reach for the Glock 19 and its magazine. Sliding the magazine in place, I go downstairs to greet my guest.

CHAPTER 19

"If you're looking to leave a threatening note, my suggestion is by the sink in the kitchen. We generally have coffee in the morning."

The intruder's head jerks up at my lazy drawl. I'm shrouded in the shadows at the top of the stairs, while the figure downstairs is illuminated by the moonlight shining through the floor-to-ceiling windows. The figure glances back toward the entrance and the stairs that lead to the first floor.

"I wouldn't if I were you." I lift my gun and direct my uninvited guest toward the dining room. "There's a car outside with someone waiting to take you to the police. Or you can take a seat, and we'll talk this out."

As if on cue, Tanner's security person pulls up. We both turn and watch the headlights flicker across the windows. With slumped shoulders, the intruder trudges over to the table.

A door slams outside and then footsteps tromp up the stairs. A disheveled Steve appears at the top, wearing a loose-fitting T-shirt and jeans. A gun is in his hand as well.

"I've got this." I scowl at him.

He merely grunts and moves into the living room. With a flick of a switch, the television pops on and he appears as if he's doing nothing more than settling in to watch a few rounds of infomercials. But it's apparent from the tension in his shoulders that he's ready to leap over the back and subdue our quarry.

As I flip on a couple of lights to illuminate the room, the intruder settles in and drags off the mask. Despite the short haircut, there is no mistaking my intruder's femininity. Steve sucks in a breath of surprise, but I'm unmoved. Tiny's earlier revelations unspool in my mind like a two-foot-long parchment.

"Table 57 doesn't pay its wait staff enough, so you've been forced into a life of larceny?" I ask lightly, setting my gun on the center island and releasing the magazine. Steve stands up, hands on his hips, and frowns at us. No one has updated him, so it's understandable he's confused.

Lauren is an attractive young lady, probably in her early twenties. Her figure is boyish, but I wonder if some of that is due to restricting undergarments and part of her disguise. Strands of reddish brown hair stick up due to static from the hat. I peg her height to be close to five-nine. Model proportions, which I can see attracting a certain percentage of male attention. Idly I wonder if her black slacks and top are also part of her restaurant uniform. Doing double duty, so to speak.

It's her turn to be shocked. Or maybe she has been all along. She sits there dejectedly, and the note she was to leave falls out of her grip and onto the table. Steve is there to grab the paper before I can open it.

"Anthrax," he grunts in warning.

"It's just a letter. I put it in the envelope myself." She sounds tired. No, that's not the right word. Defeated. Her shoulders are slumped, and her head hangs so far down I wonder if her neck is broken. Steve pulls out two pairs of plastic gloves and hands me a set. Holding the envelope up to the light, we check for signs of excess powder.

"It's only got my fingerprints," she says sullenly. "I printed it out at the local copy shop."

The envelope is cheap—the kind that bills and political flyers come in. Confident that there isn't a white powder risk, Steve slits the envelope open with his HK knife, a large wicked-looking thing. I roll my eyes at the unnecessary threat, and Lauren doesn't even look up to see it.

He hands it over when he's satisfied the letter and envelope present no danger.

"See? Nothing," she says spitefully.

"You're pretty mouthy for a girl who's a phone call away from being put in jail," he shoots back.

"You're pretty thickheaded for not listening to anything I'm saying."

"Why should I? You're all over security feeds fumbling around the house and trying to break in with a second-rate lock pick set. You didn't even see the cameras," Steve says, putting together more words in one sentence than I've ever heard him use before.

"Excuse me for not being a professional thief," she rages back. "Not all of us can go to Thugs "R" Us and buy all the cool larceny tools."

This display of instant attraction disguised as repugnance between the two would be amusing if the girl hadn't tried to break into my house and threaten the safety of Tiny.

"No glued-on newspaper letters, or is that so 1980s?" I quip. The letter has only a few sentences.

> The decline in Kerr stock could be much worse. Think about
> that when you're deciding who to socialize with. Hope you and
> your slut enjoy the poor house. There's much worse where that
> came from.

"Someone doesn't like you, Steve. Look at the insult. I shouldn't be socializing with you." I hand the letter back to him and strip off the plastic gloves.

"It's Kaga they don't like then because you hang around him more than anyone." Steve sticks the letter into a plastic baggie and sits down across from Lauren.

"True," I muse. "Nightclub business can be cutthroat."

"I'm not going to tell you anything, so you might as well just call the police." Lauren interrupts our jests. Scowling, she adds, "And it's not a fucking joke."

"You're not very good at this," Steve says. "First, there are cameras at the door. Visible ones. Second, you were noisy as fuck. We could hear you on the exterior video feed coming down the alley." He shakes his head in disgust.

"I'm a fucking waitress, not a spy," she retorts.

"You should stick to waiting tables."

"Oh, what great advice. Next time I have someone forcing me to do things, I'll be sure to tell them I'm only good at waiting tables. I'm sure that will go over swell."

"Worth a try." Steve turns to me with a raised eyebrow. "Louis?"

"No, Richard Howe, I think." My gaze hasn't turned away from her, and I see her flinch slightly. Yes, Richard Howe. Tiny needs to come down.

"Just a minute." I stride over to the stairs. "Try not to kill each other while I'm gone."

I leave the two glaring at each other. Tiny will be sorry she missed the fireworks. I saw more sparks between Steve and this stranger in the last few minutes than I ever have with Steve's sullen girlfriend.

Upstairs in the darkened bedroom, Tiny is sprawled out on the bed, her arm over on my side as if she's searching for me. The sexy hollow of her spine leads down enticingly to the rise of her ass, barely covered by the sheet. If there's anything I should be angry about, it's that I have to wake her from slumber. She should be allowed to rest after the workout I gave her. I nab her the blue silk embroidered robe.

I like it on her because there's no easier access to her tempting charms than through an ill-fitting robe. On second thought, given that we have company, the sex robe should be shelved. I pull out a pair of knit shorts and a tank. She can put the robe overtop of those two items.

"Bunny," I whisper, stroking the hair out of her face, "we have some company."

She mumbles something into the mattress but doesn't move. Her exposed back is too tempting to resist, so I place a few kisses down the column. Downstairs there are murmurs. The two are still talking. I hear a scrape of a chair and then running water. Steve is probably making tea. Aussies love their tea.

"Wake up, Tiny," I say with regret. I'd love to climb back in bed with her, but we've got an issue to deal with.

She rolls over, squinting at me. "Are we poor?" she asks sleepily.

"Poor?" I'm baffled and give her a confused chuckle.

"Did you lose everything in the Asian markets?" She sits up, grasping the sheets to her chest and looking like an adorable little owl.

"No." I stifle another laugh. "We can still afford a few homes and takeout. But we do have a guest, and I'd like you to come down and talk to her."

"Is it Sarah?" She swings her legs to the side of the bed and starts to pull on clothes as I hand them to her.

"No, it's Lauren."

"Lauren?" Because she's sleepy, it takes a few seconds for the battery leads to connect in her brain but once they do, her head snaps up. "Table 57 Lauren?"

I nod.

"Holy shit." Tiny jumps up, grabs the robe out of my hands, and runs out of the room while struggling to wrap it around herself. She hops down the stairs and skids to a stop at the sight of Steve pouring hot tea into mugs.

"Tea?" he asks, holding up the pot.

Tiny shakes her head no. I can tell by the way her gaze swings from Steve to Lauren and back again, she's not sure who is the more interesting and surprising entity in her dining room. I give her a small nudge, and she plops into a chair at the head of the table.

"I'm Victoria." She holds out her hand to Lauren.

Lauren grasps it gingerly, as if Tiny might shock her. "Lauren Williams."

"Nice to meet you. I understand you knew Richard Howe at one point. Me too."

Lauren gasps and covers her mouth. "I'm sorry," she says after a moment of staring.

"No need. I have Ian." Tiny replies and holds up a hand toward me. I grab it, standing behind her chair with my other hand on her shoulder. Lauren's eyes eat this all up, and neither Tiny nor I miss the under-the-lashes sideways glance Lauren shoots to Steve as he comes over with two mugs of tea, placing one in front of Lauren. "I know that you're in some trouble, Lauren, and we can help." She gestures around the table. Steve grunts his agreement, back to his closed-mouthed self.

"You want to help?" Lauren shoots back.

Tiny nods and leans forward. "Yes, we do."

"Then back off. Whatever it is you're doing that Richard Howe doesn't like, just stop. That's how you can help."

"We aren't doing anything. We'd have to stop existing," Tiny protests, but I cough.

"What?"

"I forgot to tell you that I've called in some of Howe's debt." Tiny narrows her eyes at me. Holding up my palms, I add, "I swear that's everything."

"They're dangerous," Lauren warns.

"They?" I ask, turning toward her.

She looks down at her hands as if worried she's given too much away. "I can't help you. I'm sorry. Just call the police."

Her implacable response reminds me of Big Guy, who refused to give anything up as well. Their silence isn't purchased by money, though. I couldn't have bought their words. They're bound by something more powerful than money.

"What happened tonight?" Tiny finally asks me.

"I saw this young person fiddling with the lock. I let her in so that I could confront her."

"God, Ian, that was so dangerous." She slaps my arm, and Steve grunts in agreement.

"I had a gun."

"You have a gun?" she asks and looks around wildly until she spots it on the kitchen counter. "Put that thing away!"

"It's not hot. There's no bullet in the chamber, and the magazine is lying right next to it."

"Seriously, can you put it in a drawer or something? It's making me nervous. What if it just accidentally goes off?"

"How?" I ask, perplexed.

"Just put the gun away, mate, and get on with this," Steve snaps.

Tiny raises both eyebrows and mouths "wow" at me. Shaking my head, I push away from the table. I drop the gun in the drawer beneath it, which happens to be the utensil drawer, and stick the magazine in my pocket. "Good?"

She makes a face at me but nods.

"Sorry," she apologizes to Lauren. "We *can* help you. Ian has more money than small countries. Tell us what the problem is, and we can solve it. It's your brother, right? Richard Howe is threatening your brother?"

Lauren sucks in her lip and then bites it, as though that will prevent her from spilling the story, so Tiny forges on.

"Your brother got into some trouble, and he's out on parole. Maybe Richard helped with that, and if your brother breaks parole, he goes back in and serves more time, right?" She doesn't wait for a response this time. The question is clearly rhetorical. "You don't want him to go back in, but since Howe got him out, he can send him right back. Howe has a cop, maybe someone on the parole board, in his pocket, so he says keep your mouth shut or your brother's parole will be revoked?"

Lauren's mouth is hanging open, and even Steve looks on with some approval. Me? I'm starting to understand why Jake thinks Tiny is wasted behind a desk.

"Can you fix this with money?" Tiny demands of me.

"I'm not into bribing cops," I admit. "That's a high-risk proposition. Maybe if we knew more about your brother's situation, we could think of another resolution."

Lauren stands up. "I see you've done a lot of investigating, but talking about possibilities isn't enough for me. I'm going to go now. Either call the police or let me leave. Otherwise, this is kidnapping."

Steve whistles. "You got some balls accusing us of wrongdoing when you're guilty of breaking and entering."

"I didn't break in." She sniffs. "The door was unlocked."

"We have you fiddling with the door. You're dressed in all black, and you've delivered a threatening note."

"What threatening note?" Tiny looks around and then grabs the plastic baggie that is now holding the letter Howe had Lauren deliver to me. I'm not sure how much of it she can make out, and I'll read it to her later. Her face takes on an ashen quality; maybe she can make it out just fine.

I glance at my watch. I need to check the markets again. "I hate cutting this party short, but it's late. Or early, however you want to look at it. Steve, you take Lauren home. Lauren, this is my card. You change your mind, let me know. I think between the four of us, we can come up with a solution to your problems."

Steve nods and reaches for Lauren, who jerks away. As she stomps toward the exit, he gives me a wave, and then the two disappear downstairs.

I turn to Tiny. "I want you to get some sleep."

"I can't sleep now," she grumbles as I lead her up toward the bedroom. "How many times do we have an intruder in the house? This is kind of exciting."

"Only you would think this turn of events is stimulating."

"I have something to tell you, and I think you're going to be mad," she says as we stop at the bedroom door. The serious tone in her voice has me pausing.

"Let's go to the office." My gut clenches.

She settles into one of the chairs in front of the massive desk, and I drop into the chair next to her instead of rounding the desk and sitting in the office chair.

"Tell me," I order. And then, because I don't want to argue, I add, "Please."

"I didn't want to tell you because . . ." She pauses to pinch the bridge of her nose, and I take the time to practice my deep breathing so I don't get to my feet and start throwing things around in frustration and fear. "Oh god, I have no good reason. At the time, I thought I had it all planned out, but now that I'm thinking about how best to explain it to you, I realize that my plans are really, really stupid."

"Please tell me," I say quietly. The even tone in my voice is a fucking miracle.

"I've got two other notes."

"I'm sorry, but I thought I heard you say that you have received two other threatening notes and are just now telling me about them." I can hear myself yelling even as I try not to, but the terror of what she's saying is breaking down all my self-control.

"I know. I'm so sorry." Her words are muffled because she's placed her hands over her face. "I should have told you before, but I thought . . . I thought I could help you. Find something on Howe, and then we could put it all behind us."

"Tiny," I say, my voice hoarse with the shouts I'm trying to keep suppressed. "We are a team. I told you about the men who attacked me. You are my fucking world. If you are gone . . ." I trail off. Her body is convulsing from harsh silent sobs. In short order, I have her on my lap. "Stop. I'm not mad. I promise."

"I'm not crying to make you feel bad for me. I'm not manipulating you." She cries, her frame is shaking.

"I know, bunny. You're breaking my heart here." I run my hands over her arms and legs and head to reassure myself that she's whole and unhurt.

"It was wrong. I see that now. I should've told you, but I didn't because I knew I shouldn't have done it."

"All right," I try to soothe her. "What's done is done. Tell me so we can figure out what happened."

It takes several minutes before she's composed enough to recount the fucking foolhardy plan that she and Sarah had cooked up and the two notes she's received. "We need to get those to Jake."

She nods and hangs her head. No doubt Jake will be yelling at her too. I'll go with her in the morning because no one gets to yell at Tiny but me.

"The bodyguard is going to come tomorrow. Promise me you will use her. That you won't go anywhere without her. That you won't endanger your life. Promise me this."

"I promise," she vows solemnly. "I promise I will protect myself because I am your heart."

"Thank you." I close my eyes and clutch her to my chest. She finally gets it.

CHAPTER 20

Tiny refuses to go to sleep in the bedroom, so we make a nest of blankets and she falls asleep on the sofa in my office while I handle international calls and watch the Asian markets. Before the morning light filters in, I get a text from Jake that the new bodyguard will be arriving soon.

At precisely seven in the morning, there is an alert from the back door. Outside I see a woman with short dark hair wearing a lightweight parka, jeans, and soft-soled shoes. She matches the picture Jake sent. Quietly, so as not to disturb Tiny, I speak into the intercom. "Name, please."

"Marcia Stephenson" is the brisk reply. I watch her for a minute, but she doesn't flinch, merely stares unblinkingly at the camera with her feet set and her hands hanging loosely at her sides. I approve, but more importantly I think Tiny will like her.

"Up the stairs." The sound of the lock releasing prompts her to enter. We meet at the entrance.

"Nice to meet you, Marcia." She has a firm dry grip.

"Marcie, please. Marcia is too . . ."

"Brady Bunch?"

"Yes," she grimaces.

"Tiny's sleeping. What has Jake told you?" I gesture for her to sit down, but she doesn't. Instead she prowls around the edges of the room, tapping locks on the windows and eyeing the layout. If she were a different kind of woman, I'd be bristling against the intense perusal, but she looks no different than Steve did the first time he walked in.

"This is a basic personal protection duty. I'm to ferry one Victoria Corielli and then ensure the safety of her person against any threats." She looks at me and emphasizes the word *any*.

"Good. She's the most important person in my life." I dump coffee grounds into the machine and start the brewing cycle. "I've read your resume, but those are dry things. Why the bodyguard business?"

She stiffens at the word bodyguard, which tells me she is a true professional. Steve doesn't like the term either. In one of his rare communicative moments, he explained in a wounded voice that personal protection services involve security surveys, advanced planning, and logistical preparation.

"I'm not a bodyguard, sir," she says with restrained offense.

I hold up a hand to forestall further explanation. "I know. Sorry."

She doesn't relax an inch. "Ms. Corielli will be my first priority."

I pour myself a cup of coffee and offer her one as well. She hesitates and then relents enough to walk over to the kitchen. "Half a cup, please."

Pushing a mug to her, I pour until she says stop, and then I empty the rest in another mug for Tiny. "Have you met her?" I ask. They both work for Tanner, so it's probable that they have come across each other.

"In passing. She's doing dispatch at Jake's, so we've all come into contact with her at some point." Her voice is neutral, not giving anything away.

I refrain from questioning her about Tiny's work because I know she wouldn't like it.

"Let me get Tiny, then." I'm halfway up the stairs when I see Tiny coming out, dressed in work clothes. She gives a grateful look at the mug in my hand and swipes it from me. After gulping down a healthy swallow, she offers her face up. Heedless of Marcie's presence, I pull Tiny hard against me and give her a long, hungry kiss, tasting coffee and the mint of our toothpaste. The very fact that I have to hire Marcie makes me a little insane. I want to pull Tiny into the bedroom and lock her away there.

"Good morning," she murmurs, breaking away. There's a slight flush on her cheeks, which stirs my blood. Neither of us can be this close to one another and not be affected. I'd like to slide my hand into the front of her pants and between her legs to see how hot I've gotten her with just a good morning kiss.

"It's a good morning now," I say, contenting myself with simply squeezing her ass. "We've got another guest."

"Another one?" she cries and tries to push her way past me.

"Run toward the abandoned house where the killer awaits you, why don't you?" I complain in an undertone which she unfortunately hears.

"Are you suggesting I'm acting like the stupid girl in a horror movie who gets offed in the first five minutes?"

"Your response to the announcement that we have an intruder is to run downstairs and confront them." I follow behind her as she ignores me and marches into the kitchen.

"Marcie Stephenson, right? I'm Victoria Corielli." They shake hands as if they've never met before.

"I know. You're working dispatch and reception for Mr. Tanner." Marcie puts her mug on the counter. Apparently drinking coffee in front of the body you are to protect is verboten.

"I've heard your voice, but we haven't met." Tiny perches on a stool at the counter, and I call in our breakfast.

"I do a lot of field work," Marcie replies vaguely.

The two chat quietly with one another. Jake has done a good job of finding the right personality to mesh with Tiny's. When breakfast arrives, I eat my share and then kiss Tiny good-bye.

Jake calls first thing. "Steve gave me an update on your nocturnal visitor."

"Did he share that he nearly boned the poor girl on my dining room table?" The opening bell for the NYSE will ring in thirty minutes. There are dozens of emails that have populated in the few minutes that I haven't checked my phone between exiting the car at the front of the building and getting to the twelfth floor. They are all demanding to know if the rumors are true. *What rumors*, I wonder.

"He left that part out."

"I feel sorry for his girlfriend," I say, scrolling through several emails that ask essentially the same thing. There are three reporter requests as well.

"Do you?" Jake asks.

"No, it just seemed like the thing to say."

"Back to Howe, do you want me to put pressure on this girl?"

"Find out everything we can on her brother. I want to know his lawyer, who prosecuted his claim, who his parole officer is, who the supervisor of that officer is. I want to know what they eat, when they piss, and who they fuck. We'll find some pressure point somewhere."

"On it."

In the twenty-second email from the top, I see a headline in the subject line. "Billionaire's Father Accused of Embezzlement." My heart starts pounding as I double click on the email. I make it to the fourth line of the blog post from a major news outlet before I call Gabe.

> On a cold winter morning in December, Duncan Kerr was enjoying a privileged life as a top manager at Lionheart Partners Ltd. By the end of March he'd be dead. Doctors' reports identify the cause as a heart attack, but sources close to him hint at something more tragic. The cause of death is a mystery, but some point to whispers of embezzlement that plagued Kerr on his way out. Those rumors are now gaining velocity as the current CEO of Kerr Inc. is purportedly accused of engaging in the same self-dealing that may have brought his father down so many years ago.

"I want to meet with the editor," I bark out.

"They aren't going to name their source," Gabe says. I can tell by his clipped speech that he's read the article too.

"We already know the source. I want them to know we are suing them for libel. Whispers of embezzlement? They're defaming both my father and myself."

"It's a blog. We'll get them to take it down today under threat of a lawsuit." This time even Gabe's steady tones aren't soothing me. I slam my hand down hard on my desk.

"Are you fucking kidding? We aren't going to threaten them. We need to sue them. The damage is already done," I thunder.

"A defamation suit will take years," Gabe roars back. "If you want to do something now, then you need to take your fucking gloves off. Cecilia has to know she sleeps with a snake. It's her responsibility to remove herself from that situation. She's not your mother."

The blood is pounding in my ears, and my hand fucking hurts. I look down and see that I've broken the hinges on my laptop and the LCD screen is cracked and ugly. Idly, I lift my hand and see blood on my palm. For years I've tried to avoid collateral damage by not going after Howe as hard as I could. But now he was dragging up the ghosts of the past. He was affecting my future and placing Tiny—my heart—in danger. So yeah, the gloves were off. Everyone standing with Howe is going to either sink with his ship or jump off.

"Consider it done. Pull in Jake. Let's review all the information. I've got their debts. I want to start placing pressure at every point. Call in the mortgage, repossess their boat. I want their credit denied all over the city. Let's topple this motherfucker once and for all." I slam down my phone and throw open my office door.

Outside is Frank, his assistant Lucy, and two racks of clothes. Shit.

"Rose," I bark. "I need a bandage." I hold up my hand for her to see and she jumps up, scurrying out of the office. Turning back to Frank, I ask, "What the hell are you doing here with all that shit?"

Frank ignores my question but instead just wheels in his two racks of dresses. Inside the office, he turns, places his hands on his hips and says, "We have an appointment."

"I don't care," I shake my head. "I don't have time for this. Get out. Please," I add to soften the blow.

Rose rushes in with a washcloth, tape, and a big bandage. I let her fix me up with one hand while I use the other to scroll through my messages. More are coming in by the minute. I halt at one and reply back to the interview request.

Yes. Will talk. Call office for appt.

I copy Gabe on the email and press send. Frank is still standing there.

"What?" I ask sharply. "I told you I don't have time."

He puts up his palm to me. "The Frick Ball is this weekend. You've put me off for two weeks now. You either see me now or Tiny goes to her first public event looking like a castaway. Is that really the image you want to be portraying right now?"

"Who's this?" I jerk my head toward his male companion who can't be more than twentysomething.

"He's my assistant." Frank frowns.

"He can't go in."

"What do you mean?"

"You're it, and I tell you it takes a superhuman effort to be OK with that."

"He's gay. Gayer than the rainbow. He probably farts glitter, don't you, Phillip?"

Phillip looks wide-eyed and nods in agreement.

"No." I'm implacable.

"I can't work under these conditions." Frank turns and rattles the metal clothes rack.

"Then I guess we'll be hiring a new stylist."

"Oh for God's sake, Ian. She's got the same bits as anyone else."

"Her bits belong to me, and no other man than you and me is ever going to be looking at them without clothes on."

"Fine. Fine." He waves Phillip into a chair and hauls the racks and other shit into the office.

I shut the door when the phone rings again. It's one of my board members, Paul Tazo. Paul has been on the board since Kerr Inc. started. I owe that man a lot, and if there's anyone I respect and look up to, it's him. He owned a small brokerage business in New Jersey and took a chance on me when I was hustling small time illegal shit. Now he's rolling in cash, in large part because of my success, but I still listen when he talks.

"Kerr, my boy." His voice is subdued. "We're going to have to call an emergency meeting. I have no doubt you have an answer for what is happening, but the others are anxious."

Jake, who has been recently appointed, and Kaga sit on the board. With me, that's three votes. There are nine board members. I'll need to swing two to my side. I'd like to think that one vote will be Paul's, but I'm not going to count on it.

"Of course. Thank you for calling. Get with Rose and we'll schedule something this week."

"I knew you would respond this way. I told the others you would, but they were concerned you would try to delay it."

"There's no need to delay," I lie. A delay would be great. I'm bleeding money now. First to buy up shares of Kerr Inc. Then exerting the financial pressure to make sure that the Howes are denied credit. And now I'm going to have to buy out at least two—if not more—board members in order to salvage my own company.

But first things first. I need to call Tiny to tell her that she needs to shuttle her ass downtown to try on dresses. I'm sure she'll love that.

CHAPTER 21

"You want me to *what*?" Tiny's outraged voice carries well beyond the screen that Frank has set up at the far end of my office in front of the ornate fireplace and two midcentury modern lounge chairs.

"It's nothing I've never seen before," Frank says with bored impatience. "Strip so we can get on with it."

"You may have seen lots of bodies before but not mine." Despite the screen blocking my view, I can visualize her crossed arms and mulish expression.

"We aren't Victorians. It's okay to show your lady parts."

"I've never met a gay man so anxious to get a chick out of her clothes before."

Marcie sits thumbing through her emails on the sofa while I alert Rose to the impending board meeting, but my interest is being drawn away by the activities behind the curtain.

"What is this?" Tiny asks.

"Underwear."

"Doesn't look like it."

My curiosity is piqued. I'm watching the trade price for Kerr Inc. and listening to the conversation at the same time. The share price is fluctuating wildly. Every time I buy a block it shoots up, but then it drops again on the heels of some whispered report. It's like playing whack-a-mole, and it requires every bit of my attention. Yet . . .

"Seriously. This isn't underwear."

"Are you the fashion consultant now? I thought you were a bike messenger."

"Emphasis on *were*," she replies, and I wince. She's still bitter about that.

I get up to wander back behind the screen and stop short. Tiny is wearing a diaphanous undershirt and a pair of pants that stop just below her knees. The fabric is sheer and matches her skin color almost exactly. Board members, accusations of embezzlement, an imperiled business, all of it recedes under the flood of red-hot heat.

Tiny's young, athletic body needs no shaping garments or corsets. Her waist naturally curves in, and her plum-shaped breasts sit high on her chest without support. I stare in appreciation at how her beautiful body is framed in the sheer silk.

The filmy cloth clings to the points of her breasts, her nipples pebbling under my gaze. The rise and fall of the fabric becomes more rapid with every breath. Slowly my gaze drifts downward. Her navel and flat stomach are shrouded by the gauze, but it clings to her hips and the soft curls between her legs. Is it my imagination or is she getting wet? Is the sheer fabric darkening from her arousal? I want to fall to my knees and bury my face in her pussy.

Embarrassed by her response to me, she lifts her arms to cover her breasts

"Get out," I order.

There's no movement. I repeat myself, louder and with more force. "Out. Now." The sheer violence in my voice sends Frank and his assistant scurrying out of the room. The door closes.

"You as well, Marcie."

She sighs but leaves. And then we're alone.

"What is this?" I ask in wonderment. Circling Tiny, I note how the shadow between her buttocks seems all the more enticing, like a forbidden valley, under the fabric.

"Frank says it's underwear." She holds out her arms, which lifts the soft swells of her breasts.

"We're buying a dozen sets." I drop into one of the chairs. I need this. I need *her* to remind me of all the good that I have in my life. I'm not the twelve-year-old whose beloved father has died or the bitter fifteen-year-old whose mother committed suicide. I am a man loved by this amazing woman. "You need to come over here right now."

When she nears, her expression changes to tender understanding. She senses my hunger. "I'm here, Ian. I will always be here, no matter what."

Emotion tightens my throat. "Show me," I say hoarsely.

"There's a slit here," she says, knowing what I require. Pulling aside the material between her legs, she displays the clever, hidden design.

If my head could have exploded, it might have. I pull her to me, enjoying the feel of the wispy fabric against my hand. The barely-there undergarments are intended to inflame the flesh, rather than support or cover. Knowing that Frank and his assistant have seen her like this makes me want to mark her. If she walks into the Frick wearing this under her dress, there is simply no way that I will be able to resist taking her into a corridor and feasting on her.

My cock is so hard I fear it will break. "Look at me," I command. I stretch the wool of my suit pants taut across my erection. "See how hard you've made me? I can't wait."

"I'll take care of it," she says, bending low.

"No," I stop her. "I need you. Put your feet right here." I pat the slim wooden slats.

"I'll break that chair."

"If you don't climb up here, something else is going to break."

She doesn't resist when I lift one foot on an armrest. The movement causes the fabric to separate and bares her cunt to my gaze and touch.

I roll a nipple between my fingers, the stiff bud getting harder with my attention. She stifles a moan and pushes her breasts closer to my face.

My ability to think shuts down, and I fumble with the clothes, nearly tearing the delicate fabric in my haste to get inside her. I find the opening between her legs and slide my thick, long arousal inside her sweetness.

Eyes closed, I savor the sensation of her walls closing around me. Gripping her waist in my firm hands, I lower her until I'm fully seated. The position is awkward for her, and she must rely on me to hold her tight.

She's loud, and I revel in it. Everyone outside the office can hear, and it makes my blood pound even harder. I want to come all over her body. I'd rub it into every pore until she sweated me. Until everyone knew that she was mine.

I want to be soaked into her essence until she can't breathe without knowing that I possess her.

CHAPTER 22

As I hold her and she comes down off her orgasmic high, I tell Tiny my plans. About Richard. About the company. About the impending board meeting.

"The company can just vote you out? It's your company." Tiny is outraged.

"It's publicly held, which means I answer to the shareholders. Everything I do must be measured in terms of the fiduciary duty I owe those who own stock in Kerr Inc.—from the janitors who invest their retirement funds in my company to the traders who buy and sell the stock for a living. Things are going to change. I'm done playing around with Howe."

"Because of the article this morning about your father?"

Jake must have told her.

"Yes, and I want to protect you. Which means we need to do a couple of things. Are you with me?"

"Always."

"For the next week or so, I'd like you take a leave of absence from Jake's."

She protests but ultimately agrees for my own piece of mind. Her dislike of the job may also have played a role in her decision-making process.

I clean us both up and let Frank back in. No one says a word about the interruption, although I'm sure that's more for Tiny's sake than it is mine.

The board meeting gets scheduled for this Friday, the day before the Frick Ball. It's perfect timing, in my opinion. By the end of the weekend, this should all be put to rest.

I spend the next few days contacting major stockholders and offering to buy their shares at a price higher than Louis is offering. His pockets are finite, and given that it's Howe behind him, they simply don't have the money to jeopardize me. The stockholders are easy to maneuver. The real danger will be if I can't swing at least two of the board members my way.

♦ ♦ ♦

On Friday morning, Tiny selects my most severe suit.

"I think today calls for a vest," she says, pulling out a black wool three-piece suit. I allow her to dress me, my mind running over the course of events that will follow. A red power tie and my father's mother-of-pearl cufflinks complete the ensemble.

"You look very powerful," she says, brushing imaginary lint off my shoulders.

"You did call me *God* repeatedly last night. That goes to a man's head." I wink.

"As if your head isn't big enough."

"Stop with all the compliments."

When we get downstairs, I see the car pull up. Steve is ready to take me to my office.

"Are you okay with the direction we're going?"

"Yes," she says impatiently. "It's your business, Ian."

"It has my name on it, but everything I do affects you now, so it's our business."

Her face softens. She's finally getting it, I think. How much she means to me. How I'll do anything she asks. How all of my decisions start and end with whether they will make her happy.

"Ian, I love you. I'm going to love you if you're the head of a huge corporation or a guy who wears board shorts and eats street tacos every night."

"I like those street tacos. I think anyone with functioning taste buds does, but I draw the line at board shorts."

She reaches up to place a soft kiss on my jaw and hug me; the warmth of her love settles into my bones.

"No matter what happens today or tomorrow, I've already won." I tighten my arms around her briefly and then release her.

"After today, I might not be able to afford you, Steve," I say as I climb into the car.

"You'll work it out," he says.

"You're so confident?"

"You're not?"

An image of Tiny leaning against the doorframe dressed only in one of my T-shirts flickers to mind. "I'm not fully invested in either outcome. Tiny and I will be happy regardless, so yes, I guess I am confident."

Kaga, Jake, and Gabe are waiting for me at my office on the day of the vote.

"You going to tell us the plan or make us go in blind?" Jake asks.

"It hinges on Paul and one more board member," I tell him. "If Paul doesn't vote with me, then it becomes problematic."

"You mean us. Vote with us," Kaga corrects.

I look at him blankly.

Kaga sighs. "You're not an island, Kerr. We're here to back you with our bank accounts, if necessary."

I glance at Jake and Gabe, who nod their heads in agreement. The three of them could easily bail Kerr Inc. out of the deep end. Jake and Kaga have family money. Gabe is one of the wealthiest lawyers in the city. The bone-deep heat in my chest generated by Tiny's love spreads a little farther. I told her that I was fully prepared for the meeting this morning, but clearly I had lied.

The strong support of these men is shaking me. It's one thing to offer verbal support, to play poker, or drink whiskey together. It's entirely another thing to offer up one's money.

This morning I was prepared for a number of things, but this wasn't one of them. "I'm honored, but you can put your checkbooks away. I've got it covered."

I share the details of the plan with them.

"When it comes down to it, you're the CEO of Kerr Inc. You get to make the call whether to wind down or keep going," Kaga states emphatically.

"I can take the company in whatever direction I want, but lawsuits could tie my hands for years while the value of the company drains away. This is the best course of action."

Nothing more is said as the other members of the board arrive. Once everyone is assembled, I address the board.

"Thank you for coming today," I begin.

Paul interrupts. "Thank you for agreeing to this. We know you could have stalled or held out for some time. This is a show of good faith on your part."

His words are said more for the benefit of the rest of the members than for me. I take a glance around the table. Will Blake will vote with Paul. Tiffany Rosien sits next to him. I invited her to join us two years ago, and she's now serving her third and last year. At the age of forty she was the CEO of a top tech firm. Now she's primarily an angel investor. She's sharp and ambitious and wouldn't want to tie herself to a ship she thinks is too damaged.

Donald Harris is an attorney with Scheff, Market, and Rutherford. He's always been adverse to risk. Dumping me is the safest route in his mind. Jeffrey Olsen is a partner in United Insurers. Insurance companies have tighter fists than Scrooge. Susan Murphy is the Vice President of Operations at Venture Entertainment. This group of three has always voted as a block. Tiffany and Paul are wildcards, but Tiffany tends to vote with Susan.

"I understand that you're all concerned about the recent rumors that I might be winding down Kerr Inc. or that there has been some inappropriate siphoning of funds away from the corporation. Another person might remind you that I've increased your financial portfolio consistently every year since the very first; that some of you would not be where you are today if not for me. But I'm not interested in looking back, but forward."

"Forward? Is that what winding down is?" scoffs Donald. "Cashing out positions and closing your doors is a backward act. An act of someone who's guilty and trying to cover his tracks."

Beside him Jeff nods slowly.

"I'm not interested in winding down the business, but I do believe that Kerr Inc. can be profitable without being as large as it is. Reducing positions isn't a sign of weakness, but of ensuring we are nimble enough to jump on great opportunities in this fast-changing environment," I explain.

"It's been an honor serving on the board, but as a board member it is my job to ensure that Kerr Inc.'s interests are placed above everyone else's," Tiffany interjects.

There is more bullshit discussion about putting the needs of the stockholders first, but the self-interest in here reeks. Everyone is concerned with their own skin.

I sit back and let them talk.

It's clear that the plan concocted by Donald, Jeff, and Susan is to force a vote that would require me to buy out their shares, or, if I can't, to hand over my shares to them to be placed in escrow to avoid further devaluation of Kerr Inc. stock. Or they could start a stockholder lawsuit, which we all know would place the company in tumult.

"I want you to feel like you've been treated fairly. For those of you who are unhappy with the way I am handling the company, I propose to buy all your shares in Kerr Inc. at the market price. In exchange, you will resign immediately from the board and waive all responsibility for board actions. This offer is open to everyone seated here." My gaze sweeps the room.

Donald blusters that he doesn't want my money, just security for the company. Jeff and Susan nod their heads. Tiffany looks to Susan for direction and nods late. Paul remains silent.

Kaga, clearly annoyed by all of this, calls for a vote. "Someone needs to make the motion."

"I move Ian Kerr will personally agree to buy out the shares of any board member in exchange for the member's immediate resignation." Jake's voice booms out. Gabe is my attorney and is not a part of the board, as it would be a conflict. He says nothing. Tiffany's eyes narrow, but my attention is on Paul. As I told Tiny this morning, the outcome is already assured, regardless of the vote.

"Seconded," Kaga says.

"Discussion?" I ask.

There is none.

"Everyone in favor say 'aye.'"

Everyone in the room, including Paul, says aye. His eyes twinkle a little bit as he loudly affirms his support for me. I nod my head in gratitude. Paul's support of me means more than he even knows.

"Motion carries. Who wants to be bought out?"

Donald jumps to his feet. Susan and Jeff quickly follow.

"Motion for Ian Kerr to purchase the shares of Harris, Olsen, and Murphy and accept their immediate resignation."

"Seconded."

"The motion carries." Kaga slams his hand on the table.

Gabe pulls out the papers I had him prepare before the meeting. "Pursuant to Article 35, subpart A, we are valuing the shares per the price at the open of today's market. Here are your checks. Please sign at the flagged pages. Copies will be sent to you via courier later today."

Donald's mouth drops open. "How can you? I had no idea you had this money! Where did you get it? If you've been hiding income, we'll prosecute you to the fullest extent of the law!"

"Why would you vote for this if you thought I didn't have the funds? Did you believe you were just going to take my portion of the company in exchange?" I shake my head. "Given that you are no longer part of the company, nor do you have shares, you don't have the right to sue me. Besides, if you thought that I had all my money tied into Kerr Inc., you're too great a fool to be on the board anyway."

Since the meeting is adjourned, I leave Gabe to clean up the details. No need for me to watch him bury them.

"They're walking away with a lot of money," Kaga observes as we exit the room.

"Not as much as they could have. Kerr Inc. stock will rebound, and I'll get it back eventually. One by one." It will give me something exciting to do in the office as Tiny learns how to be an investigator for Jake.

CHAPTER 23

"The walk-up?" I look at Tiny blankly.

Her grin falters and then slides off her face. "Yeah, I mean, I thought maybe I'd sublet it or something, but now we can live there. Do you plan to rent this out or just sell it outright? The money should keep us afloat for a few years, right? And what about the Central Park apartment? Shoot, some people can retire on the proceeds from a place like that. Not to mention that we definitely do not need a place in Long Island."

"Bunny." I shake my head, but under my skin, my heart is expanding beyond its container of tissue and muscle and bone. She truly doesn't care about all the things my money can buy her. "When I said that I was sunk, I meant that I might not be able to retain control of Kerr Inc., not that we'd have to move into a fifth-floor walk-up. We've got plenty of money. I'm not even going to make you fly commercial when we go on our honeymoon."

"Do you own your own jet?" Tiny frowns. "Because that's just wasteful."

I pull her onto my lap. "No, only sheiks own their own jets. I'm a lowly peon with a NetJet share."

"NetJet?"

The delicate curve of her neck calls to me, and I bury my nose there, inhaling her sweet scent. My palms rest against the plump swells of her ass cheeks. I can't resist squeezing them and pulling her closer to my aching groin. When I don't answer, she pokes me in the shoulder. I groan but relent. Lifting my head from its nest, I smile down at her. "It's a timeshare for a jet. You buy shares that guarantee you access to the type of jet you need within four hours. It's fairly genius. I wish I had bought it, but right now I think the market is too unstable to launch a competitor."

"I could call up today and say I want to go to Pennsylvania and the plane will be ready in four hours?" she asks in wonderment.

"Try Paris, bunny. We can be in the air by midnight. Just say the word."

"The life you lead." She shakes her head.

"It's our life." I'm quiet but emphatic.

"If it weren't for our shindig tomorrow, I'd be tempted to say yes," she admits.

"Next weekend then," I promise, and I'm not joking. Next weekend, we'll take a private jet to Paris.

She allows me to carry her into the bedroom then, and we take each other to a destination far more pleasurable than those that exist on earth.

◆ ◆ ◆

Midmorning Saturday, Frank and his team of stylists arrive to prepare Tiny for the Frick Ball. Her attire is a mystery, and as part of our punishment for failing to agree on anything he brought to my office last week, he doesn't allow us to see it.

"You'll just have to trust me," he declares.

Tiny raises her eyebrows but gives herself into his care. I barricade myself in my office to make sure all of the details are taken care of for tonight. Tiny and I went over them this morning, but one more check can't hurt.

Around noon, she sneaks into my office with a tray. Her hair is up in curlers, and she's wearing a dressing gown and not much else.

"Tell me you're not wearing Frank's infamous underwear."

"I'm not wearing that fancy underwear."

"Is that a lie? No, don't answer," I laugh. "I'm sure that Frank would gut me if I came over and messed you up."

"He would. I had to promise him I would stay at least six inches away from you."

"I'm wounded." I place a hand on my chest. "You'd have to stand farther away than that to avoid contact with me."

She smirks. "What Frank doesn't know won't hurt him."

She places the tray on my desk and slides into my lap. "Whatever you do, don't touch my hair."

"Yes, ma'am," I reply, slipping my hand under her dressing gown. She's wearing a pair of old boxers and a tank top. Easy access clothing, and I take all the advantage the loose-fitting garments afford me.

"Six inches!" Frank screeches as he slams open the door. "I knew I couldn't leave you two alone for one second."

My hand stills against her as Tiny freezes up.

"Don't ever come barging into any room in my house again," I say. The violence in my voice must be evident because Frank's eyes flare. He opens his mouth to say something, but then his instincts kick in. He realizes he is a hairsbreadth away from me leaping over my desk and pounding him. Without another word, he turns and stomps out of the room.

"Well, that was embarrassing," Tiny mutters against my neck.

"Now we know," I say.

"What?"

"That you aren't into being watched."

"Too awkward," she admits.

"Maybe it wasn't anonymous enough," I suggest. "We'll test it out."

"We will?" She arches a brow.

"Why not?"

◆ ◆ ◆

"I'm impressed."

"I'm terrified," Tiny says, holding her hands out from her sides as if she is afraid to touch her dress. Over her right wrist is a heavy gold, red, and black bangle. The diamond engagement ring winks at me. The sight of it on her finger will never fail to thrill me. It's a visible mark of my possession, and I can't wait until I wear her ring so that I can declare to all the world that I belong to Victoria Kerr.

"It's a vintage Charles James," Frank says proudly, gesturing toward Tiny with his arms outstretched and both hands pointing toward the gown.

"I have no idea who that is, Frank," I admit. Tiny gives me a grateful look. She doesn't know either.

Frank huffs. "Charles James invented the sports bra, as well as the wrap dress cut on the bias—otherwise known as the taxi dress."

"Taxi dress?" Tiny echoes.

"Yes. It was so simple you could slip it on and off in the backseat of a taxi."

I give a wordless shrug in answer to Tiny's raised eyebrow. My knowledge of fashion history is shallower than a rain puddle.

"He was the subject of the Met Ball this year!"

At our blank stares, he throws up his hands and calls us uneducated cretins.

"That's why we pay you, Frank. To make us look good."

"No doubt. This is an amazing dress. I don't even look like myself," Tiny exclaims.

Our praise soothes his wounded feelings, and he perks up. "You do look amazing, Victoria. Simply amazing."

Her lovely brown hair is parted in the middle but drapes lightly around the sides of her head before it is swept back in a sleek curve over her skull. The long strands are caught up in an intricate mass of curls that sit right at the nape of her neck.

The ball gown is tri-colored. The top portion is a severe black and sleeveless, with a neckline that cuts directly across her collarbone. The full coverage back dips into a vee right above the top of her ass. Around her waist, claret-red silk is draped and tucked and folded into a complicated structure that stands slightly proud of her hips. The side is drawn up as if it's a curtain you're peeking underneath. The underskirt is made of a straw-colored, tissue-thin silk folded into what seems like a thousand different pleats. Even though nearly every inch of Tiny is covered, the effect is shockingly erotic because it looks like she's in a state of undress. Or perhaps like an exotic flower unfurling her petals.

Blood pulses through me, dark and hot.

"Stop right there," Frank orders. "No touching, or she turns into a pumpkin."

"Her jewelry is wrong," I murmur. From my inside tux pocket I pull out a soft velvet bag. "Hand up, bunny."

She holds out her palm with a questioning look. Frank falls silent and then gasps as the jewels fall into her hand.

Chandelier earrings made of rubies and diamonds are paired with a diamond and ruby bracelet. The bracelet is a three-inch-wide flexible cuff with alternating circular and oval-cut rubies interspersed between baguette-cut diamonds. Cars are less expensive than this bracelet, but when Frank told me that I should buy her a bracelet to compliment a red dress, I knew I had to have it.

It's a warrior's cuff to be worn by a woman with strength and power. I affix it to her wrist and then lift her ringed hand to my mouth. "You look good in diamonds."

"I'm doubly terrified now," she says shakily.

"Don't be." I bend over and kiss her bared shoulder, reveling in her hiss as she swiftly draws a breath. "It has no value beyond that it looks good on you."

Frank sighs. "I want one of you, Ian. Find me someone right now."

Without removing my lips from Tiny's shoulder, I respond, "I'm not a matchmaker, but if I find a wealthy guy tonight who looks unhappy I'll be sure to slip him your phone number."

"That's all I can ask for, I guess," he says grumpily.

◆ ◆ ◆

In the car, Tiny asks quietly, "What's this really for?" as she fingers the jeweled cuff.

"Tonight we go into battle. It's just a weapon to show that you belong there as much as anyone. You may think of yourself as a dyslexic former bike courier, but I know you have the heart of a warrior. A warrior who will fight to the very end for the people she loves. Who will do anything—even go from a mansion to a fifth-floor walk-up to be with the man she loves. A woman who means more than anything in the world to me. A woman beyond price."

CHAPTER 24

The theme for tonight's ball is Scheherazade, and the entrance is a red carpet covered by a canopy of gold leaves. Inside we find women wearing filmy gowns which seem to draw inspiration from the cartoon version of *Aladdin* rather than the original tale of *One Thousand and One Nights*.

Tiny, in her structured ball gown, stands out, and there are several envious glances tossed her way. In a social setting, you want to be remembered. She is dressed as if she's risen to her place on the throne next to the sultan.

And as we walk forward and down the steps into the large atrium lined with columns, I can see her spine straighten and her shoulders go back. Her apprehension at tonight's event seems to flow down her silk-lined back to fall on the floor, forgotten.

"Game on," she breathes when we clear the entrance. The Howes are out in full force, standing on the far side of the long, oval reflecting pool that divides the indoor garden. Flowers are perfuming the air, and the tinkle of the central fountain can be heard over the lilting strings of the quartet in the corner. Father, mother, son, and daughter-in-law are talking and smiling as if a thunderstorm isn't about to break over their heads.

Around us there is a bubble of space. It could be Tiny, but I'm more certain it's me. Poverty and failure are a disease to these people, and right now—given all that's gone on in recent weeks—I'm a primary carrier for a dangerous disease. If I was the bitter, vengeful person Tiny met many months ago, I'd be marking down every snub and cut in a mental ledger, so I could punish these slights when my fortunes recovered.

But pursuing revenge doesn't interest me anymore. After tonight, I want to take a ride out to our estate in Long Island and shut the gates and the world out. I want to lay Tiny out on the big lawn and make love to her under the moon and stars until she's full of my seed and replete from my attentions. I want to fill my life with the laughter of our children rather than hate for my enemies. I've spent the better part of my life alone with only revenge on my mind.

I'd never go back to that state willingly.

"You have a fierce expression on your face," Tiny murmurs, brushing the backs of her fingers against my cheek. I catch her hand before she breaks contact and kiss her long, elegant fingers.

At the base, there is a line of hard callouses built up from years of holding on to her handlebars. They remind me of how strong and devoted she is. How lucky I am to have her as my own.

"I love you," I say.

She sucks in a breath and gives me a brilliant smile in return.

"I don't know what brought that on, but I can't say I'll ever tire of hearing it."

"I'm just thinking about what a lucky bastard I am that you're with me."

With a shake of her head, she disagrees. "It's me who's the lucky one. Look at all you've given me."

She waves a hand over her dress, the cuff bracelet glinting in the lights.

"Is that all I've given to you?" I'm taken a little aback that she measures our relationship in objects.

"No," she says impatiently. "But all the love I have for you doesn't manifest itself in things. It just is. Like an intangible."

"You're wrong. Your love is as real as the bracelet I gave you and longer lasting and more valuable. Don't get caught up in all of this. It's meaningless in the end. Look around us. Is there anyone but you willing to talk to me? Do you think, this week, that half the women here wouldn't have left me for greener pastures and half the men wouldn't have refused to take my calls? Don't diminish your feelings for me. Or mine for you."

She flushes and then steps closer to me until there's virtually no space between us. The front of her red skirt crumples on contact with the black wool of my tux, but she pays it no attention.

"I'm sorry. You're right. Sometimes it is easy to get so intimidated by everything you have that I lose sight of what you didn't have. We've found life in one another. You've given me so much that I feel almost too fortunate. Like life can't be that good to one person. Life has taken a lot from us. Let's hold on to what we have."

"Yes." I want to kiss her until there's not a speck of lipstick left on her face. But crushing her gown is all that I'll allow myself.

Finally remembering we are standing in a crowded party, Tiny steps back and tries to smooth out the wrinkles.

"I can't figure out if it's me or you they dislike more," she jokes.

I pluck two glasses of champagne off the tray of a waiter passing by.

"It's me. They don't dislike you. They're afraid that my misfortune is contagious."

Even when I first came back into the city, hungry and poor, doors weren't ever really closed to me, I thought. They were ajar, and I kicked them open the rest of the way. But for my mother? The cold shoulders and the unwelcome whispers from previous friends and acquaintances would have burned her deeply. No wonder she tried everything to get back the sense of belonging she had lost. No wonder she gave up when nothing worked. The last of my resentment toward her melts away.

"How's the tutor hunt going?" I ask. We need to kill some time before the awards part of the ball, and I want to think about something less maudlin than my mother's untimely death.

She grimaces and takes a sip of her champagne. "Not well. Most of them come off as more oriented to kids. I don't feel like I fit well with any of them."

"We'll find someone. Let's cast our net wider."

"What do you mean?"

"Look outside the city."

"I don't want to move." She looks alarmed. "And I'm not driving. I don't feel comfortable with that yet."

Downing my champagne, I cover a smile. She's with me but not fully adjusted yet.

"No, they'll come to us."

"Oh," she says. And then, "*Ohhh*, because you'll pay them."

"Yes."

I don't think she realizes that money means not just fancy dresses but actual meaningful differences in our lives. I couldn't save her mother. Sickness is the great equalizer, but for now I'll use everything I have to make her path easier.

After the last of the champagne washes down my throat, I signal a waiter for something stronger. When the waiter appears Tiny gasps in surprise.

It's Lauren, our midnight visitor. Her eyes are steely. "You're having me followed."

"Just a precaution," I say. "For your safety as much as for my benefit."

"Stop it. Just stop interfering. You're going to get someone hurt."

"Ian can help you," Tiny urges. "Let us take care of you."

"Unless you're going to buy off a city cop and a probation officer, you don't have anything on the menu worth my time. Why do you think I'm here? Because Howe wanted to keep an eye on me. Howe commands, and I respond." Lauren gives us a polite smile. "Does the lady want anything to drink?"

"Yeah, I'll have what he's having." Tiny sighs, her frustration evident in every taut line of her frame.

Lauren gives a short bow and spins away. I glance over to the Howes where, sure enough, Richard is watching the interaction like a hawk. He moves to the side, likely attempting to follow her, but someone interrupts him.

"Is that Steve's little morsel?" Kaga's come up behind us.

I nod but raise an eyebrow because these types of events north of, say, Fiftieth Street, hold no interest for him. "Who let you in?"

"Gate crashed," he responds and swirls some amber liquid in his glass. "This stuff is swill. Peasants shouldn't even be forced to drink it."

"I wouldn't know," I say wryly. "I haven't gotten my order yet since you decided to appropriate it before I could have a drink."

"It's better that way." He sniffs. "I don't want your taste buds corrupted. I've spent years training you to know how decent Scotch tastes. By the way, do you have the plague? Why is no one talking to you?"

"Poverty is contagious."

And so is success. Despite his preference for his clubs, Kaga's cachet with this circle means that his standing and talking to me is effective enough to break the ice. Men and women wanting a little piece of Kaga's empire drift closer until the invisible line separating Tiny and me from the rest of the crowd is crossed and then rubbed away by the traffic. I draw her close as Kaga and I take turns introducing her.

Society is run by a herd mentality. If the herd fears you, it stays away. If the herd believes you have food and water and shelter, it tramples its own to get to you.

"That's a Charles James, right?" One young lady dressed in a pastel green gown made up of layered sheer panels asks with envy in her voice.

Tiny nods. "That's what I was told. I'm not very knowledgeable."

"Me either, but I went to the Met Gala celebrating him, so I feel like I can recognize his work for at least the next month. Michelle Everly. I'm the Executive Director for the Women's League for the Advancement of Literary Achievement. Big title, but essentially I'm a literacy advocate."

Tiny perks up and grabs her hand. "Victoria Corielli. I'm a dispatcher for Jake Tanner's security company." Her tone is challenging, as if daring Michelle to be put off by the fact that she's just a dispatcher, but Michelle responds with ease.

"Oh, I know Jake. Actually, I know his sister Sabrina. My younger sister goes to Columbia with her."

Tiny nods and some of her tension eases away. "Jake's dreading her graduation. He complains about it at least once a day."

Michelle rolls her eyes. "Those two are troublemakers. I'll have to tell Jake that their graduating and separating is the best thing that could happen for all of us. Together they're minihurricanes. Apart, they're just minor tropical storms. Can I just say your ring is gorgeous? May I?"

Tiny raises her hand, and Michelle *oohs* and *ahhs* over it, making me feel good in the process. Their conversation turns to Michelle's work, and I can tell by Tiny's questions she's intrigued.

Kaga raises his eyebrows and then hands me a glass of Kaga-approved Scotch. "Nice," I compliment after taking a heavy sip.

He grimaces. "It's acceptable but not by much. Do you realize that this place is devoid of almost any East Asian art?"

"It's too bad that they don't have a donor who could change that," I say wryly.

He's only listening to me with half an ear. Most of his attention is directed at listening to Michelle and Tiny talk about Jake's little sister. When Kaga finally deigns to answer me, we're interrupted by Ross Fairchild.

"Mr. Kerr, I didn't realize you'd arrived. I'm so sorry I wasn't here to greet you. Last-minute details." He shakes my hand vigorously. "No hard feelings?"

Kaga raises an inquiring eyebrow.

"In order to avoid any problems tonight, I donated the full amount in cash, rather than stock options or a gift made over a several year period as we'd originally discussed," I explain.

Fairchild wilts under Kaga's stern disapproval. "He should have trusted you."

"He was doing his job." I receive a weak smile from Fairchild.

Hoping to change the subject, he turns to Tiny. "Perhaps I can take your delightful companion for a tour."

"It's me who's unfamiliar with your establishment," I correct.

"That's right." Tiny gives a small, sad smile. "My mother and I came here frequently. We weren't always able to pay, so we really appreciated the pay-as-you-can policy."

Fairchild beams. "That was the entire purpose of Henry Clay Frick's donation. He bequeathed not only this residence but the entire collection of art he and his wife curated. They bought all the art with the intention of donating it. Did you know there is another Frick museum in Pittsburgh?"

"No," she responds with interest.

"Yes, you must go. In fact, call me and let me know when you're going to be there, and I'll arrange for my colleague to give you and Mr. Kerr a private tour. Tell me, what is your favorite collection? Is it the Fragonard room? Everyone loves that."

"That was my mom's favorite," I hear Tiny say as they walk away.

"Good call on the museum thing," Kaga says. "It makes sense now. You've never been a big patron of the arts, so the fact that you were donating five million to this racket made me doubt your sanity."

"I suppose I should be grateful you waited until after my fortune was safe before voicing public concerns about my mental health."

"I'm generous that way." He slaps me on the back. "So Michelle, is it? You're part of the Everly family?"

She nods, somewhat dazzled by his sudden attention. "Y-y-yes."

"And did you go to Columbia like your sister?"

"No, Wharton."

"Good school," Kaga guesses. He doesn't know one US institution from another, unless it's Harvard or Yale. Nor does he care. "Your sister and her, ah, friend? Roommate? Are they enjoying their last year at college?"

"This fall will be their last year. They're friends and roommates."

"I can't remember my college days," he says as if he's confessing some intimate piece of knowledge. Michelle leans toward him. "Tell me your sister and her friend's most outrageous exploits. It'll remind me not to be such a stick in the mud."

"You could never be boring," she says breathily. And for the next twenty minutes, Kaga expertly interrogates Michelle on all the details she knows about Sabrina, as I watch Lauren.

She's bait tonight, even if she doesn't realize it. Both Richard and I are tracking her, and I can tell by the rigid way she holds herself that the attention is making her uncomfortable. Play with the wolves, prepare to be eaten or to bite back. She doesn't have it in her to bite back. Not like my Tiny.

As she ducks out with an empty tray, Richard makes his move.

"Excuse me," I murmur to Kaga and Michelle, uncaring whether or not they hear me or if they were even talking to me.

The layout of the ball has the caterers set up in the rear antechamber, just off the left arm of the museum. There are several alcoves where Howe can corner Lauren.

I walk quickly and with purpose, and no one stops me.

A quick survey of the gallery reveals that neither Lauren nor Howe is present. But a flash of black to the left catches my eyes. I exit left and then head down a short hall. Gotcha. Howe is holding Lauren's arm in a tight grip. Her tray is rattling against her leg as he shakes her arm.

"Didn't like your tuna tartare? I hardly think that complaining to the staff is going to help your indigestion." I lean against the wall and cross my arms. Act I of the play has just begun. This part calls for nonchalance and boredom, even though I'd like to leap forward and crush his skull between my hands.

"Kerr," he huffs and lets go, all his social training kicking in. No scandals in public. Lauren takes the opportunity to slip away.

"Have your fortunes fallen so far that you're now begging the wait staff to warm your cold bed?"

"Just following your example," Howe sneers. "I hear those girls give stellar blow jobs. They're so eager to take a step up the ladder. How's Tiny's mouth? Tighter than a vacuum?"

I nearly bite my tongue in half to prevent myself from launching at him. "Every time you say her name, the cost of your redemption goes up. I don't think you'll be able to buy your way out of this one. In fact, I'd think twice about trying to buy anything in the near future. And by near, I'm thinking five, maybe ten years. How's bankruptcy look in the polls these days? Think your father will win his nomination if he can't balance the books at home? How long will Cecilia remain married to you when her cards are declined at Barney's? Because every debt you have, I'm calling tomorrow."

Howe takes two steps forward, and I drop my arms to my side. He glances down to see my hands curling into fists and steps back.

"I don't know what you think you've done, but you'll never be a Howe."

"That would be a great comeback if I cared about that," I said dryly. "No one has wanted to be a Howe in a very long time."

His face tightens at this insult, but because he's a coward, he turns on his heel and walks away.

The curtain falls. I glance at my watch. Act II is about to start very soon.

Swiftly I return to where I left Kaga and Michelle. Tiny has returned, and she looks amused. Perhaps because she knows why Kaga is interrogating Michelle.

"Did you enjoy your little chase?" Kaga asks as I rejoin them.

"It was a good start to the evening, but I'm not going to be satisfied until I've had the main course."

I glance over at Richard's wife, who is glaring daggers at me.

"She looks unhappy," Tiny observes.

"I think her husband may have just delivered bad news about their credit."

"Ouch." She winces. "I don't want to be with them tonight."

Michelle looks avidly between us, as if she is dying to ask what we're talking about, but her own good manners prevent her from speaking.

Ross returns before she can gather up her nerve. "Mr. Kerr, Ms. Corielli, perhaps you'd like to step up to the podium."

He waves his hand toward a small dais at the center of the atrium in front of the string quartet.

Tiny gives me a questioning glance. I've shared most of what would happen tonight, but not all. And for a moment I feel a twinge of guilt. Perhaps another day and another event would be better suited for this. But I had to put this behind us once and for all. Not just for my sake, but for the future safety of our family.

I lean over and kiss her on the cheek. "Trust me."

"I do." She places her hand in mine and squeezes. Together we walk toward the dais. Howe is standing there.

"What's he doing there?" she whispers.

"He's the chair of the Frick Foundation," Ross informs her. "He'll be announcing the generous donation Mr. Kerr has made in honor of your mother."

"What?" She stops short and turns to me. "Ian, what?"

"It was a surprise." I give Ross a dark look—but then, it's really my fault. "I made a modest gift to open up the private member gardens to the public."

"Modest!" Ross laughs but at my next glare, sobers up quickly. "Yes, my dear. The gardens have been available to members only, but Mr.

Kerr came to us a few months ago asking if we would be interested in opening them up much like the museum is open, on a pay-as-you-can basis. The gift is substantial enough," he gives a tight smile as if to say that he'll call the donation whatever he wants, "to fund the renovations, maintenance, and staffing for several years. We will be naming them the Sophie Corielli Gardens."

Tiny gasps and then covers her mouth with both hands. Her eyes are wide, and I suppose behind her hands her mouth forms the same perfect circle.

"A minute," I tell Ross. He nods, his face alight with concern.

"Certainly, Mr. Kerr. Take all the time you need."

I draw Tiny behind one of the pillars. We aren't hidden, but it provides us a small measure of privacy. Sweeping my hands up to the bare flesh of her shoulders and down to the bracelet cuff, I try to rub some of the shock away.

"I would have told you before, but I wanted it to be a surprise. I see now that was a poor idea."

"Months ago, Ian?" she says with a trembling voice.

"Months." I nod. "I knew from the minute I saw you that I wanted you. If I had to buy my way into your heart, I would. It's my flaw, you know. I need you. And now, since you've foolishly fallen for me, I thought to make the donation to honor your mother. Consider it a wedding gift."

"Before my mother's death?"

"Even before then, but I upped the donation and made the naming a condition of the gift after she passed."

"I'm pretty angry with you right now," she says. I brace myself, wondering how I'll be able to talk or buy my way out of this. "Because I really, really want to reward you, and I know I'm going to have to wait."

I exhale in relief. "This'll be over in less than thirty minutes, and then we'll be in the car and I'll make sure you come twice before we've passed Midtown."

She laughs at this. "I might hold you to that."

"Do. After this is all over, I'm going to need a challenge." My smile fades then. "I'm sorry for tainting your night with the Howe business, though. I felt like this was our best chance, and I wanted to get it over with."

"Don't apologize." She brushes my cheek. "I want this as much as you. And I know my mother is probably cheering you on right this minute."

And what is there for me to do but kiss her until all her lipstick is smeared between us? Her mouth tastes like Scotch and Tiny—a sweet, heady brew. Her lips are lush, ripe fruit that beg for my teeth, and her tongue is a swift, darting thing inciting lust with every caress.

A loud cough from Ross breaks us apart. Panting slightly, she points to my mouth. Whipping out my handkerchief, I wipe at my lips and cheek until she gives me a nod and wink of approval. Leaning forward I give her another kiss. After all, I've destroyed her lipstick already. There's no point in restraint now.

"Kill him," she whispers, and it's with her bloodthirsty words in mind that I join Howe at the dais.

"Kind of you to join me," Howe says tightly. "Hope this isn't uncomfortable for you, old man."

"Not at all. I'm still feeling spry, given that I haven't even reached my midthirties yet. Are you feeling poorly? Perhaps Ross has a chair for you." I start to raise my hand to gesture for Fairchild.

Howe tugs my arm down. He is a remarkably easy target. In my mind, he's been built up as this soulless monster ravaging everyone around him, too dangerous for a child to attack. But I am not a child or even the orphaned teen I used to be.

"I'm fine." He scowls and then at a signal from his father, rearranges his face into a placid expression. "Good thing you got your check in early. Wasn't sure if we would be able to continue with the ceremony. Did this come straight from the Kerr Inc. coffers? What would your shareholders say to that?"

His voice is pitched low enough that only I can hear him.

"Unlike you, Howe, I don't need to dip into my shareholder funds. I have plenty of my own to draw from."

"That old canard? Is that what your father told you? That I borrowed some funds from a few portfolios?"

"Not at all," I counter smoothly. "I was thirteen when he died. It was you who admitted to your wrongdoing. Don't you remember?"

He pales, and I forge on.

"He came to you with a request that you return some of the funds he had lent you to cover up your embezzlement. You refused. You told him that he of all people should know that the code of the street was to eat or be eaten and that he shouldn't have let you gobble him up." I stare at Howe steadily as he turns ghostly white. The lilies lining the atrium have more color. "Want to know how I know this?" I ask quietly.

It's hard to say whether the movement of his head is a nod of affirmation or a negative shake, but I proceed on. "Because my father recorded it. I still have it." I reach inside my jacket pocket. "Shall I play it for you?"

Howe reaches for my hand. "Stop." His breath is labored and sweat dots his brow. "What do you want? You told me that my credit is no good. I assume you've bought up my debt. What is it that you want? For me to leave Tiny alone? Done."

"What I want from you, Howe, is to admit your wrongdoing once and for all." My words are barely above a whisper, but he hears every word. And so does everyone else in the audience. The buzz of the crowd has all but dissipated, but Howe doesn't recognize this. He is too wrapped up in his own panic to be aware of his surroundings—including the fact that I don't have a recorder. I brought a different piece of electronics with me today. It sits on the dais and I've just turned it on. "Confess your sins here and now, and I'll make it right for you."

He nods, slowly and jerkily. "Then all will be returned to the way it was?"

"Yes. All will be made right."

"Wh-what specific sins?" He licks his lips.

"Why not start with my family? If we have time, you can recount any others you've done wrong."

"I did turn your father away, but I want you to know I've regretted it."

"Did you regret taking the money from him? Or allowing him to cover up your embezzlement? Or did you regret turning him away?"

"All of it. It's been eating at me." He thumps his chest.

"What about the people you stole money from? Do you regret that?" He's so caught up in himself that he doesn't notice anything beyond his own nose. Not the changing expressions of the crowd. Not his mother turning pasty white. Not his father trying to charge toward the platform to stop the destruction of their family. Kaga holds him back.

"Y-yes." When he doesn't say anything further, I take a menacing step forward. He starts talking again. "I regret taking the money from my clients."

"Is that why your father's funds are so depleted now? Why he's had to rely on his friends for so many big donations? Do they know he's not matching them with his own funds because he's covering up your mistakes?"

He shakes his head. "It's an expensive lifestyle we lead." He grabs for me, but I move away from him. I don't want his filthy hands on me. He loses his balance and grabs the podium. "You know this." He raises his voice even higher. "You know this!"

"I've earned every penny I've spent," I respond. "Can you say the same?"

In an instant, his pale face turns red with anger. "Your golden goose is cooked. I made sure of that. Kerr Inc. isn't going to be controlled by you much longer, and then how many things will you be able to buy yourself and your whore?"

I might have swung at him if not for Tiny's hand at my back. She's right behind me, telling me with her touch that I should go on and not deviate from the plan.

"What else have you done? Tell me," I command.

He's too angry now to watch what he's saying. "I've fucked women for their money. Is that what you want to hear? That I've taken advantage of old hag socialites to get their accounts and slept with daughters to ruin their fathers?" he sneers. "This dick has stuck more women in the city than a porn star in the Valley. And I've made more money doing it. I don't need you," he says, straightening and trying to gain composure. "There's a hundred stupid women out there right now whose dickless husbands can't get it up. You offer to eat them out, and they're all too willing to open up their checkbooks as well as their legs. Easy pickings."

Complete silence is in the room now. His mother has disappeared and his father has quit fighting. He, unlike Richard, has realized that it's all over for the Howe family. Cecilia is gone. I haven't seen her for quite some time. I don't know when she left.

"Easy, is it?" I peruse the crowd. Howe is still bloviating. "You know what your problem is, Howe? You have no imagination. You aim low and achieve low."

"Fuck you," he grunts. "I'm Richard Howe. I can trace my descendants back to people who rubbed shoulders with Henry Clay Frick himself. You could have aligned yourself with me. My father could have put you in a position of power. Your mother didn't even know how to dress herself when she married Duncan Kerr. And now, blood tells, because you went and tied yourself to an illiterate bike messenger. How stupid can you be?"

"Not so stupid that I say indiscreet things when there's a hot mic in front of me." I tap the microphone and the *thump thump* reverbs back. It's almost as satisfying as hitting Howe in the face. Almost, but not quite.

So I turn and punch him right in the mouth so that the flesh of his lips is pushed hard against the line of his teeth. He stumbles back off the dais. No one helps him, and he falls to his knees. I jump down beside him. The crowd is rushing toward us, scenting blood. No matter how rarified the air, everyone loves a fight.

"I'm tired of you insulting my fiancée, who on her worst day is smarter than you'll ever be. Unlike you, she doesn't have to prostitute herself to make a living. Unlike you, she's not a whore."

The crowd collectively inhales. Rather than concede that he's been beaten, Richard, because he's a dumb animal, strikes out. "Like your mother? Because she tried to sell herself to me. That's where I got the idea that these stupid bitches could be screwed out of their money and into submission."

I shake my head. "You'd think you'd shut up while you could, but no."

I punch him again, and he goes down. This time his nose is bleeding as well as the corner of his mouth. Someone—Kaga, I think—shoves a handkerchief at me to wipe away the blood on my hands. But I don't want to wipe it away. The sight of his blood ignites a fire inside me. All the hate and rage I've stored up against him is roaring, and the blood is fanning the flames. Red is all I see.

Howe scrambles back as I stride toward him. Like a scuttling crab, he moves backward until he hits a chair and then a potted plant and then a wall of people. There's nothing more that I want to do than pick up a chair and bash his head in until he's not able to talk again. Not able to breathe again.

I'm reaching for the back of a cloth-draped chair when a small hand presses against my arm. "It's done. Don't waste your time with that animal." It's Tiny, and the rage recedes slightly at her words.

"He needs to pay," I say through gritted teeth.

"He has. He will. Look around you," she urges.

The yoke of revenge and hatred still weighs me down. With great effort, I lift my head. The crowd has gathered close, and on their faces I see shock, dismay, and even some satisfaction . . . which so easily could turn if I press too hard. His father is in the grip of Kaga. I ease back.

"Mr. Fairchild," I say loudly, trying to regain my composure. A handkerchief is offered again. In fact, not just one but several are being offered. This is a gesture of support, and I'd be stupid—stupid as Howe—if I didn't take it. I see one being offered by Kitty McFarland, a scion of the community. "Thank you." I bow my head in a courtly gesture.

She gives me a grim smile. "You look like you need it, son."

"I do. Fairchild," I repeat. "I think we're ready for that announcement. Since Mr. Howe is indisposed, perhaps you can do the honors."

"Of course! If everyone would gather over here by the dais, I would love to share the generous donation that Ian Kerr has made to the Frick Foundation to benefit the citizens of New York City."

I take Tiny's hand and walk toward the dais. Behind me I hear a scuffle, and we both turn back. Richard is being forcibly helped to his feet by two brawny young servers. They begin to drag him out of the atrium with Kaga directing. I give Kaga a nod of appreciation and he returns it.

Turning back, I wrap my arm around Tiny and draw her close.

"Does it hurt?"

"My hand?"

She nods.

"Yes, because I only got to punch him twice. It would hurt a lot less if I had gotten to hit him at least ten more times."

"I think the pain will lessen with each day. Didn't you once tell me that?" She's referring to her mother, and hell, maybe she's referring to mine too.

"And was I right?"

"You were. But this is the only time I'll admit it."

"Good enough for me."

We stand there then and listen to Fairchild extol the virtues of Sophie Corielli, the mother I had gained for a short time and then lost. But she left me her most prized creation, and that was a bigger gift than any monetary contribution I could ever provide. My arm tightens around Tiny's shoulders, and she leans into me, placing a hand over my chest.

"I love you, Ian Kerr."

"I love you, soon-to-be Victoria Kerr."

CHAPTER 25

Our lovemaking that night is more tender than fierce, as if we are both comforting each other.

"We're going to make a baby tonight," I swear as I thrust slowly inside her.

"Is that right?" She smiles at me, a wicked thing full of naughty promise. Her arms are stretched high above her head, and she undulates slowly beneath me, enjoying the slippery friction of our bodies moving against each other.

Her eyes are half-lidded, weighed down by desire. Through the curtain of her lashes, I see the glow of her eyes. It's a heady mixture of love and lust, of want and need, of passion and promise. Each stroke of my steel-hard desire is met with her own driving fervor.

"That's right." Bending forward, I capture a jutting nipple in my mouth and am rewarded with an arched back and a breathy moan. With one arm, I gather her more closely to me so that she is nearly suspended, pinned to the bed by my rutting cock. "I'm obsessed with you," I confess, panting slightly. The hold of her snug walls on my cock makes it hard to think. I want to just fall on her and plunge repeatedly into her soft core until my shaft explodes in a mania of pleasure. "I can't stop thinking about you or wanting you. Everything I do now and forever will be for the sole purpose of making sure that you are fucking satisfied in every way."

My words are punctuated with increasingly harder thrusts. She meets them readily, swiveling her hips and using her feet and legs to meet every press.

"I love your cock," she moans. "And your mouth."

"They love you too, bunny."

Inside the slick recesses of her sex, that cock is pushing toward a finish, and as she begins to tremble around me, I realize I am not alone. Holding her firmly against me with one arm banded around her back, I slip my free hand between us to find her clit.

With my erection hard inside her and rubbing her sensitive tissues with each stroke, she comes apart at the firm caress of my fingers on her delicate flesh.

"Oh," she gasps and then cries out, "Ian! Please. Now."

Her words release me, and I thrust inside her with jerky, uncoordinated movements as the orgasm rolls up the base of my balls. But I hold off because I want to her to come with me. I want to feel her milk me until I'm coming so hard that my brain detonates in my head.

"I will want you forever," I growl into the soft mounds of her breasts. Then, biting down on her tender skin and her plump curves, I mark her. She screams out in ecstasy, her head thrown back and the long line of her jaw exposed to my ravening mouth.

As she shatters in my arms, I jet my seed into her body while she clings to me like I'm the only port in a storm.

"I wish Mom had seen what happened at the Frick tonight," Tiny sighs, curling into me. I roll over to fold my arms around her and tuck her into my body.

"She's here with us." I stroke her damp back, lightly dusted with sweat from our bed play.

"I hope not," she jokes. "Like, I hope when she's watching me, she takes a few breaks so she doesn't see this."

"See what? Me fucking your brains out?"

Tiny rises up on her knees and pushes me onto my back. "How about *me* fucking *your* brains out?"

"Look away, Sophie," I say. "Your daughter is about to defile me. Worse, I'm going to enjoy the hell out of it."

The entire weekend is spent in bed, exploring and making sure that baby gets made.

◆ ◆ ◆

On Monday, I feel energized. And I realize that for the first time, I'm not waking up with the bitter knowledge that my family's destruction has gone unavenged. In my more rational moments, I acknowledge that letting go and moving on might have been the honorable things to do, but I doubt they would have been as satisfactory.

Page Six is full of the weekend's entertainment, but the front page is even better. Below the fold is an article mentioning the troubled fortunes of mayoral candidate Edward Howe and the speculation that he will be dropping out of the race.

Kerr Inc. stock is up when news of the blocked takeover bid by disgruntled board members is leaked by Jake to a reporter friend. That's all he had to leak to her. The rest of the information she was able to run down on her own.

On the Arts page is a write-up of the gift to the Frick honoring Sophie Corielli. It's all good today.

The phone rings all morning with congratulations and thanks and innuendos about my mother. The rumors will always dog us, but at least most of the truth has been revealed. Because Kerr Inc. stock is high, I sell a portion of my shares before lunch to start shoring up Nessie's fund. It saved my business having that fund, and I'd like to get it to solid levels again. It will take time to dig out of the financial hole I'm in, but it will happen.

I'm dragged out of my office by Kaga for lunch at Morimoto.

"It's all Kerr, all the time in the New York papers. One would think you bought off the press."

"I did. I bought them with a salacious scandal full of sex, old rivalries, and doomed political futures," I counter.

"It was an expensive night," he answers thoughtfully. He's referring to the information Howe revealed about my mother.

"That was merely the rantings of a madman." Some people will believe it. Others won't. I'll have to live with that.

Kaga dips his head slightly. He won't ask any other questions. "I've been speaking to the director of the Frick about making a donation, but I'd like to tie a specific request to it."

Now it's my turn to shake my head. "Sabrina isn't interested in being a curator at a museum."

There's hardly any change to his expression, but I sense his discomfort. I don't know that anyone's called him out on his obsession before.

"And you know this, how?"

"Because she wants to be a DJ. I believe she's expressed that desire more than once to you and Jake."

He waves his hand. "That was a passing interest when she was a teenager. She'll be graduating and wanting to enter the real world with a good career."

"I'm pretty sure that her answer to this will be 'bullshit.' Or something even more candid, if I recall Sabrina correctly."

Kaga narrows his eyes. "You know something. Tell me. Tell me right now, or I'll be forced to kill you with my chopsticks."

I feel like living on the edge, so I just smile at Kaga, willing to suffer the consequences. Given that I walk out of Morimoto's without harm, it seems like every bet I'm making is coming up aces.

◆ ◆ ◆

TINY

Marcie and I are walking down Amsterdam to pick up lunch at Grandaisy Bakery when I see it.

"Marcie!" I shout, pointing toward the street. It's unnecessary. She's already off, halfway into the street. In the middle of the intersection between Broadway and Amsterdam, there's a baby carriage. Marcie leaps in front of a cab that's screeching to a stop. Before she can get to the carriage, another car speeds through the intersection and strikes the carriage, sending it careening to the west side of the intersection.

Another vehicle swerves to avoid striking it but hits another car instead. The sounds of horns, screeching brakes and crunching metal fill the air.

I start toward the carriage, but before I can even take a step, a hand pulls me backward. Stumbling and off-balance with my arms wheeling in circles in the air, I'm pushed forward into the back seat of a black town car.

Before I realize what's happening, Cecilia Howe is closing the door.

The car takes off immediately, positioned conveniently to head north on Amsterdam and away from the scene of the collisions. Confused, I turn back to see if Marcie has saved the baby. Behind us, I see cars stopped haphazardly, and toward the southwest corner, Marcie is standing at the side of the carriage, one hand holding a phone to her ear and one hand in her hair scanning the horizon. Scanning it for me. *Shit.* I scramble toward the door, but when I try the handle it's locked.

"Child safety locks." Cecilia looks smugly at me. "The door can only be opened from the outside."

"Fuck this," I say and press down the window button, but I'm defeated in that too. It's either broken or some other kind of child safety control prevents me from rolling it down. Finally I bang on the raised privacy screen, but there's no response. "What the hell, Cecilia?"

"It's been a very bad few days for me," she says. Holding out her hands, she displays her fingernails, some of which are broken and all have chipped polish. The skin of her hands looks particularly pale and thin.

"This is a bad idea. You think Ian was mad before. He'll be like an enraged bull; everything will get destroyed."

"You have so much. You should have just left us alone." She folds her arms and looks out the window. We're heading crosstown now toward the Upper East Side.

I pull out my phone, but there's no signal. She must have some blocking technology in the car. I debate my options. Until the vehicle stops and someone opens the door, I'm stuck in the car. I have to assume that the driver is in on this. Settling back against the seat, I start to plot. Fine. When the car stops, I'll jump out and run away. I'm healthy, fit, and fast.

Cecilia took me by surprise. That's the only reason I'm sitting in the back of this car right now.

"Did you set up the carriage thing? Was there even a baby in it?" I ask suddenly.

"People are very easy to manipulate. A child in danger? That's more important than anything, even you."

Ian and I are so dumb, so shortsighted. We've never viewed Cecilia as anything more than a flighty society wife, but she obviously knew about Richard's activities. And here she created a stupid but clever diversion that separated me from Marcie and got me into the car with no violence at all. I view her with respectful wariness. Maybe jumping out and running won't be enough. I feel like I'm stronger than her. My job was one of physical exertion, cycling up and down the streets of Manhattan. Surely I could subdue her in the car.

"I wouldn't try," she says, with a slight nod downward. A small, round barrel is pointed directly at my belly. At this close range, she could hit me without even trying. I haven't ever handled a gun before. Or driven a car. Or been kidnapped. Holy Christ. I kind of want to laugh. This is all so ludicrous.

"Do you think you can shoot me and all your troubles will magically disappear? Newsflash, I don't have any money, and I highly doubt that Ian is going to give you any if you kill me."

"Of course I'm not going to kill you. Killing is very thuggish. I'm going to hurt you, Miss Corielli. And I'll continue to hurt you until Mr. Kerr provides me the means to start anew somewhere else." She smiles as if quite pleased with herself. "I only need Ian to believe that I will if he doesn't do what I ask. Oh, and when we come to a stop, Travis will also have a gun. We'll both shoot you in the leg or arm, something not terribly vital. Who knows? It'll be like a carnival game or something. Take your chances."

"I thought you needed me alive to lure Ian to do your bidding." I try to be upbeat, but Cecilia has been planning this for a few days and I'm winging it. I never thought I'd need a getaway plan from a crazy lady kidnapping me at gunpoint.

"You only have to be alive for as long as it takes him to wire me the money I'm going to be asking for."

"You'll need to send proof of life." I've watched movies, and kidnappers always send those.

"Don't you worry your pretty little head. I have that all planned out," Cecilia answers and then laughs, a note of hysteria detectable in her high-pitched cackle. I take a little comfort in that. She's not completely in control. Of course, that could mean she shoots me sooner rather than later.

"This is the twenty-first century. Don't you think this will follow you? You can't just start a new life."

"Part of the condition of your safety and well-being will be to keep quiet. I have people in the city who will enforce these rules when I'm gone.

Besides, your Ian, for all his ruthless ways, has far too many morals. He's held the means to ruin Richard for years but held back. Because of me, you know." She sounds so proud of herself. "I'd seen some irregularities in our bills. I take care of all of that. Richard is too dumb. So I planted a few seeds." She smiles cruelly. "Ian loved his mother. Adored her really, and I made sure to mention how much I adored her as well. And how I was doing all this charitable work to save women's lives. Ian was too wrapped up in his grief over his mother—grief and guilt—to want to hurt me."

"You manipulated him for years."

"I did." She's so proud, and I want nothing more than to smack that smile off her fucking face.

Instead, I praise the crazy lady so she doesn't shoot me in the car. "You should have taken that to the craps table. You're smart, Cecilia. Smarter than Richard. Why didn't you cut your losses and take off?"

She scoffs. "You know why. We have no money. We live the way we do on credit, and now that Richard is humiliated and ruined, the credit won't be extended. I'm not cut out for a life of menial shopgirl labor."

"With your connections, you could probably have run a charitable organization. That's hardly menial shopgirl work."

Before she has time to answer, we pull up to a five-story limestone townhome. The Howe residence, I presume. "Nice place you have here."

It's the wrong thing to say because Cecilia reaches out and slaps me across the face with the gun in her hand. My head hits the window. My vision is blurred, and when the door opens and Travis, a big brute, pulls me out, I'm not ready. I struggle, but Travis is too big for me. His arms band around my side, and I'm carried down into the basement.

I catch glimpses of shelving, carpet, and then I'm shoved into a wine cellar. Travis drops me into the corner, and Cecilia follows behind. The door shuts and it's just Cecilia and me. In my struggle with Travis, I still manage to dial Ian's phone. I don't know if I still have a signal down here. I can only pray it connects.

◆ ◆ ◆

IAN

When I step into my office suite, Malcolm Hedder is sitting in the waiting area looking like he went a few rounds down at the gym with some bruiser and lost. Rose raises both eyebrows in helpless chagrin.

"He wouldn't leave."

"Of course not." I open the door to the inner sanctum. "Come on, then."

He walks gingerly toward me. The surface bruises must be matched by others less visible. Or maybe he's faking to make me feel sympathetic.

I drop into my chair and gesture for him to take a seat. He does, lowering himself slowly into the chair that I fucked Tiny on. I get a juvenile sense of satisfaction over that.

"Are you here to beg for mercy? You've timed it right." I spread my arms wide. "I'm feeling benevolent."

Malcolm scowls at me. "He's gone. I told him to leave."

"Him being Mitch?" I ask, lowering my arms to the desk.

"Who else?"

"Was it you or your father who hired the attack on me?"

"Neither." He looks at me with undisguised surprise. I figured it was Richard, but it didn't hurt to ask questions when the opportunity arose. "Why would you suspect me?"

"I could say because it's in your nature to want dangerous things. Like your sister. You did try to obtain my signature on an unsavory and unenforceable contract for services in the hopes of blackmail. But the real reason I suspected you is because you love her and you didn't realize this until she fell in love with me. Pretty clichéd," I mock. "Wanting what you can't have."

He laughs then, a hollow, aching sound, and I feel almost sorry for him. Almost. "Yeah, like a sister."

"You love her," I repeat.

His face falls, and as if the effort of denying himself is too strong or he's just relieved to finally say it, he admits, "I love her."

"I'm not unsympathetic. I'm sure I would be a broken and angry man if I had as many opportunities as you did to share this with her and didn't, but she's mine now. And I'll do everything I can to protect her, even if that means limiting your contact with her. Tell me why you believe your father is gone?"

"Because I told him to go. There wasn't any point in him hanging around."

"I'm sorry you have shitty parents. It happens to the best of us." It's the most comfort I can offer.

"Maybe. Anyway, I'll keep him out of your hair as much as I can."

"Are you blackmailing him?" Because if he pays his father off once, he'll have to continue to pay, and the price will go up until Malcolm can't meet it. So clearly, Malcolm must have something to hold over his father's head that's more powerful than money. I can't imagine—no, I don't want to imagine—what that might be.

He gives me a short nod. "But I'm not telling you what I'm holding over his head, and you won't find out—not with an army of investigators."

"Fair enough. But if he comes calling again, all bets are off." There's never any peaceful end to blackmail. Why Malcolm hasn't learned this yet is a surprise to me. In some ways, he's almost as innocent as his sister, despite his criminal activities and propensity to fuck his stable of hookers.

"Did you get Sophie's things from him? Tiny will want them."

"There isn't anything. It was all a story designed to lure Tiny into his web and then get money from you."

"Goddammit." I sigh. The last thing I want to do is inflict more pain on Tiny as a result of her mother's death.

"I'll tell her, though," Malcolm so generously offers.

"With me."

"What is this? Fucking supervised visitation?" he scoffs.

"Call it whatever you want, but you don't get to see her without me being present. Ever," I reply evenly.

"She's my sister," he protests.

"Stepsister," I correct. "And you don't have brotherly feelings toward her." At his mulish expression, I continue, "Look at it from my point of view. Would you ever permit a man who loved your woman within ten feet of her alone? No. I can see by your face you wouldn't. She was never a Hedder. She belonged to Sophie and now me. She'll be a Kerr soon, and you can either be part of that world where she stands beside me and sleeps with me, or you can be on the outside. Take whatever path you want."

I stand up. Our meeting is over. Hedder rises and lumbers after me to the door. As he exits, I call after him. "She cares for you. Don't shut her out. You'll regret that."

He shakes his head but doesn't respond.

"No more phone calls," I instruct Rose. "I'm not getting anything done."

"Yes, sir." She mock salutes me.

Before I can even close my office door, my cellphone rings. It's Jake.

"Are you sitting down?"

Instantly I know it's Tiny. "Where is she?"

"We don't know."

"What the fuck, Jake?" I explode. Racing to my desk, I fumble with the bottom drawer. Before he can say another word, my line beeps. It's Tiny.

"Thank God," I say, but she starts speaking over me, and I realize she isn't talking to me at all.

"What's the point of this?" she asks.

"You need to make him stop." That's Cecilia Howe's voice. Thin and weak and . . . menacing?

"I'm not sure what you want him to stop doing. It was your husband behind the mic."

"Ian Kerr is a menace. He's bought up all our debt and is requiring us to pay within the next thirty days. The house, the cars, the cabin in the Hamptons."

I hear the rustle of paper, as if Cecilia is shaking paper in Tiny's face.

"Do you know how humiliating it is when your credit is denied, not just once but with every single card? Those saleswomen were looking at me like I was a piece of trash. Me, Cecilia Montgomery Howe! My family came over on the goddamn boat."

"Yeah, um, say it, don't spray it."

"*What* did you say?"

I press the mute button on my phone and pick up the landline to dial Jake. "Cecilia Howe has Tiny. Can we trace Tiny's phone?"

"I'm going to need to hack into her cell phone service and see if we can pull up a GPS signal. Call a car service and come here. I sent Steve to get Marcie."

Cursing, I ask. "How's the traffic? Maybe I'm better off taking the subway."

"You have her on the phone? You'll lose her once you go underground."

"Fuck, you're right. I'm leaving right now."

I don't connect the phone to Bluetooth. I'm too afraid of losing the connection. From my desk drawer, I pull out a handgun. I've had this piece since my days on the street. It's unregistered, and the serial number has long since been filed away. Tucking it into my suit coat pocket, I fold the jacket over my arm to disguise the bulk.

"Do you need me to call a car for you?" Rose asks as I sprint past.

"No time. I'll whistle down a cab."

"What about Steve?"

"He's busy." I slide my card into the panel next to the elevator bank and ring for the elevator. One appears within twenty seconds, but that's almost too long for me.

"I said, 'What is it that you want me to do?'" Tiny repeats.

"Call Ian right now. Tell him to make everything right."

"No."

At first, I'm angry that she's antagonizing Cecilia like this, but then I realize that she can't call. She's already on the phone with me and an incoming call might be heard on the other end. Tiny smartly doesn't want to take the risk. I flag a cab and clamber in, holding the phone to my ear.

"Eightieth and Amsterdam. There's five hundred cash if you can get me there in ten minutes. Five hundred plus any traffic fines." I wave the money at him, and he nods. I'm barely in the car before he takes off.

"What?" Sissy screeches.

"I'm not calling him and asking him to do that. Do you know what your husband did to Ian?"

"Duncan Kerr died because he was weak," she sniffs. "And Ian's mother. Disgusting. She actually propositioned Richard in order to make him pay off their debts."

"But kidnapping is so much better?"

Oh for God's sake, Tiny.

I'm lucky. The traffic up Amsterdam is sparse despite it being Monday. Plus, my driver is weaving in and out of traffic like he's in a Formula One race.

"What does he see in you?" I hear after a long pause.

"I give really good head."

I pound my head against the window and let out a weak laugh.

"This isn't funny," Cecilia fumes.

"I agree. I'm not amused at all, but what can I do while I'm trapped in the basement of your townhome?"

I tap the driver. "Change of plans. Take me to 64th and Lex."

"I'm going to have to navigate Central Park traffic. That will take some time."

"Double the bonus if you can make me forget there's traffic. And give me your phone."

He hands me the phone, and I give him the five hundred right then. It works because he stomps on the gas and we shoot forward. I call Jake. "She's at Cecilia's."

"I'll meet you there. Don't do anything without me," he warns.

"I'm not leaving her to stew in Howe's clutches while I wait for you."

"Do you want to have a happy life with Tiny, or one where she visits you at Riker's?"

I disconnect in response and throw the phone in the passenger seat.

"Call him," Cecilia shrieks. "Call him right now."

"Okay, but I told you he's working. You know, to save his business."

We all hear the phone ring, and it seems like everyone—including the driver—is holding their breath. It rings three times and then Rose answers. "Kerr Inc., Ian Kerr's office. May I help you?"

"Answer," I hear Cecilia hiss.

"Um, just wondering if Ian is there. It's Tiny."

"No, Miss Corielli. He just left a few minutes ago. Wasn't he talking to you?"

Oh shit. Oh motherfucking shit, no.

"What?" Cecilia shrieks and then there's a scuffle.

"How long has this phone been on?"

There's no response, and then the distinct sound of flesh striking flesh repeats itself one, two, and then three times.

I unmute the phone. "Goddammit, Cecilia, if you hit her one more time, I will end you myself."

"You're so clever, Ian Kerr. Did you figure out I was hitting her just from the sound alone? What does this sound like to you?"

There's a boom and then the line goes dead.

CHAPTER 26

TINY

Cecilia's gunshot destroying my phone galvanizes me into action. I've had enough of this farce. There are weapons everywhere in here. One strike with a glass wine bottle, and she'd be out of it. I lunge at her. In surprise, she jerks backward and shoots, but I go in low and the shot careens high. As she stumbles backward, we crash into a wooden rack filled with bottles.

"You bitch," she says, shooting again, but I've got my arms around her. The shot makes a pinging noise as it hits a wine bottle or two. There's a sharp bite in my side, but I ignore it because I've pressed the *on* button for her psychosis and it's either her or me now. One of us is going to win, and it's going to be me. I have way too much to live for. The love I have for Ian is supercharging me. I know he's coming to save me, and I'm going to be alive when he gets here.

Cecilia is strong and a few inches taller than me, but she's gym strong. She works out to look good. I've been doing the biking equivalent of manual labor for six years. The knock on my head and the bruise on my cheek only fuel me to fight her harder.

We tumble to the ground, and the ache in my side intensifies. There's liquid and glass on the floor from broken wine bottles. I roll so that Cecilia is on the bottom, and from her yelps of surprised pain, I know her back is being stuck with jagged shards. The pain makes her loosen her grip, and I wrest the gun from her. Scrambling back into the corner so I can see the door, I point the gun at her.

"I'm not much of a shot, but I bet I don't miss from here," I pant. "Sit over there." I gesture toward the opposite wall. I want her as far away from me as possible, but I need to be able to see the door in case Travis comes in. I want to look for a phone, to be able to call Ian, but I'm afraid to take my eyes off her.

"You have so much!" Cecilia cries. "You could spare a few million, and Richard and I will be out of your hair. We'll go to Monaco, and you'll never see us again."

"Don't beg." I rest my back against the wall-to-wall shelves that hold probably a hundred bottles of wine and pull my knees up. I'm shaking from adrenaline, from pain, and from fear, so I use my knees to steady my arm, never taking my eyes off her, never moving my aim. I can't shoot her, though. Not like this. And maybe not ever. I try not to let that show in my face, but holy Christ, I've never held a gun before and I've never shot someone. I don't even want to. What I *do* want is to know why, and so I ask, "Is it just about the money? Ian says that in your circle, it's either money or status. Don't you have status from your family?"

"Is this where you think I'm going to spill my guts to you like some bad movie villain?"

I shrug. "Fine, don't talk. I guess I don't give two shits why. You're going to go to prison. Imagine how your nails are going to look in there."

"You know that Ian called Richard and threatened him," she snarls at me. "Was I supposed to just sit and take it? After all I've done to maintain our lifestyle? After all the years I've spent cleaning up after Richard, did you think I'd allow you and Ian Kerr to ruin us? Besides,

Richard out on his own would have squealed like a pig. I love that man, but he's weak and useless."

"It was you behind the notes, the assault on Ian? All of it?"

"All of it," she sneers.

"You're a horrible person. You are so horrible that I'm glad you're going to go to prison and that you won't ever be able to hurt Ian again."

"You are so uncouth." Her lip curls. "Ian is as well, if all he's interested in are your sexual abilities. Like mother like son. He probably sold himself. That's where his money came from."

"Uncouth but loaded." I can't help but mock her. "Besides, his mother wasn't a prostitute. She was desperate, and your husband took advantage of her. I don't get why you stayed with him. Is he a good lay? Because he's not a good provider. You're a pretty woman with a good background. I think you could've done a lot better."

"You have no idea." She sneers. "Men over fifty look at women like me as if we are some kind of relic. We only have one role to men with money and that is to care for their children. Otherwise, there is no second chance for us. They want—and are able—to fuck teenagers and college students. Anyone over the age of twenty-five must have some kind of spectacular attribute. Big tits. Long legs. Both preferably, and those only last until we're thirty, and by thirty-five we are simply too old to be considered of any use. Richard might eat at different restaurants, but he always returns home to me. Always."

"Because you have money. Or *had* money, but once that goes, so will he," I say.

She turns away, trying to hide, but not before I see the anguish flash in her eyes.

I'd feel sorrier for her if she hadn't kidnapped me and tried to kill me. I try to calm my racing heart by taking a deep breath, but the pain in my side intensifies. I drop my hand to press against the ache, and it's red when I pull it away. Blood red.

"You shot me," I say in a stunned voice. "I can't believe you fucking shot me."

"Did you think the gun was for show?" She rolls her eyes like I'm some stupid child.

"You're a psychopath."

Eyes blazing, she retorts, "I protect what is mine. Just like your precious Ian."

"Ian held off any action against your husband for years because he didn't want to hurt you. You and he are nothing alike. You used people and hurt them—people like Lauren and her brother. Buying cops? Shooting at people? Ian would never do that. He's better than you and always has been."

"You're weak," she says. "You'll never be able to shoot me."

I fear she's right. I've never fired a gun before, but I want to live more than anything. I want to hold Ian again. I want to kiss him, fuck him, live with him until I'm old and gray and can't do anything more than sit on our little beach and hold hands. Biting my lip, I squeeze the trigger.

◆ ◆ ◆

IAN

Fear and rage are fighting for dominance. The only sound I can hear is my harsh, ragged breath. My throat is coated with bile. I clench my teeth hard to stop the shaking. I bargain with God, with Buddha, with every single higher entity. *Please. Don't let her be harmed. Let them just be talking.*

Deep breaths, I counsel myself. I need to be calm to help Tiny. Serenity is too far out of reach, though.

I open my mouth to offer the driver more money. At this point, I'm ready to buy him a fucking transportation company, but before I can get a word out, I'm thrown backward as he presses the gas down hard.

"Don't need to offer me more cash," he calls back. "I heard. I'm getting you there, stat."

We speed down the Sixty-Fifth Street transverse and catch air as we pop out of Central Park and head toward Lex. "Turn down Lex," I order.

"I know where to fucking go," the driver growls back. Barely braking, he takes a hard left on Lex and then a right onto 64th but he's not driving fast enough. There are too many fucking cars on the goddamn road. I want to howl with rage. "What side?"

"Right!" The front door looks formidable. I'm not going to be able to kick it down, and shooting the lock off in broad daylight seems risky. "Go down to the corner."

At the corner is a store that sells lotions and shit. It's blindingly white and probably smells like a florist's shop. He brakes hard, and I'm running before the car stops. Behind me I hear a door slam, but I don't take the time to look back. Throwing open the door to the soap shop, I barrel through, dodging a saleswoman and the center display aisle.

"Back door?" I ask.

One woman points behind her while another shouts, "Wait, you can't go there!"

"Don't stop him," I hear behind me. It's the driver. "His woman is in danger."

The back room is filled with boxes, and I feel like I'm running a steeplechase as I hurdle over a couple and land a few yards from the rear entrance. I don't stop running.

Outside, the alley is tiny, and as I count the houses, I encounter a tall wall, at least ten feet high. "Goddammit!" I look around for something, anything I can climb on top of. There's a Dumpster down the way. I'll pull that over. But before I can run down, the driver puts a hand on my arm.

"I'll boost you, man."

I look at him for the first time. He's slightly shorter than me, but built like a tank. He'll do. "Thanks."

He hoists me, and I'm able to grab the top and haul myself over. It's a drop to the ground, and my knees are weak with the impact, but I don't feel it. Running forward, I grab a deck chair and throw it through the glass patio doors of the Howe's sunroom. The glass shatters, and I push through it, not caring about the cuts the jagged glass is making on my arms and torso.

The interior doors on either side of the sunroom are open, and I race through them past the kitchen, looking frantically for a staircase.

In the gallery beyond the kitchen, there's a metal railing and carpeted stairs leading down to the cellar. I fling myself down the stairs. There's an open area with wooden shelves lining the walls, full of random figurines.

I pull the gun out and disengage the safety.

These city townhomes are long and narrow. Cecilia could be holding Tiny on either end of the basement. There's no blood on the floor. That could mean that either Tiny was bleeding out at the end of the room or that she'd escaped without harm.

As quietly as possible, I creep toward the door to my right. The thick pile carpet muffles any sound, although the crash of the glass and the pounding of my steps probably alerted everyone to my presence. So fuck the attempt to be silent.

"Tiny!" I yell.

There's a muffled yelp and then nothing. I reengage the safety back on the gun so I don't accidentally shoot myself. There's a door to my left and then two more at the other end of the room. I decide to clear each room methodically and take a brief moment to study the wood trim, stainless steel hinges and matching handle.

Bracing my back foot, I deliver a swift kick to the side of the lock mount, the weakest part of the door. The wood splinters, and I hear a scream on the other side. Tiny.

"Cecilia, if you touch her again, I swear I will kill you."

Another blow to the door has it completely giving way. Inside, I see Tiny hunkered down on the other side of the room against a wall of wine racks. The air reeks of spilled wine, and there are darks stains in the carpet along with shards of glass that glitter like diamonds under the low cellar light. My heart stops when I see Tiny's right hand clutched to her side. There's a viscous red liquid seeping through her fingers that is definitely not wine. Her other hand is braced on her knee, holding a gun on Cecilia Howe.

"You know how you said we shouldn't ever be apart?" Her voice is strained, but the hand on her knee is steady and she doesn't take her eyes off Cecilia once. "I'm rethinking my need for independence right about now."

"Oh, bunny." My knees are weak. Part of me wants to ask Cecilia why, but there are more pressing things to handle. While I cringe at having to hurt a woman, Cecilia is an obvious danger, and I'd be foolish not to take her out. I strike the butt of my gun against the back of Cecilia's head to knock her out. She slumps inelegantly against the side of the wall.

"Did you have to do that?" Tiny asks in a shocked voice.

"Yes, I did." Gently taking the gun from her hand, I engage the safety and then carefully lift her into my arms. "I need to get you out of here, and I can't do that if I have to watch my back because some crazed socialite is going to rise out of the cellar with a knife or something."

"Right. You're right. It just took me off guard," she pants. "God, my side aches. I always wondered what it felt like to get shot."

"You need to start having better fantasies. I'm clearly not doing my job right." Cradling her against my chest, I give her both guns to hold and then start the process of walking up the stairs without jarring her.

"No, you're doing a great job. This was just a weird thought I had before I met you. Back when my life was boring and all."

"I'm sorry for bringing this into your life." Christ, she should hate me.

"Nah, I mean, who doesn't need a little excitement in their life from time to time? I shot this gun. First time."

"To hurt Cecilia?" I ask astonished.

"No, just to scare her. It did the trick. She was yammering about how I didn't have the guts to shoot her. I didn't know if I did, but I wanted to live. I love you. Your love made me strong." Her smile blinds me.

Your love made me strong. Had I once thought love weakened me? I'd gotten it all wrong. Love made me a better person, and with Tiny, I had all the *more* in my life than one person could ever acquire. She's right. Love does make you strong.

"I'm pretty much done with excitement," I manage to joke. "I'm even rethinking the house. Maybe the Long Island Sound isn't far enough away from the city."

At the top of the stairs, I see Steve and Jake. "How'd you guys get in here without me hearing?" I ask, disgruntled. There's no question I sounded like an inept burglar when I broke in.

"Ninja skills, mate," Steve responds. Jake is on his phone.

"I hope you're calling emergency services," I say. When we reach the top, Jake gestures me toward the kitchen. Steve hurries in front of us and clears the table with one swift motion of his arm. Flowers, candles, and place settings all tumble to the ground.

"I hope that was some priceless, irreplaceable shit I just broke," Steve remarks, gesturing for me to lay Tiny down.

"No need to give speeches," Tiny jokes. "I'm not dying yet."

"Speeches?" Steve asks. He glances toward me, but I'm more interested in what Jake is doing. He's on his knees looking at Tiny's wound.

"Yeah, usually you give me only one- or two-word responses. This time you used several words. Like, I don't know, seven or eight."

"Eleven," I murmur.

"Ouch," she says. "Do you have to poke me there? I'm wounded."

"Just a graze," Jake says and stands up. He washes his hands and finds a cloth he dips in water. Offering me the damp towel, he asks, "Do you want to do the honors?"

"Just a graze?" I ask, dizzy with relief. I brace myself on the table so I don't collapse.

"Just a graze?" Tiny asks, completely affronted. "I got shot, dude. She shot me. Or actually, I kind of shot myself. But still, it hurts like a motherfucker."

"You shot yourself?" All three of us yell.

"I was struggling with Cecilia for the gun, and it went off, and it ricocheted off a bottle and hit me."

"You lucky girl." Jake begins to laugh. "I think you may have been grazed by a piece of glass from the bottle. I wondered why the cut was so jagged. Didn't look like any bullet hole I've ever seen. Don't wrestle any crazy women with guns in the future, and you'll be fine."

There's a knock at the door, and Jake goes to see who it is.

"I got shot," Tiny insists.

"Of course you did. It's a grievous wound. I think we should take a picture of it and post it on Facebook."

"Fuck you, Ian Kerr," she says grumpily.

"You have already," Steve mutters.

And with that, I can't hold it in any longer. I start laughing and I don't stop, not even when the paramedics show up or the cops, who take Cecilia away. I laugh because Tiny and I together are an undefeatable team. Strong enough to overcome hate, revenge, and loss.

We will take control of our lives together.

CHAPTER 27

Tiny allows the paramedics to load her in to the ambulance. There's no danger, but her side needs to be sewn up. At the hospital, the police show up and take our statements.

The baby carriage was empty, as Tiny suspected.

The press will have a field day with this. Several people show up to check on Tiny's status including her friend, Sarah, and Gary, the driver.

"I can't thank you enough," I say, handing him my card. "But I'm buying you a car. Pick out whatever one you want and call me. I'll arrange to have it delivered."

"Nah, man. It's all good. I can't take a car."

"You have to accept," Tiny pipes up from the bed. "Or he'll keep coming after you. He'll wear you down." She waves her ring in the air. "I kept saying no and see where that has gotten me."

"True story," I say.

With a grin, Gary takes the card and nods his head in Tiny's direction. "Seems to me that we're both getting the better end of the deal."

"Trust me, you're not." I clap a hand on his shoulder and walk him to the door.

"I should probably get going as well," Sarah says. She leans over and gives Tiny a hug. "Call me for lunch later this week." As she leaves, she pats me on the back. "Take good care of my girl."

"I will."

◆ ◆ ◆

One night, a few weeks after she recovers, we arrive at Club O2, an oxygen bar that Kaga is interested in buying. As I hand my keys to the valet, Tiny tugs at my arm.

"Isn't that Richard Howe?" she asks, pointing to the line of patrons waiting to be judged worthy of entering.

Toward the middle is a man wearing an ill-fitting suit, his hands in his pockets as he hunches his shoulders forward. It *is* Richard.

"Go inside," I say. Tiny shoots me an uncertain look but does as I ask.

I step aside and walk a little ways beyond the club so I can observe without being noticed. And then I wait.

Richard fidgets in the line, but unlike the rest of the crowd, he doesn't pull out a phone to text or read something to pass the time. It's possible that he can't afford a phone or doesn't pass the credit check for a cell line.

When he arrives at the doorman, he says something like a plea. One hand is on his chest and the other is pointing inside the bar. *I'm meeting friends. They are already inside.* I guess at what he might be saying.

The doorman shakes his head and looks past Richard. He waves the next three people inside. Richard moves toward the entrance, but the bouncer pushes him aside as if he's a pesky fly, still not looking at him. Richard starts to froth and rage. Both arms are in the air. *Do you know who I am?*

People behind him point their phones toward him and begin filming. Maybe it will be put online, or maybe no one will care about some drunken sot being kept out of O2.

Richard continues to shout and soon a NYC plainclothes policeman appears from the inside. I edge closer so I can hear.

"I'm going to have to ask you to leave," the officer says to Richard.

"On whose orders?" he responds belligerently.

The officer flashes a badge. "NYPD."

I've seen enough. Tiny is waiting for me.

"Ian. Ian Kerr," Richard calls out as I brush by the line, nodding my thanks to the doorman and bouncer.

"Do you know him?" the bouncer asks. I turn and look at Richard.

"Never seen him before in my life." Pulling a bill out of my pocket, I hand it to Richard. "Go and buy yourself a warm cup of soup tonight. Get off the street."

His face turns red with humiliation at the insinuation that he's a homeless person. The officer takes his arm and starts dragging him away.

Inside by the coat check are Tiny and Sarah.

"Everything okay?" Tiny asks.

"It's perfect," I answer. "Just perfect."

Her face turns upward to receive a kiss, and I plant a leisurely one on her that is so thorough Sarah blushes.

◆ ◆ ◆

We marry at the Frick gardens in a civil ceremony. Tiny wears an Elie Saab haute couture gown made out of blush tulle with hand-sewn Swarovski crystals and organza flowers. She complained it weighed a ton. It has an empire waist because by the time things settle down enough for us to wed she has begun to show. She looks like a glittery fae princess.

I send everyone down to the warehouse after our vows are said.

Drawing her into my arms, I whisper, "Can I take you here?"

"No, no you can't," she laughs.

"I want to come here in the future and know that I made love to you right at this spot where we promised to love each other until death parts us."

"No." She is adamant.

I gather the front of her skirt, crushing the delicate fabric in my hands as I raise it.

"Everyone can see," she hisses batting at my hands.

"No one can see a thing." I scoff. "There's enough fabric here to hide a child."

I slip one hand between her legs, enjoying the feel of the tissue thin fabric as it rubs against her skin. "See," I whisper. "No one needs to know."

"You cannot finger bang me here," she insists.

"Really?" Under her skirt she is wearing the knickers she modeled for me in my office. Her sex is swollen and wet.

"What *were* you thinking about, bunny?" I laugh, lightly caressing her delicate flesh.

She blushes fiercely.

"Stop it. We are not doing it here. I'm in the Frick gardens for heaven's sake." She sounds completely scandalized.

"Where then? Inside? In the Fragonard Room where the cherubs stare down at us?"

"That's like having sex in a church."

"How will you make it up to me?" I stroke her again. Her eyes flutter shut.

"Rooftop sex?" she offers.

"When?" My finger dips inside and she grips my arms.

"Before the party?"

"Done." I withdraw my fingers, giving her a good-bye pinch that has her leaning into me. I raise my slick fingers to my mouth and lick them clean.

"Did you just hustle me?" she asks, clearly suspicious.

"Love you, bunny." I wink. Taking a handkerchief from my pocket, I wipe my fingers dry.

"I'm going to get you back," she vows.

"I look forward to it."

EPILOGUE

Despite a few rocky moments, Kerr Inc. ended the fiscal year with a 20% increase in its stock valuation. The upward trend is positive. The dividend to stockholders this year looked to be in jeopardy during the summer months, but after rumors were put to rest and a few stunning new acquisitions in the fall—including a Japanese solar company that wowed exhibitors at a recent clean tech summit—Kerr Inc. rebounded in a decisive way.

Nearly every market investor and analyst on the street has marked Kerr Inc. stock as a buy. After all, Ian Kerr has proven time and again that he has legendary instincts for this business.

"That's a nice article."

"Is that the trash you're reading these days? I'd think you would want to enjoy a novel, rather than the gossipy financial pages." I lean over and brush my lips over Tiny's cheek as I set down a tray of coffee and pastries. Her reading skills are improving. She would still never read for pleasure—it is an onerous task, and one she mostly does only when her work demands it—but she practices, and with each day her skill increases. When we get back from our honeymoon, she'll sit for her private investigator's license and be a full-fledged field agent for Jake. Likely the only one with her own bodyguard, but still.

Jake is getting two investigators for the price of one. Tiny objected at first, but when I wouldn't budge and then poked her in the side where her scar was, she acquiesced.

I suspect that Marcie will do quite a bit of their paperwork, but the important thing is that Tiny doesn't feel so disempowered anymore.

"The financial pages are rather boring," Tiny admits. She takes a long sip of coffee. "Ahh, this is so good. I don't think I'd want to be pregnant if I had to give up coffee."

I glance at her belly. The sight of her rounded stomach makes me instantly hard.

"Oh no," she says.

"What?" I murmur, distracted. The skin of her belly is soft. I can't stop touching it. "Is our son asleep?"

"For now." Her hand joins mine. "But the coffee should wake him up. If not, you will. I recognize that look on your face."

Leaning over, I press a kiss against her hand and then against her belly. "I love you, son," I whisper.

Still holding her hand, I tug the sheet lower until I've exposed her completely. She's naked from our earlier lovemaking. "Are you too tender?" I ask, sliding a finger lightly along her lower lips.

"No." Before I can test the veracity of her statement with my tongue, she stops me and tilts my chin upward to look me in the eyes. "Do you think we can love too much? Too deep? Too strong?" she asks, widening her legs for me in clear invitation.

"How can loving someone be a bad thing?" She looks vulnerable and concerned.

"I'm afraid we have too much. That we're too happy." With one hand, she rubs the taut skin stretched across her womb.

"*Are* you happy, Tiny?"

"Happy is not the word I'd choose. I feel like I could float with the joy that's inside me. But part of me feels like I should be scared, too, because it can all be taken away so quickly."

She's thinking of her mother. Or maybe my mother. I understand her fear. We both lost our parents too early, and she worries about the future of our child. "Our children will not grow up alone, Tiny. We'll live a healthy life. We'll be safe."

"Can you guarantee that?"

"I can't," I admit. "But I can tell you we can love each other every day, and that love will be remembered. Don't you feel Sophie with you always?"

She nods slowly. "Yes, even more so since I got pregnant. But it's weird because I miss her more, yet I don't know that I've ever felt more in tune with her."

"I have legendary instincts. The paper just said so. And those instincts tell me that we are going to live for a long time and watch our children's children grow old."

"Yeah?" She smiles and then lets out a little laugh. "You do have good instincts. I'm going to trust them just like the gossipy financial paper told me too."

"Good, now are you ready for something different?"

"What do you have in mind?"

"Breakfast."

A soft laugh correctly interprets the kind of meal I'm referring to, but before I can move down her body, she lifts my face gently until we're lip to lip. As her mouth slowly parts, I give her a good morning kiss, curling my tongue around hers and lazily stroking the interior recesses of her mouth.

I could kiss her all day, but there are other parts of her body I'm just as anxious to place my lips upon. One hand tangles in her hair, angling her head for deeper penetration, while the other roams her beautiful body. There is the growing curve of her belly and the extra lushness in her breasts. A slight brush of my fingers against the tips of her nipples wrests a gasp against my lips.

"Tender, are we?"

"Mmmm," she purrs.

We touch each other until the night recedes around us and there is only Ian and Tiny and the fruit of our love.

"I love you, Ian," she finally sobs. "I love you so much. Make me yours."

"I love you too," I gasp into the delicate shell of her ear. "You are mine. Forever. Always. Mine."

Then we are both shuddering as the cataclysmic pleasure crashes around us. Behind my closed eyes, I can see her face thrown back in ecstasy, her eyes glowing with desire and love. The purity of her heart shows through everything, making this coupling a reverential event. Our mouths find each other repeatedly, and we kiss until our lips are tender and bruised.

"I adore you, Mrs. Kerr."

A smile more transcendent than every work of art in this great city appears on her face. "You love saying Mrs. Kerr."

"You have no idea."

"Maybe I do. Because I can't stop saying I love you, Mr. Kerr, my man, my lover, my heart."

Did I say love made you weak? I was so wrong. I could conquer the world so long as I have Victoria Kerr at my side.

◆ ◆ ◆

When we get back to the city it is much the same—loud and vibrating with energy. While Paris was beautiful and we enjoyed our time there, particularly our private early morning tour of the Louvre, it is good to be home. Unsurprisingly, Tiny liked the Orangerie, a small museum in Paris's Tuileries Garden, better than the Louvre. It reminded her of the Frick in scale.

Sitting in the oval rooms surrounded by Monet's Water Lilies was peaceful and captivating at once. We'd held hands as we sat on the bench and she'd told me of the first time her mother had taken her to the Frick.

"I was ten and I hadn't wanted to go. Museums were boring and I hated everything I thought was educational because school was so painful for me. But we tagged along behind a tour guide and as I listened to her explain how each piece of the museum was acquired and how I could look at the paintings and learn, museums became one of my favorite places," she'd explained.

"I'm surprised you didn't become an artist," I'd said.

"You have to have skill to be an artist and since I can barely draw stick figures, I decided that being an admirer of the arts was good enough."

"And now you are a patron of the arts."

She'd traced the veins on the back of my hand before answering. "I find that incredible," she'd admitted.

"You are in charge of the art acquisitions for our homes, now," I'd reminded her. The return look of love and amazement and wonder made me want to impregnate her all over again.

We've moved into our new townhome. Tiny insisted we keep the warehouse but we're renting it out for the time being. Together we found a five-floor townhome on the Upper West Side close to Jake's office. Tiny bikes to work most days with her bodyguard Marcie. I've hired two replacements for Louis, deciding that the work/life balance I am espousing couldn't be easily achieved under the work load that Louis had toiled under alone.

After marrying Tiny, after learning of our impending parenthood, I reached out to Louis thinking to forgive and forget. In the intervening months, my fortune had righted itself. Gains overcame losses, and filled with misguided benevolence, I thought I would lend a helping hand to Louis. I'd heard that he was selling refinancing mortgage packages in Jersey.

But whether it was shame or anger or a mixture of both, Louis refused to meet with me and I let it go.

Today it's Saturday and Tiny and I are going to take a trip to the Central Park Zoo and have lunch at the Boathouse. It was the first date we'd shared. Tiny argues it wasn't a date but that I'd horned in on an outing with her mother.

Semantics.

We ate lunch together and I took them home. That's a date.

♦ ♦ ♦

"We should have dinner with Steve and his girlfriend," Tiny says as we head down Central Park West.

"Steve broke up with his girlfriend so that would be challenging and awkward."

"What? When did this happen? I feel out of the loop with Marcie. She doesn't gossip at all."

"And Steve did?" I ask incredulously.

"No, but I was getting to learn his Sphinx-like ways. Marcie is impenetrable. She could give lessons to those British soldiers in front of the palace. What happened?" she asks. "And don't leave any details out."

"He said it wasn't working out. That's the complete story as told to me by Steve." I grin at her wrinkled nose. "Maybe you can kidnap him, tie him to a chair, and torture the details out of him. Actually, no, you shouldn't do that. Tying him up sounds vaguely sexual."

Tiny rolls her eyes. "Are you always going to assume that every man wants me even when I'm eighty, wrinkly, and my boobs are near my knees?"

"Yes and every man that doesn't is simply not right in his head. I won't be able to get enough of your geriatric ass."

She laughs and my heart squeezes at the sound of her joy. Hugging her closer, I press a kiss at her temple. We don't make it another two feet before she yelps in amazement.

"Look at that!" she says excitedly.

At the corner of Central Park West and Seventy-Second Street, a young woman is folding her bicycle into a compact arrangement of steel and rubber. Tiny hurries across the street, barely noticing traffic.

By the time I catch up, Tiny is already bent over inspecting the bike.

"I can't believe how small it folds. And it's comfortable you say?"

"I'm not going to bike any triathlons but it gets me places the subway can't," the girl responds. She flicks her gaze upward to acknowledge my arrival and then doesn't look away. Her long perusal of my T-shirt-and-jean clad body is almost discomfiting. Tiny's attention is, of course, still on the bike.

"Look at this Ian? Isn't it cool and see how lightweight it is? It's gorgeous." She lifts her shining face toward me.

"I see something gorgeous," I murmur softly. Tiny blushes under my gaze. Lifting the bike from her, I heft in my hand dutifully. "It's very light."

"I guess I don't really need something like this," she admits and hands the bike back to the girl.

"I'll trade you the bike for your guy," the girl says.

Tiny laughs in surprise and the slides her arm around my waist. "No, sorry. There's only one Ian Kerr and I'm not giving him up."

"Not for all the bikes in the world?" I joke.

"Not even for all the bikes in the galaxy," she says and raises her beautiful face to me.

That's a proper declaration.

Leaning forward, I kiss her to give her my own declaration of love. When I draw away, we're the only ones on the street corner. The bike and the girl have left. And it's just Tiny, me, and the sunshine. And the little one growing in Tiny's belly. My life could not be more perfect.

ACKNOWLEDGMENTS:

Thank you to all the bloggers for their support and promotion of these books. Being a blogger is a true labor of love and I salute you.

The creation of a book does not happen in isolation. It comes about through the endless patience of the author's family and friends.

I would never be able to finish a project without my husband who never hesitates to help me with anything—big or small. My daughter's sweet hugs and words of encouragement are indispensable to a healthy mind.

If the inboxes of my friends such as Meljean Brook, Jessica Clare, and Katy Evans would ever be closed to me, I'd have to pack up this writing gig. Knowing that I'm not alone in this writing world is immeasurably encouraging.

The day after Father's Day I got a call from my brother that my dad had passed. He suffered from mantle cell leukemia, a rare disease that is often late to be diagnosed because of the generality of symptoms that accompany the illness. I recall standing by my living room window thinking that it couldn't be true because I'd just seen him yesterday. I had bought a cashmere blanket for him to use during treatment because it got cold during his long days of dialysis and chemo drips.

But it was true. He was gone. The next time I saw my father was in a casket. I lived some distance away and I told my family not to wait for me to pull him off life support.

I don't always remember that he's gone. Sometimes I still think of him up north, tending his huge garden, going to the shooting range, and fishing in his favorite stream.

I guess he still is doing all of those things, just not in this realm.

Love you, Dad. Miss you so much.

ABOUT THE AUTHOR

Jen Frederick is the *USA Today* bestselling author of *Unspoken*, part of the Woodlands series. She is also the author of the Charlotte Chronicles, which appeared on the Kindle Top 100 list. She lives in the Midwest with her husband, who keeps track of life's details while she's writing; a daughter, who understands when Mom disappears into her office for hours at a time; and a rambunctious dog who does neither.